Life's Kipper.

By
Susan Delaney

Table of Contents

Chapter One

Crystal Blake was extremely pretty.

'Too pretty for her own good,' Mary, her mother, told anyone she happened to be discussing her daughter's peccadillos with.

The conversation was usually an opening line at the bingo hall, pub lunches, or various clubs she attended. Mary's gossip buddies would dutifully tut and shake their heads disapprovingly. They had heard this so many times before. But if nothing better to talk about, Crystal's antics were always a good fallback, as it was that day in the coffee shop just off the high street.

'Her father's the one to blame,' Mary claimed, raising her eyebrow disapprovingly and clucking in judgment of her daughter's latest fad. 'I mean, what's wrong with the name Sarah! It's what we christened her. But no, it's not good enough. She prefers Crystal! I ask you, what sort of name is that? Her soppy husband doesn't help. Spoils her rotten. I tell you, one of these days, that girl will come unstuck. Life has a funny way of biting you on the bum,' Mary continued, encouraged by her audience's attention.

'Was he named after that poet?' Jane, her closest, but not brightest friend, asked.

Mary stopped talking and furrowed her brow. 'Poet? Poet? Who? What Poet?' she fired back at Jane.

'Err usband.'

'Whose husband?' Mary was confused and becoming agitated that Jane was changing the subject when she was on a roll.

1

'Your daughter's!'

'I don't know what you're on about. Honestly, Jane, can you never keep up? I'm talking about my daughter and you've drifted to poetry.'

'I think… what Jane means… is William Blake, the famous poet,' Janet, another friend of the little gang, added.

'What's that got to do with my daughter?' Mary snapped.

'Will, Crystal's husband. He has the same name as the Poet,' Jane said, shifting on her seat uncomfortably as everyone's eyes were pointing in her direction and Mary's irritated tone.

'Well, I know that! But what's it got to do with my girl?'

'Anyone want another coffee?' Simon, who always tagged along, offered.

Mary was right; Will, Crystal's dutiful husband, who was fifteen years older, did spoil his wife with anything she wanted. He regularly arrived home from his office with another carefully thought-out gift. He adored Crystal. Nothing was too much trouble for his Princess, the same pet name her father had used.

'You're a fool, Will!' Mary told him regularly as she flashed a look of disgust at each offering, usually pointing a glass accusingly in his direction, filled with a large cognac from his precious collection.

Will would give a small guilty smile and shrug. He knew as Mary did; it was to keep his wife amused and to stop her wandering. The gifts were reminders of the good life they shared. She would struggle without the wealth if she ever did 'up-sticks' and leave. He had been sensible enough to make Crystal sign a prenuptial agreement before they married. Not that legally it meant much, but he knew his wife would not know that.

2

Although spoilt, Crystal and Mary came from a relatively poor background. After the tragic death of Mary's husband, Crystal's dad, David, she had managed to wiggle her way into their home. This was a large Tudor house with two double garages, five bedrooms, three bathrooms, and an indoor swimming pool situated on two acres of grounds. The three of them lived relatively peacefully. Except for Mary's scathing opinion of her daughter, life jogged along OK.

Will was right; twenty-three-year-old Crystal quickly became bored. She would be off like a shot if it weren't for the money and status. In her opinion, her husband was dull, his hair was receding rapidly and he was overweight. After five years of marriage, life was monotonous. She longed for bright lights, late nights, lots of friends, and a bit of flirting here and there. The gifts Will produced held no interest for her. After admiring the latest glittery jewel or item of clothing, it was usually tossed aside and forgotten.

Crystal did not work; she never needed to. She was happily ignorant about most things in life. With her thick black hair, perfectly symmetrical facial features, full lips and large brown eyes, she didn't feel the need to know much that went on in the world. Men flocked around, eager for her attention. From a young age, Crystal knew she would go places. Her adored father told her she would.

'Nothing's too good for my Princess.' David always said when each payday, he showered his daughter with yet another gift, causing Mary to shake her head disapprovingly at her spoilt only child.

He was right, Crystal mused; even as a small girl, she knew her life was not destined for the dreary council estate where she grew up.

She had met Will in a café one miserable winter day. Crystal had sat at a table with her date, Christopher, a boy from her school. He had been begging to buy her a coffee for ages. She relented when there was nothing better to do. She found boys her own age uninteresting. Stifling a yawn behind her hand, she spotted a man staring. Grinning at him, she flicked her large, pretty eyes, indicating boredom of her companion. Will laughed and pulled faces. He wore an expensive suit and looked sophisticated, mature, and very handsome. His hair was blond and combed neatly, with a slight wave escaping over his forehead. His body was trim and muscular at that time, unlike seven years later.

Crystal had just turned sixteen. She was readying herself to leave school and had no idea what to do afterward. Her parents tried to encourage her to learn, attend college, and possibly, one day, university. Although clever, she had no interest. Learning and university were for stiffs, not people like her, who didn't need to bother.

Before she left the café that day, Will had sneakily handed her his business card. "Ring Me!!! Please?" was written on the back. She did the very next day and soon, her life became a whirlwind of expensive restaurants, clubs, business functions and theatre shows. Crystal had no idea what his business was; she didn't really care. It had something to do with exports or similar.

Will bought her the finest gifts of clothes, shoes, and bags, keeping the wardrobe hidden from her parents at his apartment so they did not suspect their sixteen-year-old daughter was involved with a man, almost old enough to be her father or older brother, as Will preferred.

Life became fun as Crystal discovered a new world she had only fantasized about in glossy magazines. She boasted to her school friends about her new romance. They poked fun at her. Will became known as "Pedo." She didn't care, knowing they were jealous of her fancy life.

After Crystal left school, she confessed her relationship to her parents. They were not too pleased and forbade her from seeing him anymore.

'What's wrong with boys your age?' David, her father asked. 'He's too old for you.'

'But daddy, they're so silly and dull,' she answered, pouting her lips, which usually won her battles.

They had no choice but to relent when their stubborn daughter began staying out at weekends. There was nothing they could do. At least if they accepted Will, they would know where she was. When he overcame the age difference, her father got on well with him. Everyone did; Will was bubbly and easy-going. He laughed a lot and always found a joke to make them grin.

When Crystal was eighteen, the couple announced their engagement and set a wedding date for the summer of the same year. Will paid for the elaborate day, plus a luxury honeymoon in Las Vegas. He also found them a suitable house, which Crystal instantly fell in love with.

Soon after the wedding and so unexpectedly, David died. He suffered a massive heart attack at the factory where he worked as a supervisor. The small family were beside themselves with grief. Mary struggled to cope without her husband, sinking into a deep depression.

'My Grandmother used to say,' Will said, to comfort mother and daughter, 'It's just another of life's Kippers.'

Both stared at him, not finding him amusing at such a terrible time.

Not to be put off, he continued, 'Just when you think life is OK, a big Kipper comes along and slaps you right around the chops.'

Giving up her home, Mary moved in with her daughter and son-in-law, relishing the luxury of her new life.

Will took the new addition to his family with good grace. After all, he had the biggest prize: a beautiful young wife and was the envy of all his friends. Crystal was good for business when he took her to meet potential clients.

'When can we start a family?' he begged her often.

'Oh Will, I'm far too young for all that mummy stuff. Let's give it a few more years yet,' she would plead, flashing those big brown eyes that would win her anything she wanted. He would sadly agree to wait a while longer.

For their fifth wedding anniversary, Will came home from work excitedly. Mary was in the kitchen as he slapped a large envelope on the granite worktop before Crystal.

'Happy anniversary,' he announced, a wide grin spread almost from ear to ear.

'What is it?' she asked, staring at the brown package and feeling guilty; she hadn't got him anything.

'Look and see,' he laughed, jiggling from one foot to another, eagerly anticipating her response.

Gingerly opening the flap, she pulled out the contents, meeting his eyes questioningly.

'It's a holiday, my Princess. Three weeks in Panchaea, one of the phantom islands.'

'The where?'

Will grinned, 'It's a cluster of beautiful islands in the Indian Ocean.'

'Oh! Thanks,' she responded, with the same slight enthusiasm as she did all his gifts. Crystal could think nothing more boring than being stuck for three weeks with Will. At least at home, she could go shopping and to the gym, which she attended regularly. Or meet with friends, mainly Wills' associates' wives and girlfriends, where they indulge in gossip and giggle.

'When's it for?' she thought to ask.

The week after next,' he informed her, deflated at the lack of response. 'I've got some business there, so I thought we could make it a holiday of a lifetime. It really is a beautiful place. It's a retreat where people go to relax. They have a spring-watered pool, jacuzzi, sauna, open-air hammocks and a beauty parlour. Oh, and a gym you can spend time in. I thought you'd like it,' he said in a last attempt to draw some enthusiasm from her.

'Told you!' Mary scoffed, 'she's spoilt. Any other girl would jump at the chance of a luxury holiday. Not err.' She poked her glass in her daughter's direction.

Well, used to her criticism, they ignored her.

'Isn't there a war around that area?' Mary asked, furrowing her brow, trying to recall where she had heard this.

'There isn't on the islands,' Will answered. The mainland had some rumblings, but it's all just handbags.'

'Handbags?' Mary laughed. 'What does that mean?'

'Just a few little arguments between the two countries, Buranda and Carbombya. The islands are situated in the Ocean between them. They have been considered part of Buranda since the early nineteen hundreds when they were discovered. But now Carbombya wants ownership of them. The islanders themselves want independence and are stuck in the middle of it.

'What a stupid name, who's ever heard of the Phantom Islands? Have they got ghosts in sheets floating about?' Crystal smirked, finding her joke amusing.

Will laughed, 'No, my Princess. It's because a legend was talked about by sailors, who claimed to have seen them in the sixteenth century. Then, in the early nineteenth century, they were rediscovered, and a civilization of people lived on them. Panchaea, where we are going, is the largest of the islands. It's supposed to be exceptionally beautiful.'

Her expression had glazed, 'Oh,' she responded flatly. 'How riveting.'

Crystal felt miserable for the rest of the week and was not in the best of moods. She constantly snapped at Will and her mother. Neither could do anything right. They tiptoed around her, trying to make light of her temper and sarcasm. Her mood deteriorated further the closer the holiday drew.

'I'm pregnant,' she confided to her best friend, Layla, when they met for lunch at their favourite pub a few days before the date.

'You're kidding!' Layla gushed, her eyes widening with delight. 'That's fantastic news.' She had just become engaged to a man she had met through her work in a chemist.

'I don't want a baby,' Crystal confessed. 'I can't think of anything worse, stuck at home with smelly nappies and my mum.'

'You'll feel different once it's born. I can't wait to have kids,' Layla confessed.

'I'm thinking of having it aborted. But Will's booked this silly holiday.'

Layla gasped, 'You wouldn't? Surely not. Kill a baby? That's terrible.'

'I can't help it. The thought fills me with horror. I can't imagine how this has happened. I take my pill regularly and rarely have sex. In fact, I can't stand him touching me.'

'But he's your husband.' Layla was shocked again.

'He's more like my dad and I think he's vile.'

Layla, a kind, gentle girl, stood up. 'So, you only married him for the money and you're using him? Do you know what? I think it's you that's vile. How can you talk about Will like that? He's such a lovely man. Your mum's right, you're spoilt!'

With those words ringing in Crystal's ears, her friend stomped from the café. It seemed to end their friendship and she was sorry. They had been together a long time and Layla was her closest and only friend left from her school days. They had been like sisters, growing up on the same estate and their mother's friends since childhood.

But not to be put off, she paid the bill and walked into the park. Putting her hand on her stomach, she imagined her trim waistline swelling and distorted into a bulbous bulge, ready to burst. She had seen women with baggy bellies and stretch marks at the swimming pool. Crystal vowed never to get like that, the same way she promised never to be seen without makeup, beautiful clothes, or get fat.

As the date for the holiday drew closer, Crystal resentfully packed a suitcase. She was undecided about an abortion. Layla's words had disturbed her; what if she told Janice, who would then tell Mary?

After too many Cognacs, her mother could not resist telling Will. Once the holiday was over and she was sure no one knew, there was still a little time to scrape one in. By that time she would know if Layla had kept the secret. Maybe the plane journey would cause a miscarriage, saving her the headache of being found out.

Will was excited about the holiday. 'You'll be all right when you see how beautiful the place is,' he reassured.

Crystal sighed and gave a minuscule smile; she doubted it.

All too soon, Mary was waving them off from the front of the house and they were sitting on a plane, ready for the long journey ahead.

Will leaned over from his seat and nudged her. 'Bet she's asked the cronies around for a party,' he smirked.

'Who? Mum? They'd better not trash the house,' Crystal huffed before turning her attention to the view outside the small window.

It had started raining as they had taken off. Tiny houses, pockets of lakes, and a snake river weaving through landscape cubes of fields could be seen. Turning away, she pulled headphones from her bag and turned on music to drown out the whirl of the engines. Closing her eyes, Crystal gave a loud sigh to demonstrate to Will how she was not pleased about the never-ending flight. He did not notice as he was already engrossed in a film.

The plane took eleven hours to land on the mainland of Buranda. It took another hour to collect their luggage and get through customs. While Will dragged the cases, Crystal escaped through the airport doors, thankful to be away from the mayhem. The air outside was stifling and hot in her lungs. The temperature must be well in the thirties, she figured.

Will appeared beside her, huffing with the effort of tackling the swing doors, hand luggage, and the two heavy cases. 'Wow, this is the life!' he breathed.

Crystal flicked her eyes in annoyance at his cheerful attitude. She was tired and not in the best of moods. 'Why are there so many armed soldiers?'

'Just a precaution, Princess,' he reassured, squeezing her arm protectively.

'I hope you're right!' she snapped.

A car was waiting to drive them to the harbour. From there, a speed boat would take them for the rest of the journey. They waited almost two hours for their name to be called. After the long flight, Crystal was not happy, especially in her heavy, English-weather clothes.

The enthusiastic boat driver began to shout a rehearsed guided tour along the way. Crystal yawned; only so much information could be given about islands that all looked the same.

Will listened eagerly, intently, soaking up the information like a sponge.

'There thirteen islands, three, with people living on them. Panchaea, where you staying, is largest. Approximately thirty by nineteen Kilometres - almost size of Isle of Wight. Approximately eight thousand people live on island, which has twenty-one small villages…'

Crystal yawned again, laying her head on Will's shoulder; she closed her eyes, trying to block out the engine's drone and his voice. Delighted at this show of affection, Will pulled his arm around her and kissed her forehead, receiving a spoonful of hair.

11

The hour's journey seemed to take seven until the driver pointed out the island in the distance. Will was right; it was beautiful, Crystal observed. The vast mass of floating rock seemed to shimmer and glow in the setting sun. She could see why it was called a phantom island, as it looked ghost-like. The enormous orange ball of sun was hovering over the sea, which mirrored its beauty. Reds, magentas, and lilacs, flecked with scatterings of gold, littered the sky and water. The glow illuminated the thin silver clouds strewn across the purple setting above the hills, looking more like mountains to Crystal as they were huge.

'Wow! What a magnificent sunset,' Will breathed.

'Lovely,' Crystal answered, her voice deliberately monotone and flat. 'I'm too shattered to notice.'

When they arrived, the harbour was a buzz of people. Little shops and restaurants glowed in the evening dusk, ready for the night ahead, lights shining on the goods on sale, intensifying the colours. The buildings were bright and welcoming, with tempting menus or various goods decorating the walls and doorways. A few brightly lit hotels sat along the coastline, looking welcoming and exclusive. Behind the harbour, the silhouette of lonely steep hills could be seen, haunting the darkening skyline.

'At least the port looks civilised,' Crystal mused, attempting a signal on her phone.

'I'm sorry, Princess, your mobile won't work here. These people haven't got that far in life yet,' he grinned sheepishly.

Crystal threw him a look of disgust as she hurled her phone into her bag.

Will found the car waiting to drive the twenty-minute journey, three-quarters up the hill.

'I'm not getting in there!' Crystal whispered, staring suspiciously at the shady-looking fellow, who looked nothing like a taxi driver. His rusty old car certainly did not look like the cabs, she knew.

'It'll be fine,' Will laughed.

The lights of the harbour faded into the background as they drove into the dusky night. Crystal waited for the car to stop and for the driver to produce a gun, shoot them, and steal their belongings. Their bodies would be dumped and never found again as they bumped along a path that was nothing but rocks and dust.

For once, Will chattering to the driver was comforting; he could not speak much English but did not sound like a criminal. As they swung around yet another bend in the road, glimpses of lights could be seen a short distance ahead.

'We're almost there now, Princess.' Will put his arm around her, giving her a small kiss on the ear.

'What the hell are those?' Crystal demanded with distaste as they arrived. Large tent-like cabins were dotted around the site, lit by small lanterns. A few larger lights shone on timber buildings, suggesting visitors' gathering areas.

'They're called yurts,' Will laughed nervously.

'What? They're tents! Don't tell me you expect me to stay in one of them?' She flicked her hand towards the monstrosities to demonstrate her disgust.

The yurts were clumsy and round, with bamboo latticework covered by canvas walls. They were built onto wooden platforms, each with small doors underneath for storage. Olive trees were scattered around the site, most with hammocks tied between them.

'There is absolutely no way I am staying here! You do what you like; I will call a cab and check into one of the hotels!'

'Please, Crystal,' Will begged. 'It'll be fine. You'll see. It looks dismal in the dark. Once the sun's shining tomorrow, you'll love the place.'

She huffed but reluctantly nodded her head in agreement. 'Only until tomorrow!'

Will breathed a sigh of relief. One of the retreat workers stood close by, holding out a cocktail to welcome them with; he looked confused, not knowing what to do or say and feeling sorry for the poor husband with his spoilt brat of a wife.

Chapter Two

The retreat worker wheeled their cases and led them to a yurt near the back of the camp. It had three steps up to double glass doors, which were open to reveal the large, round inside. The four-poster bed dominated the centre of the room. A mesh curtain was scooped around the top to keep insects at bay while they slept. The canvas roof was pulled together in the middle, leaving a large hole that looked into the blackened sky.

'You watch stars,' the worker pointed upwards. 'Very romantic,' he grinned and winked suggestively.

Will smirked and Crystal flicked her eyes in revulsion. She walked to the bamboo wardrobe and pulled open the doors. Inside was a small fridge.

'Look, there's even a shower room,' Will marvelled, disappearing through a door.

Crystal clonked in heels across the highly polished floor to see. Inside the small room was a shower and a toilet. She fleetingly wondered how they could plumb something like this into a tent.

It was too dark to explore the site. The same member of staff who had welcomed them brought food on a tray. He looked dubiously at Crystal as he laid the meal on a little table with two chairs on either side. After propping a card against the condiments, he shuffled away. It was an invite to meet the other guests at the Treehouse bar in an hour.

Will was delighted as he lifted the lid off the plates. There was soup, a large salad, flan, and potatoes, followed by fruit and cream.

'It's all organic and homemade,' he enthused, stuffing a potato into his mouth as if it made any difference to her.

Crystal was tired, dusty, hot and wanted to go to bed. However, hunger getting the better, she sat down and began eating her soup. It was delicious, not that she would admit that to Will.

After the food and a shower, her mood improved slightly. Crystal agreed to go to the treehouse for a while. She was curious about how a bar could be balanced in a tree.

It was almost as the invite said. However, one side was built into the rock, and the other finished into a large tree. Eight wooden stilts held the building up at various vulnerable points. The outside area was lit by the same-coloured lanterns that hung from the olive trees and yurts. The pool, which they passed on the way, looked inviting. It was kidney-shaped, surrounded by white lights that caused the water to twinkle and sparkle welcomingly.

They climbed the stairs to the bar and were greeted by seven other guests who had arrived earlier that day. The seating was a range of armchairs. different-sized cushions and bean bags. Short tables stood in front of the clusters. The bar was at the far end, with a smiling waiter standing behind, ready to serve any requests.

'A large white wine,' Crystal asked demurely.

As Will went off to purchase the drinks, she smiled around at the other people, noting a few reasonably good-looking men, most unfortunately in couples. One was very handsome, a little older than herself, and, disappointingly, also with a partner. Crystal managed her warmest grin for him, suitably satisfied once the man grinned admiringly back.

Not wishing to engage in chit-chat, she soon made her apologies, taking her wine, returned to the yurt, leaving Will to make friends. She flicked her eyes to the sky in annoyance, hearing his barking laughter echo around the blackness. Unlike her, Will was very sociable. People liked him for his easy chatter and laughter. He was always ready to help anyone who might be having difficulty.

Arriving at the yurt an hour later, Will woke Crystal.

'You aren't really going to a hotel tomorrow, are you?'

'I'm tired. Just go away!' she snapped.

'Not till you promise me you'll at least give the Retreat a go.'

'I hardly call this dump a Retreat. But whatever. Now GO AWAY!' She hissed, turning her back to him with an exaggerated thump.

They were up early the next day, ready to explore - at least Will was. Crystal wanted to find the gym and then laze by the pool with her latest novel. She had never eaten breakfast and had already had two coffees made from the little packages in the room. The fridge in the yurt was packed with bottles of water. There were also some snack bars in a little cupboard above.

'It's all so well thought out,' Will enthused, admiring the people who created such a place. 'It was built by two Burandonian brothers,' he told Crystal, pulling back the double doors to admire the view over the hills. He inhaled a very exaggerated, noisy breath. 'It's not cheap, but wow, what a glorious place.'

Curious, Crystal walked over and stood beside him. They were midway up one of the clusters of hills that surrounded them, between rocky terrain. The tops were high, more like mountains, as their soft, wavy peaks intruded into the thin white clouds, making them appear suffocating and solitary. At various points, small stone-built cube houses were dotted about. A more extensive cluster resembling a village was high in the distance.

'Who'd want to live up there?' she shrugged and returned to her coffee. 'Really, Will, do you not think you could have found a hotel near the bay or something better than a tent?' Crystal huffed, picking up her book, she flicked a page with annoyance and lifted it to hide her face, hoping this would dismiss him.

Will sighed, disappointment veiling his eyes. 'I'm going for breakfast. Do you want any?' he asked, knowing the answer before he had spoken.

Crystal huffed and raised her eyes in annoyance. She felt sick and was glad when he left so she could dive into the toilet before he noticed. Afterward, grabbing her bag, she went for a stroll around the camp, carefully staying away from where breakfast was being served. She spotted the area in the short distance and again heard Will's raucous laughter as he bonded with his new friends.

The dining area had a lengthy table, and guests sat around it. It was outside one of the wooden buildings, which was used as a kitchen. A pergola with thick grape vines covered the area, creating a shady canopy for mealtimes. The same waiter from the night before stood, ready to serve.

Will was, as always, the centre of attention. Crystal suddenly felt very left out. She considered joining them and then dismissed this, again not wanting to make friends amongst these people. They were probably anoraks, as she thought of them and as dull as Will.

A wooden building just to the left of their yurt was a very primitive gym. Next to it were the sauna and steam room. She searched for the beauty Parlour, which was easy to find in such a compact place. At that moment, it was closed. The menu outside offered various treatments at extortionate prices. Crystal mentally ticked off a list of the ones she would try, once it was open.

'A massage a day keeps the doctor away,' she smirked and went to find a sun lounger.

The pool had a fabulous view over the hills down to the harbour they had arrived at. The sun's reflection was glistening on the sea. Fishing boats were bobbing on the gentle waves. Ant-sized fishermen could be seen preparing for a day at sea. Larger boats sat waiting for holidaymakers to board for day trips. Tiny people could be seen lazily strolling along the promenade. It all looked typical of a holiday destination.

Will found Crystal an hour later, kissing the top of her hat in greeting.

'Listen, Princess. I've got to return to the harbour for a meeting at Eleven. Would you like to come and look around the shops or stay here?'

'A meeting?' she asked, surprised.

'Yes, I did tell you I had some business here. Not too much and the rest of the time is ours.'

Crystal debated what to do. It was extremely hot already and it was still only early.

'We could have lunch somewhere if you come,' he suggested.

'OK,' she decided. And went off to change.

It was fun trawling around the little shops. Crystal managed to find some interesting clothing items. The things Will bought her were not really what she would consider wearing. She also found a new hat to keep the sun off her face.

They met for lunch at 1 o'clock and enjoyed a bottle of wine before taxiing back to the retreat. Crystal then headed for the pool while Will went for a nap.

'Don't you fancy… you know… a cuddle?' he asked, hopefully, biting his lip and waiting for the usual rejection.

'No, I do not!' she snapped, disgust filling her eyes. She stomped off, leaving Will looking like a lost puppy. The last time she had allowed sex with him, look what had happened - she was pregnant.

The rest of the week passed quickly. While Will attended a few business meetings, Crystal spent time by the pool or in the beauty Parlour, enjoying a massage or facial. Although the building was dated, the beautician was highly skilled. She advised many treatments to her client, not sparing any expense; Crystal tried them all.

She also began talking to one of the guests, Sonya, who bravely came on holiday alone. The two struck up a friendship as they sat by the pool, sipping cocktails. Sonya was nineteen and very pretty. Her hair was long, wavy, and red. She had penetrating blue eyes that sparkled as she laughed, which, like Will, she did easily. Crystal felt envious, wishing she could find life so amusing.

Her new friend was single, having just split with her boyfriend. She did not want another romance. Instead, she longed to go backpacking around Europe. Crystal thought it sounded exciting but then decided it was not for her; sleeping rough and thumbing lifts was maybe not that great.

'What do you think about the sex god?' Crystal asked as they gave the camp men marks out of ten as a pastime.

'Oh, at least a ten,' Sonya giggled. 'What about the sexy waiter with the glossy black hair?'

Nine.'

'Only nine?' Sonya was surprised. She thought the waiter was at least a twelve and told her new friend so.

'But we're only going up to ten,' Crystal laughed.

'Exactly.' And they both giggled.

After a few days, she decided the holiday was fun. The biggest drawback was the giant insects. Will explained, that the heat and moisture caused them to be larger than usual. Goodness knows why that made a difference, Crystal mused.

There were huge spiders that built web caves, not like the fragile webs in England. These were like thick cotton and the inhibitor was apparently deadly if it bit. Massive green things, like grasshoppers but seven times larger, hopped around the dusty ground. The flies were four times the size of a British fly.

A few skinny cats lived there, too. If there was no better offering, they could sometimes be seen crunching an insect or two.

Sonya found one of the thick black spiders on her bag one day. Almost touching it, she screamed so loud the entire site, including staff, came running. Seeing the spider's size, Crystal screamed too, as Sonya, in her effort to get rid of it, flicked it her way. They both danced around in a frenzied paddy until rescued by Stuart, the hunky, sexy one of the group.

Crystal threw herself into his arms hysterically, feeling his muscular body fold around her own. It was the first time she had experienced sexual feelings. From then on, her daydreams were about Stuart making love to her. Wills' flabby body and clumsy lovemaking revolted her even more.

For the rest of the holiday, Crystal flirted outrageously with Stuart. Her attention flattered him, but his wife, Judy, was not pleased. In Crystal's opinion, she was a dull little thing who liked cooking and homemaking. Probably knitting and crocheting, too, she decided. Judy was plain and wore no make-up. Her clothes were frumpy, and she was no threat to Crystal, who ignored her disapproving stares. There was no guilt as she giggled with Stuart, rubbing her leg against his, as they sat in the tree house sharing a small table.

Will tried to ignore his wife's flirting, but a muscle in his jaw twitched with jealousy and hurt. Before they were married, Crystal had flirted with him the same way.

As he returned from one of his meetings at the beginning of the last week of the holiday, Will told Crystal they were leaving the next day. He had arranged a boat to take them to the mainland.

She guessed it was because of Stuart. 'No! I like it here. You go; I'll wait until the due date,' jutting her chin with determination.

'You don't understand, Princess. The two neighbouring countries are going to announce war. We need to get home before it's too late.'

Her eyes grew large with fear. 'War? But you said it was alright before we came. I believe the term you used was people hitting each other with handbags!'

At breakfast the next day, he told the others they were leaving and that they needed to do the same.

'They are going to announce war. We have a boat waiting to take us to the mainland. Any of you are welcome to share a ride.'

'No, no, the manager objected. 'No War. You safe. No panic. No hurt you.'

'The military from Carbombya are threatening to invade the island and kill the tourists,' Will told them, his eyes blazing with the seriousness of the situation.

'No kill tourists,' the manager, who they called Garson as a joke, said. 'You safe.'

Will, ignoring Garson's reassurance, instructed Crystal to pack.

'Sonya, please, come with us?' Crystal begged. 'Will said Garson is wrong; we must get off the island.'

Sonya gave her friend a hug, 'It's OK, Crystal. I'm due home in a few days. Nothing can happen that fast. They haven't announced a war yet. You know what governments are like all mouth and balmy air. Once I'm home, I'll call you,' she promised.

Crystal gave Stuart an extra-long hug, much to Will's annoyance. Not to draw attention to her affection for him, she resentfully hugged Judy and the others. They all promised to keep in touch. Sonya said she would set up a social media group, once she had gathered phone numbers, so they could.

When their farewells were over, the waiting taxi took them to the harbour. Crystal was sad leaving Stuart and Sonya, wishing they had left with them. But Will was outnumbered, as all the group felt he was overreacting. No harm could come to them; they were just holidaymakers. Crystal thought Will was overdramatising, too, until they reached the harbour. Then she became frightened, and the seriousness of the threatening war became a reality.

The waterfront buzzed with frenzied people. Unlike when they had first arrived, there was no longer holiday excitement rippling the air. The atmosphere was heavy, anxious, and full of fear. People crowded by the water's edge, pushing and shoving with luggage, desperate to be on boats to escape the island. The shops and cafes were no longer lit; they were closed. A few armed police were trying to create control and order. They were unsuccessful, as there were so few of them. People were aggressive and panic-stricken. Some screamed at others, and fights broke out amongst random groups, all frantic to be on boats.

'Keep close!' Will shouted over the noise. He grabbed Crystal's hand and began to drag her through the crowds to the jetty.

'I can't keep up!' she shouted back.

He ignored her and, in urgency, elbowed people out of the way to be at the front. Will had arranged to meet a boat, which had cost him considerable money. He had a right to be there. However, the driver he had paid was nowhere to be seen.

'The conning git!' he yelled, frustratedly throwing his case handle on the floor.

'What's wrong!' Crystal was alarmed; Will was scaring her.

'Come on,' he picked up the handle again and continued to battle with the crowds.

Only a few boats were tied to the jetty; obviously, having heard the news, many had already carried passengers to the mainland. Cash was changing hands to gain seats on the few boats there. Will tried again, waving money in the air, to find spaces for them. He was unsuccessful as the few overcrowded boats began to leave.

'Next time!' a few shouted back; others ignored the irate, panicking people.

Some hours later, Crystal, frustrated and distressed at being kicked and elbowed, pulled her hand from Will's and fought away from the crowds. She slumped onto a wall a safe distance from the madness, exhausted and with her head ringing.

Will wasn't giving up; he hardly noticed her absence. As other boats returned, he tried again to buy a ride. It was impossible; too many people got there first. Some leaped onto the moving crafts even before they reached the shore. A few fell into the water and had to scrabble out, hurling wet luggage after them. More people appeared and many islanders seemed eager to reach family on the mainland. Their belongings were packed into bundles. Some dragged protesting children and older people.

Early in the afternoon, Will admitted defeat and left the chaotic waterfront. With sagging shoulders, he fought through the crowds and slumped next to Crystal.

'Let's go back to the retreat,' she said despondently, 'I'm hungry and tired. Maybe Garson's right. I'm sure he will arrange something for us. Or we could try again tomorrow when people have calmed down.'

Seeing the unhappiness in her eyes, Will relented, smiling, he squeezed her hand. It took another hour to find a willing taxi. Again, he paid an exorbitant amount to take them back.

'What happened?' Sonya ran to the car, as did Judy and the rest of the group.

When they explained what the harbour was like, a heavy silence filled with alarm fell amongst the group.

'We need to go tomorrow and try and find boats off this island,' Stuart said, putting a protective arm around Judy.

'It OK,' Garson assured. 'Brother has boat, take mainland. Make safe.'

That pacified them until, at sunset, a group of six planes flew over. Their shadows, heightened by the lowering sun, were vast and threatening as they rumbled over the hills. All nine of them ran to the edge, near the pool, to follow their trail. They stared in horror and disbelief as bombs were released, one after the other, onto the harbour. The explosions shook the ground and the buildings around them rattled in protest; rocks crashed as the tremors loosened their hold. Crystal squeezed her eyes shut, thanking God they were no longer amongst the screaming crowds.

26

The squarks and squeals of frightened birds and other animals were almost as deafening as the eruptions. Mushrooms of thick black smoke drifted up, one after another, dispersing to thinner black clouds that changed the colour of the sky and stung their eyes, making them stream. Boats and ant-sized people could be seen burning as they flapped their arms to rid themselves of the torturous flames. The jetty was reduced to splinters of wood, bobbing on the water. People were frantically trying to swim from sunk boats back to the shore, shot down as the planes circled and fired guns along the coast and into the water. Ships carrying soldiers drifted in from the sea and more gunfire echoed. The screaming and crying drifted upwards, bouncing around the rocks. More explosions boomed and the sound of gunshots penetrated their ears.

The guests and staff watched, too traumatised to speak in the horror of those moments that went on most of the night.

'Get things together! We go, first light,' Garson admitted, rapidly changing his tune. He looked white-faced and huge-eyed despite his tanned olive skin.

'How?' Will said, 'the bay is crawling with Carbombya soldiers.'

'Pack cases. Please, everyone, we get to mainland. You, safe. Soldiers not come hills.'

All that night, they watched in terror for more disruption down at the bay. Sometime in the early hours, everything went quiet.

'We need to rest,' Will advised them. 'It will be a long day tomorrow.'

'Are we going to die?' Crystal sobbed once they were in the yurt.

'No way, Princess. I promise you. No one will harm a hair of your beautiful head.

Chapter Three

The morning sun rose, mockingly cheerful, welcoming a day full of hope and optimism. The enormity of the night's bombing hit; not one of them had slept. The reality struck that without the bay and a boat, they were stuck on the island - in the middle of a war.

They met at the food table early, even Crystal. There was no breakfast and the kitchen door was locked. The site seemed empty except for the nine of them.

'Everyone's gone and left us!' Sonya's eyes were wide with fear.

Without speaking, Will and the other men searched for the staff while the others speculated about what was happening. In the panic of the moment, their stories became more elaborate.

'There's no one here,' Will announced on his return.

They remained silent until the other two men came back, agreeing with Will's findings. Judy began to cry; Stuart put his arm around her and kissed her forehead affectionately. Despite the dread of the situation, Crystal felt a pang of jealousy.

'What shall we do?' Sonya asked, looking at Will, who seemed to be in control. 'What if Garson doesn't come back?'

One of the guests, Aaron, suggested, 'We could head for the other side of the island.'

'And swim to where? It's probably crawling with soldiers,' Stuart raised his eyes in annoyance at the stupidity of the suggestion.

'We'll wait. Garson promised to help us. He's probably gone to make arrangements and will return soon.' Will's voice sounded more confident than he felt. There wasn't really any other choice. So, each nodded in agreement.

Stuart went to the kitchen and kicked the door. It broke easily, disappearing inside, he soon returned, loaded with croissants, rolls, ham, and cheese. 'Breakfast,' he grinned, trying to make light of the bleak situation. 'Least we won't starve. Not for a while, anyway.' Laying the load on the table, he returned to find the coffee pot.

The others talked about the war and for once, Crystal listened. The enormity of the situation intensified her interest.

'It's all about religion,' Stuart speculated, unloading the mugs he was carrying. 'Half of them are Christians, the other Muslims. So, they fight for each to dominate the other.'

'No,' Will snapped; he disliked Stuart after his wife's flirting. 'The two countries argue about who owns the islands.'

'But why would either want the financial strain of them on their back? You can't tell me the small amount of tourism brings in much cash?' Geoff, an older man of the group, argued, unconvinced of Will's explanation. 'They've belonged to Buranda for years.'

'The islanders want independence; they don't want to belong to either country. So, there is some internal argument,' Will began to explain. 'Of course, they are a bit small and vulnerable to be self-sufficient. About three years ago, a seismic vessel ran off course into these waters.' He wiggled two fingers on each hand to indicate brackets, insinuating this was on purpose. Seeing the confusion on many faces, he explained in more straightforward detail. 'It's a ship that maps the area. It uses sound waves to find oil on the seabed. They discovered a few large pockets around the islands. There was a lot of trouble from the inmates about the poaching. It makes this area unbelievably valuable. Of course, if there are a few pockets of oil, then there could be more.'

'There's much poverty in Buranda; these islands must be such a drain on resources. Surely oil would bring wealth and a better life for them?' Judy added, her eyes wide with interest.

Crystal huffed and stared harshly, showing her dislike of the woman. What would she know about such things?

Will answered, 'The islanders would not be the ones to reap the benefits. Plus, they do not want this. They are peaceful people. If they start drilling, it could pollute the waters, killing sea life. Fracking can release dangerous carbons. These people rely on fishing for survival.'

'What's fracking?' Crystal asked, without thinking, as everyone stared at her, surprised she did not know. Her face glowed at her ignorance.

'It's what they do to extract oil,' Stuart said. 'Basically, they inject fluid into the area to make the opening wider, to get the oil out. The fluid is mainly water and sand. But dangerous chemicals are mixed in as well, which can escape. And some companies have been caught dumping these into the sea, causing pollution.'

'Until now, it has just been a political argument,' Will continued. 'Now, it seems Carbombya has attacked Buranda, and war has been announced. Of course, I'm guessing the world will be told it has started for another reason and much propaganda used to cover the real reason,' Will added after seeing the concern on their faces. 'I wouldn't think this will affect us though. I'm sure they will allow our release from the island back to the mainland so we can go home. They would not want to drag other countries into this for fear of retribution.'

'They've just dropped bombs on tourists!' Stuart pointed out.

'How do you know all this, Will?' asked Crystal, trying to absorb the information.

'Because I do!' the tone of his voice suggesting she be quiet.

'More likely he is involved somewhere along the line. I mean, what were those business meetings about?' Stuart accused Will, as his know-all attitude was beginning to annoy him.

Judy elbowed her husband to stop him.

'What's that supposed to mean?' Will bristled and stood up, his chair falling behind him.

'Stop it!' Judy shouted. 'We need to pull together, not argue.'

Will picked up his chair and sat down again, but the two men glared at each other.

Crystal sloped away and went for a walk around the camp. The voices began to dim in the background. She went to the pool edge and peered down at the bay. It was crawling with soldiers. Burned debris bobbed on the ocean's soft waves. Everywhere looked black and sooty, no longer a buzz of people and islanders. The little shops and hotels were now piles of rubble. She felt sad and dismal, wondering if people were under them.

The silence was broken as a deafening explosion shook the rocks, which began to fall again. Crystal threw herself to the ground in fear; she could hear screams from their group. Another mushroom of smoke rose somewhere in the hills and birds began to squark again wildly and in panic. More gunfire echoed; it was hard to tell where from. It seemed the war was now in the hills and the harbour.

The group, except Crystal, sat around the table all day waiting for Garson. By late afternoon, it was clear no one was coming to rescue them. There were a few more small explosions, but everywhere was quiet. They met in the tree house in the evening and sat in a gloomy, depressed silence. Someone had lit the lanterns so they could at least see in the darkness. The area looked peaceful and serene; no one would have imagined the horror surrounding them.

Geoff loaded the tables with wine and beer so they could at least drown out the bleakness of their situation.

'What now?' Will said, breaking the heavy silence.

'You're the one with all the answers!' Stuart snapped aggressively.

Will threw him a look of distaste and everyone fell silent again.

'What if we do what Aaron said, head for another coastline? We might find a boat there,' Sonya suggested.

'And who is going to sail it to the mainland? It's miles away!' Fiona, one of the guests, snapped.

'It's not a bad idea,' Stuart smiled at Sonya.

'But who is going to sail it?' Fiona repeated.

33

'Has anyone any sailing skills?' Geoff asked, hopefully.

No one responded, lost in their own thoughts of ways to solve their situation.

'At least here we have food and water for a while,' Geoff finished, trying to find something optimistic.

'I think Sonya and Aaron are right; we head for another coastline. There must be islanders who will take us to the mainland if we pay well. Let's go tomorrow, either early morning or late afternoon when it isn't so hot,' Will suggested.

'I think late afternoon,' Geoff agreed. 'We need to prepare. We must take water and sort baggage, so we aren't carrying too much. The rest of our stuff will have to stay here.'

'But I've presents for the grandchildren,' Pat, Geoff's wife, objected. 'I can't just leave them.'

'You've got to be practical, love. We can only carry a little. Under the circumstances, the grandkids will understand. It may be a long walk. We've no map, so aren't sure. It will be hard enough without carrying a heavy load.'

Pat nodded sadly in agreement.

When Geoff was talking to Will, she whispered to Sonya and Crystal, 'I'm not leaving anything behind! Especially not for them skumbags to get their hands on my stuff!'

The girls giggled.

The next day, Crystal woke with a thumping head, having drunk too much wine. Not fancying a long walk with a hangover, she fumbled in her case for her costume, figuring a swim might help.

Stuart was already in the water. 'You're up early!' he called.

'My head's thumping,' she confessed, lowering herself into the coolness with a slight gasp. 'I figured a coffee and swim would ease the problem.'

He laughed and waded over to her. 'You're a very beautiful lady.'

The warmth of his eyes caused her stomach to flip as she blushed and demurely lowered her gaze. Crystal had been told this many times by men. But coming from Stuart, it meant much.

'I'm sorry Will was rude to you,' she apologised.

'What are you doing with him anyway?' he blurted out. 'He's old enough to be your father! A beautiful woman like you needs to be loved properly, not by some flabby old man.'

Crystal put her hand on Stuart's. She leaned forward, finding his lips with her own. For a few seconds, he returned the passion, before pushing her away.

'I love my wife,' he told her gently.

Crystal was mortified as she shrank away. Seeing her hurt, he added, 'If I wasn't married, though…'

Feeling a presence, they both turned, shocked to see Will standing behind them. The look on his face was thunderous and deadly.

'Get out!' he hissed at Crystal through gritted teeth.

Shocked at his temper, she hurried from the water in an instant.

Stuart also leaped from the pool. 'Leave her alone!' he snarled.

Will brought back his fist and thumped it into his face. Knocking him off balance, Stuart splashed back into the pool. Grabbing Crystal's arm, Will dragged her roughly back to the yurt and unceremoniously threw her inside.

'Will, please!' she cried in fright.

'You, Crystal, are a spoilt, nasty, selfish little bitch! I've done nothing but look after you and try to make you happy. I've even taken in your whining, miserable mother. But nothing is ever good enough, is it? All you have ever done is take me for granted and use me. Well, you listen here. When we get home, we are finished! You and your mother are out on the streets. How dare you treat me like that!'

'But… Will… Please…I…'

'You nothing! We're finished! Do you hear me? FINISHED!' he roared, turning to walk out of the door.

Crystal had never seen him this angry before; she was frightened.

'I'm pregnant,' she called, pathetically.

Will stopped and slowly turned back; the anger diminished and was replaced by tears that bulged behind his eyes.

'Ten weeks,' she breathed before he could ask.

'Why didn't you tell me?' his mind darting from one question to another.

'I wanted to get my head around it first. I thought it was too soon for me to be a mum. It was so unexpected and not planned.'

'I need to think.' He walked away, heading towards the path that led out of the camp.

Crystal threw herself onto the bed and curled herself into a ball. How much had Will heard of the conversation with Stuart? Now, she would have no choice but to keep the baby. She remained in the yurt for the rest of the day, not daring to go outside and bump into Will or Stuart. She could not face them.

The rest of the group sat around the table, feeling some comfort in being united. They clarified plans to leave in the late afternoon as soon as the sun dropped slightly. It was far too hot at that moment. They had prepared their baggage, which was minimised to one case between the couples.

'It's still too much,' Geoff said, shaking his head. 'We've not even loaded water or food yet.'

'I'm not leaving anymore behind!' Pat's eyes blazed, daring him to argue.

Knowing he was beaten, Geoff said no more.

'Stuart fell by the pool,' Judy quickly changed the subject, as the swell on his cheek was rather red and ugly.

No one had asked, but the questioning stares made it clear they were curious. Joining the group, Will said nothing about the earlier incident. Having calmed himself slightly, he would soon find Crystal; they needed to talk. But first, he would let her stew. The conversation between his wife and Stuart had hurt him deeply.

It was late morning; while revising their plans, a vehicle rumbling up the road could be heard. Relief flooded, as they were sure to be rescued at last and they would be saved from the long, arduous walk. Staring towards the road bend, they waited in anticipation. Tomorrow was their flight day. All of them just longed to be home and out of the horror of the war. When the vehicle appeared, they were horrified to see it was a lorry packed with enemy soldiers. They jumped down and pointed their guns at the small group.

'Please,' Will said, stepping forward. 'We're holidaymakers waiting to go. Can you help us?'

An officer walked forward, thankfully speaking English. 'How many of you?' he asked.

'Nine… Eight. There was a staff member, but he disappeared yesterday,' Will thought quickly and lied, not knowing why he had excluded his wife from the number. 'We don't know what's happening,' he added.

'Stay here,' the officer waved his gun, indicating they sat.

They did, silently, not wanting to argue and antagonise the military.

The officer flicked his head at his men and a few went off, guns pointing, to check for other people.

'You American?' The officer asked after they departed.

'English,' Will replied. His voice was surprisingly calm.

Crystal, hearing the lorry, suddenly felt panicky after the bombing. She feared the soldiers with their hard faces and cold, dead eyes that held no emotion. Thinking quickly, she darted from the yurt and climbed into the storage area below the wooden platform. It was dusty and stuffy, as her breath came in small gasps and her heart thumped.

Not finding anyone else in the camp, the soldiers began reappearing, each shaking their head to indicate no more people. The officer spoke to one of the men. Then, made to leave, leaving four behind, pointing guns at the terrified group.

Will jumped up and ran after the officer. 'Please,' he shouted, 'can…'

His words were lost as one soldier jabbed the butt of his gun into his stomach. He staggered backward, more from shock than pain, although it did hurt.

'Sit!' The soldier yelled.

The officer did not glance back as he ignored Will and climbed into the lorry. They left, continuing up the road.

'What shall we do?' whispered Judy to Will once he sat back at the table.

'No talk!' the soldier yelled again.

One of them left and went into the kitchen. Soon, he appeared and threw cans of cold beer at each of his associates.

Will asked if they could have some water.

'You sit!' the soldier shouted angrily.

Two hours later, the lorry appeared back from the road. The soldiers stood together, speaking quietly. The group strained their ears to listen, which was pointless as none spoke the language.

A decision was made. Four shovels and a pickaxe were taken from the back of the lorry and handed to the men of the party. They were led away, leaving the rest in more fear and speculation.

The lorry left again, this time leaving six soldiers behind.

'W… w…hats happening?' Judy dared to ask the soldier who was left to guard them.

He stared blankly and did not respond. The sun was at its highest and sweat ran down their faces. The thirst sucked their throats dry. It was sometime later when a voice called to the soldier guarding them. He flicked his gun in the direction of where the men had gone. The little group reluctantly got to their feet and began to walk.

'They're going to kill us!' Sonya hissed.

'Don't be silly!' snapped Judy. But she feared it was true. Her head buzzed; she could not think properly.

When they reached the men, the terror in their eyes confirmed it was true. They stood by a long pit, which they had painstakingly dug into the dusty, dry ground. The heap of dirt by its side had the now redundant shovels standing in.

Pat began to scream hysterically but stopped rapidly as a soldier crashed his gun into her jaw, knocking her from her feet. Her husband and Stuart helped her up as blood ran from her mouth and broken teeth. Will's eyes glistened with sadness from unshed tears. He would never see his baby born or hold it. He looked drawn and filthy as dirt had clung to sweat. They dutifully and bravely stood along the edge of the hole with their backs to it. Arron fell to his knees and began to beg the guard, who looked with distaste at his weakness. The soldiers lifted their guns and began to fire. The shots echoed around the cliffs as each fell, with a dull thud backward into the grave.

Crystal trembled and cried out when she heard Pat's agonising scream and then again when she heard the shots, guessing the fate of the party. She pulled her hands over her ears to block out the blackness that descended over her life. Her friends, Sonya and Stuart and her lovely Will, who, until that point, she had not realised the feelings she had for him. It was too late; she had caused him so much hurt. He must have died believing she did not love him.

It was dark when she woke from a murky stupor, not knowing where she was. The thick blackness was engulfing as reality hit her thumping head. Crystal decided she was dead and encased in a coffin. She remembered the gunshots. Will and the group were dead and she was alone. There was no noise; the soldiers must have gone. Hysteria rose inside of her and she felt the scream bubbling through her body as she fought to control it. Images of a large jug of cool water dominated her mind as the thirst was overwhelming. Never in her life had she felt so dry. Cramp forced her to move her aching limbs. She scrambled out of the storage cupboard. It was so dark that not even her hands were visible. The banana-shaped moon only offered a slight glow. The lanterns in the trees were not alight, but there was a blaze illuminating the tree house.

Crystal could hear the soldiers laughing and chatting - they were still there. Stumbling, she groped along the edge of the yurt with her arms outstretched. Reaching the front, she gingerly felt for the steps with her foot before silently sliding open the patio door. Inside was just as dark; not daring to turn on a light, Crystal grappled for the fridge. The small bulb sparked as she eagerly grabbed a bottle of water. As the coolness flooded her throat, it was the best drink she had ever tasted. Looking around, the faint light showed the place to be ransacked. Their clothes and belongings were strewn across the floor. The wardrobe was pulled over in eagerness to find valuables.

Figuring the soldiers were unlikely to come to the yurt, Crystal first noted the direction of the bed before closing the fridge. Flopping onto it, she lay there, not knowing what to do. The enormity of what had happened was too much to digest.

After a few fitful dozes, she opened her eyes with a start. Daylight was beginning to break. Her mind was clogged and buzzed with the effort to think.

Chapter Four

Peering out of the yurt door, Crystal strained to see if any soldiers were about. All was quiet, so gingerly, she stepped outside, her heart racing and palms sweating with fear. A noise nearby caused her legs to almost give way. She held her breath, but it seemed to be a creature of some sort scuttling through the dirt. Crystal realised she had forgotten to take water, so returning she grabbed two bottles. Then, squashing herself back outside the tent, she attempted to study the area's safety. Another noise sounded. Without hesitation, Crystal opened the doorway to the storage cupboard and darted inside. She carefully eased the door closed just as someone appeared before her. Holding her breath again and screwing her eyes shut, not knowing what else to do, she began to pray. The soldier walked away and called to his colleagues, who obviously shared some banter with him.

The day ticked slowly and painfully past. It was terribly hot and stuffy, as Crystal stayed squashed there. All sorts of odd items were stored around her: outside chairs, tables, and some disused furniture. By now, she had drunk her water and was thirsty once again, berating herself for not grabbing more. She was also ravenously hungry and desperately tired. Curling herself into another ball, she fell asleep.

The rattling sound of a lorry along the road woke Crystal sometime later. The soldiers made a lot of noise as they all seemed to be shouting at once. At last, they may leave the site. But they didn't; she could see through the wood slats they had parked up. Many more climbed down from the lorry. They seemed to be having a party as crates of beer, bottles of spirit, and boxes were unloaded. They had obviously decided to make a camp there, as items were carried to a room near the kitchen.

Footsteps on the floor above woke her again from dozing. The squeak of bed springs told her someone would sleep there the night. Crystal could not believe her bad luck. It was dark again, and her body was cramped, stiff, and sore. Her head thumped painfully as dehydration had now sucked the fluid from her body. There was no way she would survive another day without water. Quietly, pushing open the door, a crack, Crystal peered into the darkness. This time, there was light from both the kitchen and the tree house. Crawling on hands and knees, she made her way to the back, of the camp, away from where the soldiers were situated. To the right was the next yurt. Finding her way to the canvas, she groped for the storage cupboard, hoping no one had taken up residence in that yurt, too. Slowly and carefully pulling open the door, she cringed, as even on the dirt, the noise seemed to echo around the site, but it was probably more her heart thumping in her ears than the creaky door. Crawling into the hole to allow time to assess the situation, her leg caught something, and the toppling noise caused a scuttling nearby. She stifled a scream by clamping her hand over her mouth. There was no movement above, so there was hope that no one was there. Did she have the nerve to look? The constant image of a long, cool drink drove her to venture out. Scrabbling up the stairs to the door, she pulled it a crack and peered inside. The light was so dim that it was hard to tell, but there did not seem to be anyone there. Quickly grabbing the only bottle of water from the fridge and an uneaten snack bar, she ran back to her bolt hole.

The next day, the sun seemed hotter than she had known since being on the island. Crystal was trembling and almost delirious from hunger and thirst. Her stomach ached, and she felt faint. Falling into a deep sleep, her dreams were vivid, full of blood, with Will crying, holding his hand out to her, gore dripping down his face. Noises nearby caused her to wake; her eyes were heavy and swollen. She did not want to open them fully. Maybe death would have been easier than the torture she was suffering, alone and frightened, not knowing what to do. She had to pull herself together and live. Deciding it was about mid-morning, Crystal dared to open the door a crack. The camp was quiet, but the lorry had not moved. Carefully, she crawled out and ran back to her own yurt. No noise came from inside, so bravely, she pulled open the door and went in. Grabbing eagerly at the water bottles, she drank one. It went down well, as she relished the coolness of it in her swollen throat.

Stepping out of the shorts and pulling off her t-shirt, Crystal quickly replaced them with a loose top and cotton trousers. She pushed her dirty clothes under the bed before scooping up a few practical items, considering sunscreen, a sheet useful, and the last of the snack bars, still uneaten. Greedily eating two caused her to gag because of the sudden food in her empty stomach, making her cry out.

There were footsteps on the wooden stairs outside. Crystal darted into the bathroom, beads of sweat from the panic wetting her top lip and hands. There was nowhere to hide except the shower. Would the soldier notice the disturbance inside the yurt? Particularly the sheet missing from the bed and her bundle of items in a heap? Sickness rose in her stomach as she visualised a bullet being blasted into her body. Would it hurt? Her breath and pounding head were so loud in her ears that he must be able to hear it.

The soldier clonked around the area, seeming to push things around, maybe looking for something. His heavy boots vibrated the floor, and the bathroom door handle was being pushed down. Thankfully, he was distracted as another man's voice spoke. They began to talk, and then one of them laughed. The voices then left their boots heavy on the stairs outside.

Crystal ran from the bathroom, found a carrier bag, and stuffed the items inside. Quickly leaving the hut, she crawled safely back under the yurt. She knew Will had hidden their flight bag under there, but at that moment, she could not see it in the dim light. Inside were their passports and some hidden money for emergencies.

It was another long night trying to sleep with the sheet pulled over her. Whenever she closed her eyes, the images of bodies came out of the darkness, jolting her awake again.

Something brushed her hand in the early hours and again, she stifled a scream. Realising it was a cat and not a rat, she relaxed a bit. The cat cuddled onto her sheet with her. Its warmth was strangely comforting, as she raised her hand and petted it. The cat began to purr contentedly. Its large stomach suggested it was heavily pregnant. Crystal realised it was the tabby she had seen scrounging around the camp. Guilt flooded her for not dropping a morsel for the desperate mum-to-be. Now, knowing what hunger was like - it was her payback.

At first light, she awoke with her head slightly less painful after the amount of water the day before. How she longed for a cup of coffee. The cat, rubbed around her, looking eagerly at the water. Cupping her hand, Crystal poured some into her palm. The cat lapped and purred gratefully, its rough tongue tickling her palm. Its stomach was huge. It looked ready to produce very soon.

'Sorry, I've no food for you,' Crystal whispered to the sad, desperate eyes.

Feeling something crawling up her leg, she saw one of the cave spiders making its way to the edge of her trousers. Yelping without thinking, she widened her eyes in horror at her stupidity. Seeing the spider, the cat sprang, killing the intruder in seconds.

No one seemed to have heard her, so she bravely pushed at the cupboard door, allowing a beam of dim morning light to flood in. The bag was there, to one side, a lump of wood on top to hide it. Inside were the money and passports. Crystal wondered if she could reach the kitchen without being seen; it was that or starve.

The camp was quiet at that moment, guessing soldiers rose early, if she was going, it had to be now. Scuttling out of the hidey-hole, Crystal bolted silently and carefully to the other side of the retreat. A soldier was standing at the edge of the hill overlooking the bay. Another was at the entrance of the camp. It would be difficult to get into the kitchen without being seen. The guard, obviously watching for approaching enemy, walked a little up the trail. It gave her enough time to run for the doorway. In an instant, she was inside, with the door closed behind her.

The cupboards and fridge were packed with food. Crystal grabbed a cooked chicken and some cheese. Finding a loaf of bread, she filled a bag, adding tins that would open without an opener.

'So much for home-cooked organic,' she whispered, grateful the owner had lied about the cuisine.

Waiting for the guard to turn away from her direction, she bolted as quickly and quietly as possible.

Once safely inside the cupboard, Crystal broke the chicken into pieces and gave the cat breakfast. It scoffed, choking on the food, as its body shook with the effort. At the same time, Crystal ripped off some bread, wrapped a lump of cheese in it and gobbled at her sandwich, gulping it down with water. It was the best food she had ever tasted. Rations needed eking out so there was no more food for a while.

The soldiers left late in the afternoon that day, leaving just two behind. They loaded some weapons onto the lorry before disappearing down the hilly path. Crystal wiggled out to watch them go, her head bobbing from around the corner of the hut, trying to see the location of the remaining soldiers. They obviously would be back, but she was partially safe for now. The two remaining guarded the entrance, making access to the kitchen difficult.

Crystal made for the tree house to gather as many soft drinks as possible instead. Thankfully, she was back at the yurt when the two soldiers, obviously bored with guard duty, headed for the bar. Luck was on her side, dragging her suitcase to the kitchen; she began filling it with more tins of food, water, and anything useful. After, she ran from one hut to another to scavenge for any useful item. There was little left after the soldiers pillaging. In one, she found a pen knife and took a blanket. More bottles of water filled the suitcase. As a treat, she made a welcome cup of coffee, which made her feel sick.

The strange rancid smell turned out to be the bodies beginning to rot. Crystal gagged, sickened by the realisation, and more so when a group of dogs appeared and jumped into the pit. Quickly gathering her meagre belongings, Crystal began to leave. As she walked away, the pregnant cat appeared and began to follow.

'Shoo!' she shouted.

It looked alarmed and hurt, as it turned and began to skulk, dejectedly, back to the retreat. Crystal felt terrible. Dropping her case handle, she crouched and called to the cat. It looked delighted and rushed back to rub around her legs. She picked up the case and headed off, keeping well clear of the road in case the soldiers returned, the cat following closely.

It was safer to head along and further up, than down the hill. Soon, the heat became unbearable to walk in. The cat swished her tail against the onslaught of flies that crawled over her. In the short distance were two of the cubed buildings. They looked derelict, but they should offer some shade. Her assumption was right; inside, the first was overgrown with brambles. The second was slightly more habitable. There was a stone staircase leading to a room above. How could people live in such miserable, small places, Crystal wondered, looking around the tiny, dismal bedroom. There was no bathroom or toilet. Half of the roof was still intact, offering a small shade.

They both sat on the dusty floor, lying out the blanket. The cat stretched herself out and began to purr, seeming to appreciate the slight comfort. At least from upstairs, Crystal could see along the main road from the small window.

After feeding the cat a tin of Tuna, she drank a cold can of soup. They both had some water and lay down for a rest.

Once the sun dropped, the dense blackness fell like a blanket over the island. The trees and bushes came alive with wild animals. The sounds were deafening as they echoed around the blackness. Some of the movements sounded like large creatures. Crystal was terrified, wondering if bears or wild cats lived on the island. A few times, the cat growled and flattened her ears against her head making the noises more sinister and frightening as they rippled in the air. A slight breeze cooled the humid temperature, causing goosebumps on Crystal's skin.

The cat, whom she began to call Puss-Puss, or just Puss, for short, did not seem too bothered, apart from the odd growl; she seemed contented, purring gently to ease her fear.

'Who's looking after who?' Crystal smiled, caressing the soft fur, grateful for the company, as she was terrified and had never felt so alone. How she missed her mum, dad, and even Will, who had always protected her.

Sometime in the night, it began to storm, the first since being on the island. Will had told her a rainy season was due and that it went on for months. A loud crack of thunder scared her so much that she pulled her arms over her head, thinking it was an explosion nearby. Within minutes, the rain came crashing down in bucket loads. Both were soon drenched, freezing, and miserable.

For the first time since the shooting, Crystal began to cry and then howl like a wounded animal, the thunderous rain diluting the sound. Puss, bedraggled, pushed her wet body into her, trying to offer comfort. This made Crystal feel worse, having previously been so mean to cats. Now, one was trying to look after her, which caused her to cry harder. She felt no better after the tears subsided, being drenched, miserable, and unsure of what to do.

After a terrible night, the sun burst through the clouds, which soon dispersed, leaving a clear blue sky. Puss and Crystal managed to dry themselves in the heat. There was nowhere else to go but to stay there.

Early in the afternoon, the cat lay down and pushed her first kitten into the world. Crystal had no idea what to do as she watched helplessly. She gave Puss useless words of encouragement as she strained to push forward the new life. The second came an hour later, and the third two hours after. The last kitten appeared as the sun sank again, promising a long, miserable night ahead.

As it was, Crystal, exhausted, slept peacefully and did not wake until the sun was so unbearably hot it forced her eyes to open. Sweat wetted her body, and she smelt terrible.

It was amazing to find Puss had six kittens now: three black, one grey, and two little gingers. Sadly, two of the black ones were dead. Crystal took them away and tried her best to bury them under a bush, brushing leaves and earth over the shallow grave. The cat seemed to cope well with the loss as she washed and purred to the remaining brood.

'Thank goodness humans don't have litters of babies,' Crystal stroked the silky fur while Puss glowed and looked proud.

The next few days brought more scorching heat, causing her to long for a wet, cold, English winter day. Red, sore lumps covered her legs and arms as bugs fed without mercy. As she tore at them constantly, blood dripped from the wounds, encouraging more bugs to feed. Her hair hung in greasy tails, causing her scalp and neck to itch.

Random explosions and gunfire could be heard in the distance. At regular intervals, the smell of burning wafted into the little house.

Puss's ears pricked in the early afternoon on the second day. She was staring towards the road.

Alarmed, Crystal ran to the window. 'What is it, Puss?'

The cat looked terrified. With her ears flattened, she began moving the kittens to the corner of the room, shrinking into the brickwork and pulling the babies close to her stomach, hiding them with her paws.

Soon, a rumble of lorries could be heard, bumping along the road. Crystal crouched in the corner with Puss, not knowing what else to do. Lowering her head, she began to pray, again asking God to protect her and promising from now on that she would be a good person if he did. It worked, as the lorries bumped past without stopping. Running to the window, Crystal watched until they disappeared around a bend. They were safe for now. A few hours later, the sound of gunfire and explosions could be heard once again, indicating more death and destruction.

Despite rationing food and water, there was none left after three days. Crystal had no choice but to return to the retreat and try to find some. Leaving Puss behind with her brood and the suitcase, she set off back to the camp, desperately hoping the lorries that had passed were the soldiers moving on from the retreat.

She dodged behind some brambles when the site was close and studied the area. There was no sign of soldiers. Not even any guarding the area, so she ventured forward. The gentle breeze rippled over her sweating skin also brought the stench of rotting flesh. Crystal gagged a few times, trying to keep hold of her limited stomach contents. She found another case in one of the yurts and filled it again from the kitchen and the tree house. The food source was getting low with what the soldiers had eaten. Going back to the kitchen, Crystal raided the freezer, knowing the food would not last long, but needs must. Surprisingly, in a top cupboard was an old flask. Gratefully, she boiled the kettle and filled it with coffee and sugar, no longer worrying about her figure.

The sound of a lorry approaching could be heard just as Crystal was having one final look at the cupboards' contents. Panic-stricken, her eyes darted for a place to hide. The door was in clear view of the road. There was no way of running out without being seen. However, taking the chance, she darted around the back of the building with the precious case before the lorry pulled up outside.

Crystal was safely behind a large bush just in time. Her body shook with fear as she heard the chattering close by. Some of the soldiers also began gagging at the smell of rotting bodies. Two of them took shovels and, thankfully, went to cover the grave.

Crystal was not religious but tried to say some words, hoping Will and the rest of the group's souls were now free. She felt wretched that their lives were taken in such a cruel brutal way.

Chapter Five

Crystal backed away, knowing she could never risk returning to the camp again. The case, full of tins and bottles, was clunky and heavy, requiring much effort to drag it over bumpy ground. The journey back to the cube house was painfully slow.

Puss purred when she spotted her. Not leaving her babies, she stared into Crystal's eyes as if begging for something.

'It's OK, I got you food too,' she smiled, opening a tin of some sort of fish.

But it wasn't the food Puss wanted. Another of the kittens had died. Crystal felt sad; lifted the little body and took it to join its dead siblings. After, she poured a precious coffee into the mug she had thought to bring.

'We can't stay here, Puss. We'll have to move on soon. We need to find supplies elsewhere.'

Two days later, they were ready to leave after packing the larger of the two cases with food and water. Puss looked worried as Crystal carefully lifted the kittens onto the load, already cushioned by the sheet and blanket.

'I've got no choice, Puss,' she said to the large grief-stricken eyes.

They set off mid-morning along the dirt track. Again, the journey was slow and difficult with the heavy case. Many a time, she tore her skin on brambles, causing it to bleed. Along with the insect bites, her body stung and ached. Never would she take luxury for granted again.

The path ahead looked dismal and lonely. Often, when the landscape became more open, smoke could be seen, bellowing from distant areas. Guessing, it was where soldiers were destroying villages and people; the view was sickening. What were once beautiful, scenic hills now seemed vicious demons, piercing the skyline and the soft peaks like daggers, poking into hell.

Puss suddenly ran into a bush; the sky darkened, and rain thundered. The bucket-sized droplets bounced on the dry ground like thousands of balls released from heaven. Crystal was drenched and, without preparing, found no nearby shelter.

Within minutes, the rain turned off, and the sun turned on. It was as if the fall never happened. Crystal would think she'd imagined it if not for the enormous puddles in dips or the large bulbs of water that fell from trees, her body, and her hair.

'What the hell just happened?' she asked Puss, who skulked out from the nearby bush. 'You knew it was coming, didn't you? Next time you run, I do too,' she laughed.

They continued the journey, Puss's eyes glued to the case, which she sniffed at every pause. Going further up the steep hill seemed silly as the land panned out into bleakness, but Crystal did not know what else to do.

By lunchtime, it was too hot to go any further. She found a slight clearing, with shade under some trees, and stopped. Puss was grateful to be reunited with her babies. She washed them repeatedly as they suckled greedily on her, padding their tiny paws on their mum's tummy. The sun's heat had long since lapped away the puddles. Crystal laid the blanket on the dusty ground and fed Puss a tin of fish, which she scoffed in seconds. Opening another, which seemed to be soup, she sniffed the contents and wrinkled her nose. It did not smell very appetising, but it was that or starve. After consuming the contents, they lay and dozed under the meagre shade. Puss was pleased to have her brood close to her tummy, where she could guard them closely.

When the sun began to sink a little, Crystal carefully packed the kittens into the case, and they moved on. All that lay in front was dust, a few clusters of vegetation, and stones of all sizes. Some were large, requiring careful coordination to clamber over, which was difficult with the case containing kittens. A few times, little squarks of protest came from inside, causing Puss to throw looks of anxiety.

'Sorry!' Crystal grimaced with guilt.

Other stones dug into her canvas shoes, causing her to wince with pain. They were already becoming raggy and filthy. There was no evidence of the rain that had fallen so violently. The landscape was desolate and dry, with no sign of life ahead. That night they spent in another clearing Crystal managed to find before the dense blackness sunk over them. Never in her life had she experienced such darkness. Although it was too dangerous to carry on, she felt exposed and vulnerable, sleeping in the open. She lay on her back, willing sleep to come. Puss and her babies cuddled next to her, their lives offering a small comfort. Not that they could do much to fight off intruders, but Crystal did not feel so lonely and scared.

The sky became a blaze with winky stars. They were incredibly intense, without the lights of the earth diluting them. As a distraction to the jazz groups of bush noises that were becoming louder and closer, she wondered, which were planets amongst the powerful glows? The darkness heightened the noises as the creatures prowled around. Crystal contemplated that leaving the derelict house was a mistake. All night, she lay, eyes wide, waiting for what sounded like dinosaurs to flatten them.

In the distance, the gunfire and more explosions thundered, destroying any human left alive except soldiers. Survival was impossible; it was only a matter of time before she was discovered and shot, too. Either that or the now infecting wounds, dust path, or starvation would get her. It was the first time she had thought about the growing life inside her belly. Was that dead, too? She was surprised at the pain in her heart at the thought. There had been no evidence of a miscarriage. So, there was a chance it was still growing.

The next day, another kitten was dead, and Crystal, again, put the body under a bush.

'I'm so sorry, Puss,' she told the pitiful cat, who seemed to be counting the few babies left.

Determined not to give up, they continued along the path, which, at that moment, was climbing higher and higher up the steep incline. Once exhaustion had taken its toll, the terrain became kind, and the path petered out into a large area of flat ground.

After an hour or so, Crystal noticed they were heading downwards, and there was an opening in the rocks where a view of the sea burst through. She longed to jump into the cool water and be carefree again. Venturing nearer, no longer noticing the brambles ripping at her, she sat in the gap, staring into the vast, endless ocean. Nothing was in her mind but blankness as the gentle waves embraced the coastline. They showed no sign of the ugliness that lay behind, as they eased her mind of some of the misery, just for those moments.

Puss nudged her hand and let out a tremendous howl.

'Is it feed time?' Crystal stroked the silky coat before reuniting the cat with the remaining kittens.

In the far distance, along the rocky face, she focused on something shimmering. Squinting her eyes to see clearer, it looked like villas, with blue oblong swimming pools at the front. Maybe they were owned by holidaymakers. Were people still there? They were well hidden; perhaps they had been safe from the soldiers. Crystal could just make out the white brickwork under a grey slate roof. That is where she would head for; it seemed a long way away, but at least it was a destination. It was a big decision to approach, but it was worth taking the chance.

'What do you think, Puss? There may be people who will help. They might have lots of food and water. And maybe a moored boat to take us to the mainland so I can get home.'

Puss looked intently into her eyes and mewed.

'That's settled then,' Crystal smiled and stroked the soft coat, feeling guilty because Puss would be left behind if it were true.

The villas were located much further down the cliff face than they were. Heading in that direction was hazardous and getting there meant climbing further up before down again. The case, every so often, needed the wheels freed from tangles of branches and stones. This caused the kittens to squeak and Puss to become fretful. There must be a path down or a road, but it wasn't apparent. Bursting out to the edge once again, now lower down, a calm, beautiful beach was visible. Tufts of green grass poked around sandy rocks, dotted along the yellowy-white sand. Another time, this setting would be idyllic.

The pathway suddenly twisted away from the coast towards the hills again. Around the next bend, the ground spanned out to more rocks and, despite the rain, shrivelled scrubs. At the farthest point where the land became flatter was a house. Drawing closer, it appeared to be a farm. Chickens clucked and scratched at the ground. Two goats were tethered behind a back wall. A tied dog lay on the ground in front of the house, making it impossible to pass without being seen.

Crystal sunk behind an area of growth to hide, too scared to go further. If the dog barked, she was in trouble. It appeared to be asleep, as it didn't move. There was no sign of humans, so leaving the case hidden, she ventured nearer after opening the zip so Puss could feed the squawking babies. Darting to the next bush, she hid and watched again. Puss was mewing behind her, afraid to be left. Noting the back door was closed, Crystal edged closer to look through a window into a ransacked kitchen. The body of a woman was slumped on the floor, blood surrounding her head.

There was a small barn on the far side of the house. The dog still had not moved; it appeared dead, too. Pulling the backdoor, it sprang open. Crystal slammed it closed again, deciding not to face the body of the woman or the smell of rotting flesh that burst from the opening. After carefully looking around, no one else seemed to be there. The chickens ran to the mesh on seeing her, despair evident in their small, beady eyes. The goats began pulling on their tethers. One's legs buckled, and it fell into a heap. None had food or water; with the heat, they would soon be dead. Feeling wretched for them, she looked for a tap. After giving the hens some water in a trough, she opened the mesh gate to free them. The goats drank eagerly from the refilled bucket. They seemed grateful once the tethers were untied. The lifeless dog lifted an eye and began to weakly whimper. Crystal returned to the tap and offered water to him. He did not have the strength to stand and drink. Under the black and white fur, the skin felt strangely hard. Dipping her hand in the water, she trickled it into the dog's mouth. Its dry tongue appeared and slowly began to lap. Feeling encouraged, she repeated it again. Untying the dog, she carried him to the barn to shade from the sun. Wetting a discarded cloth, she ran it over his coat before wrapping it around his neck. Finding more cloths, Crystal did the same for the goats. Nearby was a bag of grain, which she emptied onto the ground for the chickens. They pecked frantically. The goats looked unimpressed with the offering but made their way, on wobbly legs, to the barn and began chewing dolefully on a bale of hay. The dog had lifted his head and was eagerly lapping at the water. When he licked Crystal's hand in gratitude, she felt overwhelmed.

There was no choice but to face the house to see what food she could gather, and the thought sickened her. Putting this off for a while longer, she returned to the overgrowth to pick up Puss, the kittens, and the case. After leaving them in the barn, Crystal returned to the house and tried the front door. It was open, so she gingerly went inside. Two bodies of young children lay at sickening angles. One was on the stairs, and one was in the hallway. Dried blood splattered around their bodies. One child was around two years old, and the other was possibly four or five. Turning from the horror, sickness heaved in her stomach at the callous slaughter; she ran from the house, gasping lungful's of clear air. There was no way she wanted to find the husband of the family also dead.

Returning to the barn, Crystal gave the dog food from her precious collection. It wolfed it greedily and then threw it up again. The goats and chickens had now taken up residence alongside the dog. They stared hopefully, their eyes begging for help. Puss had her fur puffed and stood on tiptoe as she gawked wide-eyed at the animals, daring one to attack her babies.

The sound of a lorry approaching sparked Crystal into action. She quickly looked around for somewhere to hide. The barn was not safe. Grabbing the case in record time, she hid it under the straw. With the kittens grasped carefully, she ran for the safety of the overgrowth. Puss followed, and after standing on wobbly legs, so did the dog.

The insects no longer worried her, as a large green grasshopper crawled up her leg. They were less frightening than the soldiers. She brushed it away and continued to stare through the leaves. The soldiers stopped at the house, and two jumped out. One called to the others. She guessed it was to tell them they had already done their damage there. But they ventured forward again. She could hear the chickens squawking and the sound of the goats. Her tears fell when their bodies were flung onto the truck, their blood wetting the dry earth.

Once the lorry left, Crystal gathered her case, trying not to dwell on the fresh, bloody patches on the ground. It suddenly occurred to her that she had cried for the slaughtered animals but never shed a tear for Will.

The dog, too weak to walk, insisted on following, much to Puss's disgust, who arched her back again and puffed out her fur so the skinny white bone of her tail underneath was visible. The dog was too weak and sick to notice as its legs wobbled and gave way. He sunk to the floor, whimpering.

'I can't look after a dog as well as Puss and her kittens,' Crystal told him.

Ignoring her, he pushed himself along on his stomach to follow. Crystal relented, carried the dog to a clearing, and fed him more soup by dipping her fingers and allowing him to lap. He did greedily, whining each time for more.

'You need to do this slowly,' she told him.

Puss looked on, disgust creasing her face, before turning her attention to her kittens and ignoring the dog.

It was a dark, long night, but Crystal felt slightly less lonely with her now two companions cuddled into her. Eventually, Puss decided the dog was no threat and accepted its arrival gracefully.

By the morning, the last two kittens were dead. The cat looked mortified as she nudged at the bodies to encourage them to feed. She began washing them in an attempt to inject life back into the lifeless babies before letting out a heartbreaking howl.

'Oh, Puss!' Crystal sympathised, putting one hand on her stomach and the other stroke comfort into the cat.

Although slow and wobbly the next day, the dog was slightly stronger. After more soup and water, he stood ready to journey wherever they were going. He clung to the kindness shown, having known little in his life.

In the late morning, they heard the rumble of the lorry engine as they darted into some greenery not to be seen. It was the same lorry as it bumped its way back past. Crystal was thankful; they were no longer at risk of bumping into them along the way.

By late afternoon, the sky opened again, and water crashed to the ground. This time, Puss had been unprepared for the onslaught; her fur dripped, as did the dog's coat and Crystal's hair. The noise roared as the water bounced on the ground, hitting them like pellets for the second time. Taking shelter under an overhanging rock was pathetic, as the shots still flew at them. Still, the three flattened against the edge for protection.

'What the hell? There's just no warning,' she shouted loudly over the noise. Her companions looked mournful in agreement.

The three of them dripped and steamed the rest of the journey until dried by the sun, which insultingly popped out from behind black clouds.

The first villa's sparkling whiteness was welcoming after the gloom of the grey cube houses. It was securely locked, and, dismally, no one was there to help. It appeared untouched by the soldiers though. There was no way of breaking in, as the French doors were double-glazed. Even after kicking and then hitting with a rock, they would not break.

Crystal sat on her case and put her head into her hands despondently. The dog nudged her; its big sorrowful eyes looked weepy, making her laugh despite the dismal situation.

In her mind, inside were cupboards bursting with glorious food, where they could feast until their stomachs burst, a big bathtub, where she could wash herself, and a bed to sleep. How wonderful that would be. There must be a way, she figured.

There was another villa nearby, but that would be locked, too. In the end, she decided to try. The dog clearly could not go any further, and there was no way Crystal could carry him. Ultimately, there was no choice. She scooped him into her arms, grappling for the case handle, and they set off. Even that short distance was a struggle, as the skinny dog felt like carrying an elephant.

Once they arrived, Crystal, in her frustration, hit the window with a rock again. The sound echoed, and she bit her lip in anticipation of soldiers bursting out of somewhere close by. She waited a few minutes before whacking the glass again and then again. It was hopeless as the rock bounced, and shockwaves rippled painfully up her arm. It suddenly occurred to her that not all the windows were, probably, glazed. She headed to the next, then the next. Reaching a smaller obscured window, assuming it to be a toilet, she crashed the rock into it, and a crack appeared. With more hard hits, the glass shattered into minuscule pieces and crumpled. The window was small, and it took some manoeuvres to wiggle herself through the space, using the case as a stool. She scratched her legs on the jagged glass, but thankful for a toilet on the other side to step onto, she gained access.

Crystal swung open the front door. 'Enter my little furry friends.'

The two plodded dubiously in, sniffing at the air. Puss appeared to have forgotten her dead babies as she raised her front paws and sharpened them on the plush white sofa. Worse still, the dog lifted his back leg and weed up it, receiving a harsh stare from Puss.

Crystal opened the kitchen cupboards despondently. Apart from crockery and other kitchen paraphernalia, there was little in the way of food: a couple of tins, one peach and one pea, plus a packet of salad seasoning, were the only offerings. There was a jar of coffee, though, which she kissed. Turning on the electricity was an ordeal. Will had always dealt with such things; she had no clue. A cupboard in the kitchen had a boiler, so hot water was possible.

In the hallway, she found what seemed to be the electric meter. Flicking a red switch, the fridge buzzed to life. Crystal danced at her cleverness. The boiler was more of a challenge to get working. Luck was on her side when she found instructions in English in a kitchen drawer. She plopped on the sofa with a mug of black coffee and a tin of peaches to study them.

The ignition lit after a few swear words, and water could be heard filling and heating,

'A bath!' she breathed. Then she sang the words out loud, dancing again around the living room. This caused the dog to wag its tail and bounce around, thinking it was a game. Puss ran under the table in fright.

Chapter Six

Crystal searched the bathroom. There was not much in the way of toiletries, only some hair-covered soap, which she would have cringed at once. Now, she handled it like a precious lump of gold.

After putting two bowls of water on the floor for Puss and the dog, she made another coffee, which, although it made her feel slightly sick, was sipped like nectar.

As the dog and cat slurped at the water, Crystal lay back on the sofa, closed her eyes, and relished the luxury. She was so hungry that her tummy rumbled in protest of the coffee. Running into the toilet, with the broken window, the lot came up again.

The bath was incredible; the putrid smell of blood, dirt, and sweat that clung to her skin was washed away. The warmth of water soothed the sores and aches. The bath was so filthy that the bottom was no longer visible. Crystal ran it away and refilled it for a second time. Scrubbing at her hair, without shampoo and conditioner, was going to be frizzy and crinkled once it dried. It did not matter; it was just fantastic to be clean. Her body felt lighter and better than it had for a long time. Winding her hair in a towel and wrapped in a sheet, she warmed up soup and fed some to the dog.

Washing the torn, dirty garments was a challenge. The stains smeared, and the blood would not shift. Once dry, they were stiff and scratchy but did smell slightly better.

Puss wouldn't eat the soup, which was all that was left. Crystal painfully picked out pieces of meat and handed them to the cat, who sniffed suspiciously, hunger taking its toll, eventually ate. There were only three tins left of the supplies. She boiled water and let it cool, filling all the empty bottles to the brim.

The villa did not have much of any use, but it did have a bed. Fearing putting on a light to alert anyone, she remained in darkness that night. It was again a luxury to sleep in a bed with clean sheets. Puss and the dog, which she began to call Diesel after one of her favourite shops, slept with her. Again, she felt great comfort in their presence. Before going to sleep, Crystal hid her belongings and any evidence that she was there, just in case someone came by.

The morning light awoke her, and for a moment, she could not work out where she was. It was the best sleep she had had for some time. In the distance, gunfire crackled, and more random explosions sounded.

After feeding Diesel and Puss, Crystal sat at the kitchen table and drank coffee, wondering where to go or what to do. With little food, they would not survive long.

The villa would be a lovely holiday location under normal circumstances. On one side, it looked across the hills; they were serene and peaceful, with lush trees and coloured flowering bushes, which peeped out smiling faces of flowers, of pinks, yellows, and purples. On the other, the ocean edged with the sandy beach; the sun, hitting the water, shimmered invitingly. If it wasn't for the war and bloodshed, this would be a perfect place, she pondered, trying to block the horror of her trap.

The sun glistening on the swimming pool caught her attention. Would it hurt to swim? she wondered. Crystal pulled open the French doors and walked outside. Stripping off her clothes and dropping them in a heap, she lowered herself into the coolness. It was glorious as she swam underwater to the other side and back again.

Lifting her head, she could hear Diesel barking. Alarmed, Crystal pulled herself up to the pool's edge, and her heart almost flew from her chest. A soldier was standing looking down at her with a pointed gun. He waved the end, indicating for her to get out. The fear made her feel so cold that she began to shiver violently.

'Please. I've no clothes on,' she protested.

'Out!' the soldier looked angry and fierce as he waved his gun aggressively.

Not arguing, Crystal climbed from the pool, berating herself for her stupidity. The soldier pointed his gun at Diesel, who was still barking and made to fire.

'No!' she screamed and snapped at the dog to stop. He cowered and sank down, fear also clouding his eyes.

Shivering, Crystal tried vainly to cover her nakedness with her arms as the soldier studied her body. He waved his gun, directing her into the villa and up the stairs to the bedroom. She knew what was coming next as he threw her to the bed and dropped his trousers, sinking his body on top of her. This was nothing like a rape should be. She almost smiled at the thoughts flashing through her head, which was surprisingly calm. When you are being violated by a bulk of a soldier and going to die, it did not seem right to be assessing the moment instead of screaming hysterically. But Crystal had been through so much, and her mind no longer seemed to process as before. It did not seem to process at all. Inside was an empty blackness that just strove for survival. To her surprise, the soldier did not force himself on her after all. He slumped, his weight heavy and uncomfortable. She did not move while awaiting her fate; every thought of death whirled through her mind. How far she had come? It seemed criminal to die now, and what would Puss and Diesel do without her? The soldier rolled away. After doing up his trousers, he slumped into a chair. To Crystal's astonishment, he put his hands over his face and wept.

'Sorry,' he sobbed, using good English.

Pulling the sheet around her, Crystal sat up, surprised by the emotion. Soldiers always reminded her of robots programmed to kill. But this one seemed human.

'I thought you were going to rape me. Did you have issues with your… whatsit? Are you going to kill me now?'

'Get dressed!' he snapped.

'You speak good English.' She wondered why she was so composed and talking as though what had occurred, had not.

'I went to school there,' he told her, lifting away his hands so she could see his brown eyes.

'Are there lots of you?' she asked, wondering why he seemed alone.

'No. I'm going home. I don't want to be part of this bloodshed.' His voice was surprisingly gentle. 'I'm going,' he told her and made to leave.

'NO! Please don't leave me,' she cried urgently, knowing she sounded weak and needy.

Not seeming to hear, he carried on down the stairs. Tugging the sheet from the bed, she ran after him, tripping on the length.

'Please, I need help. I don't know what to do. Don't leave me.'

The soldier turned at the bottom and stared at her, not speaking. He was contemplating; she could see thoughts flickering in his eyes.

'I cannot help you,' he said, walking towards the door.

Crystal flew down the stairs and grabbed his jacket.

'I need help. I've no food and don't know what to do or where to go. I'll be killed if I stay here.

He was contemplating again, his eyes flashing with doubt. 'Get dressed!' he snapped.

Crystal ran to the pool and quickly pulled on her raggy clothes.

'Come,' he instructed and walked away, expecting her to follow.

Quickly shutting Diesel and Puss inside, she ran to catch up. They walked along a path leading to a street with more villas. Then, through an alley which led to another street and a small shop. The soldier broke the locked door with the butt of his gun and kicked it open. It sold all sorts of holiday fripperies, but also food.

'You're OK now. Just hide yourself at the villa, and you should be safe, ' he said, turning away.

'Where are you going?' Crystal asked.

'Home. To my family,' he said quietly, more to himself than to her. He marched off, disappearing in a labyrinth of alleys.

Crystal gathered a pizza from the freezer and meat for the animals. To her delight, there was a rail of summer clothes. She needed her case for a proper shop, but for now, the food was adequate.

Later that day, after they had eaten, Crystal returned to the shop, where she had a fantastic time grabbing much-needed goods from the shelves. There were even hairbrushes and scrunchies to keep it tidy. There was not much to choose from in the toiletry section, but there was shampoo, conditioner, and shower gel. The clothes rail was a disappointment as there was not much in her size. But she did find a tunic top and loose trousers. Dropping her own dishevelled clothes in a heap, she changed, feeling fantastic to be out of her torn, stained rags. Finally, she filled the case with food and left. They would survive for a while now. She had just reached the inside of the villa when the sky opened, and the rain fell like rocks thrown from heaven. This time, it went on for hours. After packing the food into the cupboards and fridge, Crystal watched the large droplets dancing on the concrete; the noise was almost musical. Large puddles formed, and the pool looked to overflow.

'You didn't get me that time!' she shouted at the rain, pleased she was dry and clean.

It was late that evening when the soldier appeared at the French doors. They sat in darkness, not daring to turn on a light. He scared Crystal half to death, his shadow silhouetted in the moonlight. After her heart stopped pounding, she asked if he was hungry, and he nodded, looking like a lost wet puppy. Glops of water fell from him, leaving a puddle on the floor.

She made him a sandwich by the dim fridge light and took it to him. He ate hungrily as though he had not eaten for days.

'Why did you come back?' she asked.

71

'Guilt,' he shrugged.

His name was Ayan; his school friends in England called him Ali for short.

'My name's Crystal,' she told him.

He gave the slightest, uninterested nod. That night, he slept on the sofa while she went to bed with Puss and Diesel. It was even more comforting to know someone could take charge.

Ayan spoke little the following day as she pottered about making breakfast. It was so good to eat and even have a choice.

'When do we leave?' Crystal asked, placing toast and orange juice in front of him. Marvelling, as she would never have dreamed of waiting on Will. He got his own breakfast, while she pretended stupidity of cooking. She could cook, as she had learned the basics at school. But she also learned never to admit this.

'The place is crawling with soldiers. It is dangerous out there.'

'I guess you could be shot for deserting by your own people?' she said flippantly and wished she hadn't as his eyes turned angry.

'I am not a coward!' he shouted, thumping his fist on the table. 'I do not like this war. It is wrong.'

'Of course. I'm sorry. I didn't mean to upset you.' Her voice sounded pathetic, but she was frightened he would leave her.

He calmed himself, 'It's OK. It's true. I'm in danger of being shot. We both are. So many Brits have been slaughtered, and Americans and Germans, just holidaymakers, murdered, and none left that I know of. Some could be hiding, as you were. Even my own people have been killed, children, old people, and women. Villages destroyed. Apart from soldiers, the island is almost empty. The army is using it as a base. I need to get my family away from here. That's if they are still alive.'

'But why did you join the army in the first place?' Crystal asked, feeling sickened at the thought that everyone was dead.

'We were lied to. The islanders have been wanting independence from Buranda for years. We were promised that if we joined the military in Cambombya, the Islands would be given over to our people. So many of us believed this and joined up, my brother, uncles and cousins, even young boys and older men. It was all lies. They wanted control of the Islands and began dropping bombs and destroying the people and villages. So many of us were shot trying to escape the army and get back to our families.' He fell quiet, his eyes full of trauma; it was clear he did not want to continue.

Crystal looked at her hands as she absorbed Ayan's information. 'Where will you take your family?'

'To another island. One where they will be safe.'

They remained silent after that. Both lost in their own thoughts.

Later that day, they returned to the supermarket and gathered food, which was practical to travel with, filling Ayan's rucksack and the case. Crystal marvelled that the shrubs and plant life seemed greener since the rain fell, as though they had a good wash. Puddles, this time, were not stolen by the sun, although they had shrunk.

'Tomorrow, we leave,' he told her.

Crystal nodded in agreement, anything not to be left alone again. That night, as she climbed the stairs. She turned towards the sofa. Ayan was already settled for the night, with Puss on top of him.

'You could share my bed?' she suggested, her face glowing hot with embarrassment, even more so when he did not answer or move.

It seemed like an eternity that she stood waiting for a reaction. In the dim evening light, all that could be seen was the sofa's silhouette. Crystal turned away from the heavy tension and went to the bedroom, where she could thankfully close the door on the humiliation. An hour later, she was still awake as the door opened, and Ayan's weight sunk onto the bed. He did not speak as he took Crystal in his arms. Their lovemaking was passionate and left her wanting more. She had never experienced anything like it, certainly not with Will. Ayan was not clumsy and awkward; he was experienced and seemed to know instinctively what would please her, and he did. She felt like a hussy when she woke him two hours later and asked for more. He laughed lightly and obliged for a third time in the morning. Crystal felt content, and despite the awful situation, a small part of her felt happy and safe.

'The animals stay here,' Ayan told Crystal when he noted her intention of taking them.

'NO! They stay, I stay!' she jutted her chin in determination, with her arms on her hips.

He shrugged and made to leave. Not used to not getting her own way, Crystal was at a loss for how to argue. She began pleading with him, which always worked with Will. But Ayan was different; there was no give, as his stubborn jaw was set and his eyes nonplused.

'They stay,' he said firmly.

'NO! I'll stay with them then,' she flopped on the sofa.

Ayan shrugged again and walked out of the door. Gathering Puss under her arm and calling Diesel, she grabbed the case of supplies and followed him. Ayan ignored her and kept walking; his pace quickened, so she ran to keep up.

They could hear a lorry rumbling along the road a short distance ahead. They dashed into the undergrowth until it had passed. It was filled with armed men. Not all had uniforms this time. Some looked elderly, while others were still boys, confirming what Ayan had told her. Once out of view, they carried on walking. Puss had been left to walk alone and agreeably followed with no objection. Diesel contented himself sniffing here and there and cocking his leg up random bushes on the way. Only a dribble of wee came out, which Crystal thought odd.

By midday, the sun was at its fullest. It was too hot to travel, so Ayan stopped, and Crystal followed him into the shady patch he found.

'My women would never disobey a man,' he said, distaste hardening his features.

'Could we make love again?' she asked, elated that she had won.

He laughed, and the harshness softened as warmth returned to his eyes, which she noted were stunning.

After lying side by side on the sheet she had packed, still naked, they dozed. The light breeze rippled their skin but did not help cool them. The stifling air felt like a hairdryer in their lungs. Thick clouds drifted over in minutes, and the cruel rain fell again in buckets. Crystal squealed as the water was freezing on her bare, hot skin.

Diesel and Puss seemed to laugh as they dashed under a bush just in time. Ayan quickly pulled his army jacket over them for protection, laughing at her squeals.

'The rain shows no mercy here,' he shouted over the roaring noise. As the sun began to sink, they continued along the hilly path. The view of the other side of the island was clear now, showing a coastline that was no longer sandy beaches. It was rocky as waves crashed against cliffs, sending fine spray into the air and froth, decorating the verge. The sun, still hot, dried the wetness in seconds.

As they walked, they could see remnants of cube houses in the distance, tumbled and blackened by fire and bombs. The people who had lived there probably murdered, or maybe some escaped and hid in the hills. Ayan's mood was heavy and dark as he stared, shocked at the devastation of the island he loved so much. Not long after, they heard voices nearby.

'A camp!' he hissed, looking as worried as Crystal. 'They are here because they can easily see if any boats sail in.'

'Surely boats would find it hard to arrive on cliffs?'

'There are coves along the way; it would be easy for them to get through if they know the waters,' he explained.

'How far is your home?'

'It is on the south side of the island. Not far, half a day. But with avoiding soldiers, it'll take much longer. There are caves nearby. We can go there for the night.'

They had to be quiet to pass the camp. Ayan carried the case, which was less risk of noise. Crystal scooped Puss onto her shoulders and lifted Diesel. He was heavier now, so was a struggle. They passed the soldiers with Crystal's heart beating so loud, she was sure they would hear. Safely on the other side of the camp, they made their way down the cliff face. It was a climb that Puss, Diesel, and Ayan managed easily. Crystal slid into her now raggy canvas shoes. She tried not to cry out in fear but was terrified of falling over the edge and crashing to her death. The caves were invisible, and anyone not knowing they existed would never see them. After the airy climb down, they had to climb up again. Ayan went first and took hold of Puss and Diesel as Crystal passed them up. Then she heaved the case with all her might, which was not easy as it was so heavy. Lastly, putting up her hand, Ayan pulled her up with ease. The cluster of caves was hollowed into the side of the cliff. Most had small entrances. Ayan, knowing them well, took them to the third cave along. It was slightly lower on the cliff face. The opening was still small, but on hands and knees, they could crawl inside. Once through the narrow entrance, the cave opened into a large cavern. The air inside was cool after the heat of the day. Crystal shivered and pulled her arms around herself as she entered the darkness.

Chapter Seven

Once inside, safe from the military, Ayan flashed a torch around the perimeter.

'Wow! Crystal breathed as she twisted in a circle to follow the beam.

The colours that glowed in the light were breathtaking, as unique stones shone from the dull grey walls. Purples, greens, and yellows met her eyes. Gold veins glittered as they snaked their way through the cavern. Stalactites hung from the ceiling, and stalagmites grew from the floor. To one edge was a small pool of water, from which a tiny trickle cascaded lazily down from somewhere in the rock, gently splashing into it.

'This is amazing,' Crystal gasped.

'It's a secret place. There are many throughout the hills. It is rumoured that my great-great-grandfather found treasure in one of these caves when he was a boy. It was said that it was left by pirates. I'm not sure if it's true, but on a dark night, the story is told over and over to the youngsters of our people.'

'What happened to the treasure?' Crystal asked, her eyes wide with fascination.

'We don't know. But his father bought a few fishing boats and a fish shop on the mainland. He sent my grandfather's children to school in London. We assumed it was with money from the treasure or how else had he such wealth. It was said he hid the rest. But no one ever found out where.'

'But your family could have moved to another country, like America or Australia, and bought a big house; they could have been wealthy.'

Ali laughed, 'You mean if the story was real? But if it was, why? We are happy here; it's our home. You Westerners are poor compared to us. I hated London, with its plastic people. Women with false big lips and bottoms. They live in plastic bubbles and don't see life as we do.'

'In your opinion, what do you mean poor? That's rubbish. I have a big house with a swimming pool. Lots of designer clothes and anything I want.'

'And if that's what makes you happy, then that's good. So does it?'

'Well... I... I... guess so.'

Ayan laughed. 'Exactly, you were unhappy with your fancy clothes, house, and false friends. That was not real. Look at this cave. That is real. There is beauty, peace and mystery in nature. You Westerners make everything so complicated. We see beauty in old age, wrinkles, sagging bodies; it shows wisdom and experience.'

'Well, I think your way of life stinks!' she huffed. It's boring. Marriage, children, old age, and death are pointless. Life is for adventure. There is so much to do and so many places to explore. Who would want to be a prisoner of dull routine?'

She turned her back on him until he handed her bread and cheese for dinner, sitting silently while they ate. They shared a bar of melted chocolate washed down with orange juice for dessert.

Diesel and Puss tucked into two tins of meat each. After, both curled together to keep warm.

Crystal felt a little guilty about offending his way of life, and she tried to mend some of their argument.

'It must have been wonderful growing up on such a beautiful Island,' she admitted, clearing away the empty packages.

'Yes. It was easy, free, and non-complicated,' Ayan confessed, his face lighting with thoughts of his childhood. 'I've two sisters, my brother, cousins, and even an uncle of similar age. We had great games and times running riot here. There was never any danger, robberies, muggings, or murders. We were contented and happy. Tourists came about ten years ago. We built villas for them, and many outsiders moved here. Things for us changed; we no longer had peace.'

'But how did you survive with no shops or jobs? Surely not just by fishing?'

'My grandfather, father and uncles fished. We kept our shop stocked and sold some to others. Much of the fish was sent abroad. We supplied both the countries, who now argue. Tourism is hard for us to cope with. Most of my people do not like it. They resent the intrusion and changes outsiders bring.'

'I guess so. 'Crystal thought how different their lives were. 'Why did you choose to go to school in England?'

'My brother and me lived there for seven years with my aunt and her family; I hated it,' he laughed before continuing. She left the island many years ago when she met and married an Englishman; she lives in Oxford. I was going to be a doctor. My family struggled to pay for us. I felt guilty letting them down. But I was so unhappy. There were too many people, so unwelcoming. They are like robots- not warm and loving, as my people are.'

'What about your brother, did he come back too?' she asked.

'He stayed a year longer. He began getting in with the wrong people and was constantly in trouble. Eventually, my parents insisted he come home. It's a shame; he was training to be an engineer. Not much use for it on the Island.'

After the intense heat, the cave felt cold and dank; Crystal shivered all night. The warmth from Ayan's body did not help much, or his jacket, which he kindly put around her shoulders.

The next day, he disappeared to see if the soldiers had moved on and it was safe to leave. He was gone so long that Crystal began to panic, thinking he had left her behind. Dutifully, he returned after what seemed like hours.

'We need to stay here. It's not safe,' he announced. 'The place is crawling with armed enemy.'

'What will we do?' she asked, hoping he had the answers. 'I mean, if they don't go.'

He shrugged and busied himself, making lunch. Which was a cold tin of meat and some disgusting thing from another container. She could not decide what it was. Ayan was reluctant to feed Puss and Diesel, wasting precious supplies on animals.

'They will hunt to feed themselves,' he told her, looking annoyed as she opened tins for them.

Ignoring him, she placed the food on the edge of the case as a makeshift bowl. Diesel scoffed his own and then pinched Pusses, who ate slower. He received a telling-off from Crystal. Although shamefaced, the dog wagged his tail, not perturbed by the chastising.

Ayan shook his head in disgust. 'You need to obey a man, or you'll never find a husband!'

'What makes you think I want one? I certainly would never obey a man if I did!' she snapped, thinking of the easy-going Will. Crystal never realised how lucky she had been. Guilt flooded in her head, as up until now, she hadn't given him much thought.

'I did have a husband,' she burst out. 'He was killed by the soldiers.

Ali looked shocked and then, like Diesel, shamefaced. 'I'm sorry.'

'They shot all the people in our group, leaving their bodies in a pit.'

'How did you escape?' he asked.

'I heard the soldiers coming and hid.'

They remained silent after that, Crystal thinking of Will and what a good man he had been. Guilt flooded her again for the way she had treated him. At least she had told him about the baby, which consoled her slightly.

The day was long; minutes ticked by like hours. Ayan would not let Crystal warm up in the sun for fear of giving away their position. Her fingers and toes throbbing with cold and dampness were painful.

They were asleep that night when a massive explosion went off nearby. The cave shook, and large stones and rubble rained down on them. Some of the stalactites fell like daggers. Which was sad after the years it took for them to grow. Puss and Diesel shot out of the cave-like darts from a pea shooter. Crystal screamed in fright, covering her head and curling against the onslaught. Ayan poked his head out of the entrance; he could not see for thick smoke. The smell of burning flesh was putrid. Screaming could be heard, children crying, and animals wincing in pain and terror. He shook his head and looked sickened, devastated at such mass slaughter of his people. The explosions went off most of the night. They could hear gunshots and more screaming. Crystal pulled her knees up to her chin and squeezed her eyes shut, trying to block out the awfulness.

'There is a village close by.' I'm guessing they bombed it. Ali's voice was broken. 'I have family and friends that live there.'

The bombing continued over the next few days in different directions. It was not safe for them to leave. The food was running low, and Ayan complained about giving the dog and cat precious rations again. Crystal began sneaking them food from her own portion. Causing Ayan to throw her some harsh stares.

'What I don't understand,' she chose her words carefully, not wanting to sound stupid or upset him again. 'How did Carbombya recruit Island people?'

Ayan studied her for a while, his eyes clouding as he answered.

'The arguments between the two countries have been rumbling for years, but the last two were becoming more serious. We knew war was coming, and there were plans to attack the Buranda government. The Islands were stuck in the middle. Most of us did not want to become involved with either side; we are peaceful people. Although we wanted independence, it was impractical; the islands were too vulnerable and needed some defense and protection. Carbombya promised independence but would still protect the Islands if we joined them. It would be a political war, not involving innocent people. They would give funding for schooling and health care. So, many of us signed up, believing the lies. Then Buranda sent planes and bombed Cambombya. Of course, there was retaliation and a full-blown war began. I have sisters living on Buranda.'

'But why allow holidaymakers to come to the island, knowing there was a strong threat of war? Why would they do that?' Crystal's voice was angry.

Ayan shrugged, 'I guess foreigners bring money. That's why they are killing and pillaging?'

'It still does not make any sense.'

'Does war ever make any?'

Crystal thought. 'Will, my husband, did not think they would kill holidaymakers. He said it would involve other countries if they did.'

'Your husband may have been right,' Ayan agreed.

'How long have you been away from the islands?'

'Too long, six months or so.'

'Will said they fight about the oil in the sea around the islands. That it was discovered a few years ago.'

'Yes, he was right. All this is over oil and greed. That is why the soldiers are taking over the island and killing all the inhabitants. It will become their army base.'

'What happened to your brother?' Crystal asked.

Ayan shrugged, 'I never saw him once we signed up. I can only hope he managed to get away like me.'

With little else to do, they spent their time talking. Crystal told Ayan about her life with Will, including trips to the gym and clubs, her clothes and belongings, her friends, and even Layla. And their life growing up on the council estate.

He, in turn, shared stories about his brother and sisters and their antics when they were growing up, the mischief and scrapes they got into. Crystal loved to hear these stories, which were much more exciting than hers, so she listened intently. Puss and Diesel did too, as they dozed and huddled for warmth in the cold cave. It was amazing how the dog and cat had become close friends.

Ayan was a good storyteller; he made her laugh. She began to feel affectionate towards him, as he seemed to her. At night, all four of them cuddled together while they slept.

After three days, the bombing noise quietened slightly. Ayan ventured out and claimed it was still not safe. More soldiers had arrived and made a camp on the clifftop above them. Their food had run out. Thankfully, they still had water from the little pool.

'We've no choice but to move,' he stated. 'We'll do this at night, but climbing the cliffs will be slow and hazardous, especially with no light.'

Crystal was afraid, but what choice did they have? They no longer needed the case, so it was to be left behind. They had few supplies to pack besides a sheet, so that was also left. Bottles of water were carried in Ayan's backpack. He grumped at Crystal, who wanted to take her toiletries. In the end, she relented and only took her precious hairbrush.

They moved once the sun had sunk and a skimpy moon appeared. Ayan held her hand as they began the dangerous journey along the cliff face to avoid the camp above. Crystal slid and fell often; it was dark, and Ayan held her firm and pulled her along. Her legs and hands were grazed and bleeding, but she never complained.

With their precise night vision, Puss and Diesel negotiated the climbing quickly. Both bounced along, often overtaking Crystal and her slow progress. Ayan sighed and tutted often; he knew he would have been home long ago without her. Once they reached the track, the pathway was less bumpy. They walked that night for miles. The gunfire and explosions, thankfully, a dull sound behind them. Only the occasional rumble could now be heard in the distance.

'It won't be long before they start on this area,' Ayan predicted. 'We need to get people away.'

In the early hours, Crystal could no longer walk. Ayan relented, and they stopped to rest. The dog and cat snuggled up to her, and the three were asleep in seconds.

Ayan shook them awake at sunrise. 'We must keep going,' he clipped. 'We have far to go yet.'

'But you said your home was only half a day's walk. We've walked over that by now.'

'It would have been if I was alone. You're slow,' he grumbled, walking away and not allowing time for her to wake properly.

Hunger hurt Crystal's stomach, and Diesel whined for food. Puss had caught some sort of rodent and happily crunched away, causing Crystal to cringe.

'I've nothing for you,' she told the dog, sadly, feeling guilty at the desperation in his eyes.

'It's useless!' Ayan stared at Diesel with distaste. 'It's been mollycoddled. It should be hunting food, not relying on us. It needs shooting,' he huffed, disgustedly.

'Over my dead body!' Crystal snapped.

'That could be arranged,' he answered coldly and walked ahead.

They reached a wooded area that had been seen in the distance. The thin trees towered over them, which was safer not to be seen. The shade was more relaxed to walk through, but they grew at high points up the steep hill, making the climb exhausting. The higher they climbed, the thinner the trees became, until there again were just rocks and more hills in front of them.

'We need to rest,' Crystal moaned every step she took. 'I'm tired. My feet ache. It's OK for you, you've got comfy boots.'

'Soon, we are almost there,' he pacified each time he heard her groaning.

Even Puss and Diesel looked worn out as their heads hung and their legs dragged. Puss cheekily jumped into Crystal's arms and climbed onto her shoulder, where she stretched herself to take a rest.

'You're not silly, are you?' Crystal couldn't help smiling as she raised her hand and rubbed the cat.

She could not see anything in front but more rocks and more rubble. Ayan suddenly disappeared, one minute in front, the next gone.

'Ali!' she called, wishing she had been watching his trail, not the ground.

He had left her. The trees were a ploy so he could dodge away. Crystal began to panic as she twisted in a circle, looking for him. He appeared once again through a gap in the rocks, unusually smiling. Grabbing her hand, he dragged her through the alley of stones, which weaved and twisted. Ayan then pulled Crystal in front of him and gently pushed her through a larger opening. He was smiling, waiting in anticipation for her reaction.

'Oh… my…god…' she gasped.

Ayan was suitably pleased and proud as he pulled back his shoulders and held his head high.

Chapter Eight

Another world lay before Crystal's eyes. 'It's magnificent,' she breathed.

A large plateau spanned in front of them. The area carpeted in lush, soft grass. All colours of wildflowers were dotted amongst the green. Bees buzzed as they busied themselves collecting nectar from the array of plants, shrubs, and trees that sprang in various clusters. Birds sang .out-of-tune magical music. At the far end, a spectacular blue rock pool could be seen, purple water raining into it from a waterfall cascading from the cliff border. Some of the rock sides had skilfully carved faces and animals. There were also paintings depicting stories of times gone by. A massive stone structure stood in one corner, offering a large, shaded area with climbing greenery, grapevines, and coloured flowers; underneath were gold tables with wooden chairs scattered. Trees were in abundance, offering fruit or olives and palms with coconuts dangling. Golds, mauves, and reds of precious stones sparked from the rocks, catching the sunlight, and prisms danced around the ground.

Crystal ran to one tree and grabbed a mango. Without pealing, she dug in her nails, ripped it open, and devoured the fruit in seconds. Then another and another. Ayan did the same. They were so hungry that neither cared that juice dripped down their chins onto their clothes.

Puss and Diesel ran to the water edge and began to drink.

Ayan stripped away the layers of his clothes, dropping them in a heap until he stood naked, his brown skin glistening in the sunlight. His rippling muscles and flat stomach caused Crystal to gasp and forget about the fruit. Ayan's body was perfect. She thought these

89

men only existed in her novels or on television. Despite their lovemaking, she had never really looked at his body before.

'Thirty out of ten,' she giggled, then felt sad remembering her game with Sonya, now dead at such a young age.

She watched his muscly buttocks as he walked to the water's edge and jumped into the blue depth, disappearing below the surface, leaving ripples of intrusion. Puss and Diesel ran from the splash but were soon back to drink again.

Ayan appeared seconds later, wiping the water from his face. 'Come?' he beckoned.

Crystal, feeling in awe of the surroundings and Ayan's body, began peeling away her clothes. She also jumped into the water. It was surprisingly warm and felt amazing next to her skin as it caressed the sores, infected bites, and scratches from brambles.

'It's healing?' he smiled, causing his eyes to crinkle at the corners, enhancing his handsome features.

'Yes, I could stay here all day. It's incredibly beautiful.'

Diesel found shallow water and paddled his sore feet, bravely going further to cool his belly. Thinking them all silly, Puss sat at a close distance and watched.

Ayan swam to the edge and climbed out of the pool. He disappeared into an assortment of greenery, returning carrying a cluster of red, strange cone-shaped flowers. He handed some to Crystal, and the others squeezed over his head. A liquid came out. His body and hair lathered; he moved under the waterfall and washed.

'Soap,' he grinned at her expression, 'none of that chemical stuff you use.'

She was amazed. Doing the same, moved under the water flow and scrubbed herself clean. It felt wonderful not to smell.

'See, we may be poor but have many riches.'

'What is it?' Crystal was astonished. Her skin felt oiled, and her hair was like silk, no longer brittle from the sun.

'It is Zingiber. Soap flower.'

After, they lay on the soft grass to allow the sun to dry their bodies. They made love without a care in the world. The blood and slaughter, for those minutes, were forgotten.

'What is this place, Ali?' Crystal asked as they lay dozing.

'It is a gift from our gods. It is our church or sacred temple,' he smiled. 'It is where islanders meet every few months for gatherings. We would stay for the weekend and have parties with plenty of food, drink, and music. We danced, held plays, told stories, bathed, and made love.'

Ayan jumped up and disappeared into the jungle of plants once again. Crystal had fallen into a sleep when he shook her awake. He was loaded with strange roots, leaves, and fruits she had never seen before.

'We eat properly,' he said, laying the food on the ground and showing her how to peel the strange fruits and roots.

He kindly threw food to Puss and Diesel, who were so hungry that they scoffed every bit. The food tasted strange but not unpleasant. After a few mouthfuls, Crystal began to like the new tastes. Although she was so hungry, she would have eaten anything.

Once they were full, Puss and Diesel found new energy and began to play. At least Puss did. Hiding in the undergrowth Diesel had to search for her. The dog jumped and barked in protest as the cat leapt out, giving him a fright. This resulted in a game of chase to get his own back. Crystal giggled as she watched; Puss came running over on hearing her. Her thin tail pointed towards the sky like a pencil.

'Why is the waterfall purple and the pool so blue? I have never seen anything like it,' she asked Ayan, stroking Puss's fur as the cat snuggled and purred herself into a doze.

'The pool's surface is clay, which causes it to look intensely blue. Come, I'll show you.'

He grabbed her hand, leading her towards the fall. Still naked, they walked behind the water on a thin ledge. Crystal gasped again, and her eyes widened with amazement.

'Amethyst!'

The rock face behind the fall was purple, with gold flecks, making the water appear the same colour. Ayan continued to lead her behind, where a large opening led to a massive cavern. The inside was magnificent and breathtaking. Every colour imaginable glittered and glistened with the reflection of sun and water that showered down the entrance. A large, green stoned altar stood at one end. A gold chalice, two bowls, and various other little jugs and pots containing ash stood on top. Crystal ran her fingers over them as though they may break under her touch.

'But all this gold? It must be worth fortunes.'

'Yes,' Ayan nodded. 'It's not gold, though. It is pyrite, I believe you call it - fool's gold. It's valuable to Westerners in large quantities. This is a sacred place where we join, which is the same as marrying, naming babies, and holding burials. It is where we talk to our gods. Ask for help or celebrate. We have sex rituals here, too. If Westerners find this, we'll lose our temple and our culture.'

'Sex rituals?'

'Yes, I can show you.'

'No, thank you,' Crystal bristled but then was left wondering what a sex ritual was.

It was true; this would all be pillaged and taken. It would be heartbreaking to destroy such beauty, she thought.

'Our island has many treasures. We have lived this way for hundreds of years. Without it, our lives, as we know it, would be ruined. You must never tell anyone about this place when you get home,' he warned.

'What if the soldiers find it?'

'This is why we do not want outsiders in our country. Not because we do not like them. But we do not want our lives too change. We do not want poison – phones that you carry. Internet. Televisions.'

'Everything in life has to change, though. It's progress. Things move on,' Crystal said.

Ayan looked sad, knowing she was probably right. 'Until the world becomes a blob of ants. Everyone the same. Fighting for power and greed until they destroy each other… Come.'

He took her hand and led her from the cave to the table under the stone canopy. Pulling a root from the ground on their way. Grabbing the knife and lighter from his backpack, he began to chop it into tiny pieces. Disappearing, he came back moments later with a few leaves. Rapping the pieces of chopped root inside, Ayan rolled them into a cigarette shape. Leading Crystal to a shady tree, he lit it.

'You sit and take a big puff,' he handed her the cigarette.

She looked at him, her eyes worried and questioning.

'It'll not hurt you. It'll show you. Keep the smoke inside as long as you can.'

He sat down beside her and demonstrated, drawing on the cigarette and noisily sucking the smoke into his lungs. Crystal cautiously took the tube from him and did the same. She spluttered and gagged as the smoke met her lungs. Ayan laughed and told her to try again. Nothing happened at first, so she did it again. Her head began to sing, quietly at first, then louder and louder. The sun snubbed out, and blackness descended. She felt herself falling and falling. Until a hand reached out from the darkness and pulled her upwards. It was Ayan, his strength incredible. She opened her eyes and saw he was smiling, causing his face to light up, and the kindness in his eyes made her feel safe.

'Look,' Ayan waved his hand around.

Crystal looked beyond him. The lights were so bright that she squeezed her eyes shut and turned away.

'You'll get used to it. Open your eyes. You're safe.'

The blaze of colours that met her was incredible. Everything was the same as before but enhanced, powerful and overwhelming; the intensity of colour radiated from the ground, trees, water, and flowers.

'I don't understand. Is it a drug that makes lights brighter?'

Ayan laughed. 'No, it is what we do not see with our earth's eyes. It is always around us, but our mind blocks it out. Humans radiate energy like the planet. Look at the sky.'

She did. Bright lights shone down: white, yellow, orange, red, lilac, blue, and green and colours that had not yet been named or seen before. They circled and spun like vortexes blasting into the earth.

'They are our gods,' Ayan said. 'They are powers of the universe that spin to help us live. Now you see, there is so much more to life than money.'

Crystal looked around, mesmerised, the lights hypnotic, warming and healing her soul. She walked forward, lifted her arms, and looked down at herself. There they were, penetrating points in her body. Spinning from the sky into her core and, in turn, her own light, from her body radiating and becoming as one with the universe. She felt like a goddess, and the peace was so absorbing it could surely never end. Crystal looked at Ayan; his body was the same, the lights apart of him, his fingers and toes glowed as did the centre of his skin to the crown of his head. A fire of deep blue circled his whole being.

95

He held out his hand, and she reached for him. Electric charged into her at the touch, sizzling up her arms and into her heart. Crystal knew at that point they were as one for the rest of their days.

The energy was exhilarating but exhausting. Ayan lay down under the tree and pulled her into his arms.

He kissed her forehead tenderly. 'We shared our souls. Became joined,' he whispered gently into her ear. 'It is like a sex ritual.

Crystal felt warm and safe; love flowed from her for this wonderful man, who could be brutal but so kind and tender. They slept then, still holding each other, their bodies united.

'Princess!' it was not Ayan's voice that called, pulling her out of the blackness of sleep; it was her father's.

Crystal opened her eyes, and he stood in front of her.

'Daddy!' She untangled herself from Ayan's body and jumped up, throwing herself into his arms, with tears streaming down her face. 'But you're dead. I'm dreaming.'

'I'm always around you. It is just you have opened your mind to see me. We never die, Princess. We just moved to another place.'

He was younger, and the worry lines that Crystal had not acknowledged in his life were no longer there. He was handsome, and his hair was no longer grey but raven black, as it was when he was young.

'I never realised,' she said through tears.

'Realised?'

'How ill you looked before your heart attack. Seeing you so well now, it makes me realise. Was it me that caused you to die?' It was guilt that she had carried since his death.

'Of course not,' David told her. 'It was my time to go. We have not got long on this earth.'

He pulled away, gently, reluctantly letting go of her hand. Will stood behind him. A younger Will. He was no longer balding; his body was trim and much more youthful than Crystal remembered him. She fell into his arms and kissed his face. Her tears wetting his cheek.

'Oh, Will. I'm so sorry for being an ungrateful, selfish bitch. You were the best husband a woman could hope for. I did love you.'

'I know, Crystal. You were young. I shouldn't have expected you to settle for an old codger like me. You had so much life to live. I should not have taken that from you. I want you to know I'm safe and happy. I've seen Sonya. She's OK too. It is beautiful where we live. Take care of our son, Billy. Be happy, never be sad or lonely. We are here, watching over you. But I need to tell you, I am sorry.'

'Sorry for what?' You did nothing wrong,' she said, surprised.

'I did. Do not think bad of me. I wanted the best for you. But I should not have done what I did. You'll be OK. Hold onto that when things are dark.'

'Princess, we must go,' her father said.

'Be happy, Crystal,' Will called as they drifted into the distance, and the blaze of lights swallowed them up.

Crystal opened her eyes. It had been a dream. She was still lying on the ground, with Puss and Diesel curled beside her. Ayan was watching, his brow crinkled with questions. He reached for her and pulled her into his chest as she sobbed.

'A bad dream?' He said gently as he stroked her hair.

'No, just a sad one. I dreamt of my father. And of Will, my husband. It was all so real.'

The lights were beginning to fade, and the brightness diminished. Nothing would ever be as beautiful again, Crystal thought.

Ayan nudged her, 'Come, we need to go.'

She never wanted to leave that beautiful place where she felt so at peace.

'Was that marijuana?' Crystal asked, having never tried it before. 'That made us see those lights.'

'No, it was not that stuff you smoke in your country. What you saw was real. We use it to learn. There is more than we mortals will ever know. But we must go now.'

Sighing, she pulled on her raggy, filthy clothes and ran to catch Ayan as he began weaving through the rocks to the dullness on the other side. She knew colours would never look the same to her after that.

'I did not realise you carry a child… A son.' Ayan suddenly said.

'How did you know? Did I say it out loud?'

He laughed, 'let us just hope you are no longer going to be a selfish, ungrateful bitch,' he finished.

Crystal gasped, blushed, and found escape in her filthy shoes.

'But it was a dream; how did you know that? Was I talking in my sleep?'

Ayan smiled knowingly and kissed her head. 'Those visions are not always dreams, Princess,' he winked and chuckled mockingly.

He walked away, leaving her staring after him.

She had so much to think about but now was not the time. What did Will mean, he had done something wrong?

Chapter Nine

After another hour of walking, just when Crystal felt she needed to collapse with exhaustion, they saw a village in the distance at the bottom of the steep hill; they were almost at the top of it.

'Is that your home!' she squealed, not containing her excitement.

'No,' he answered. 'It is a neighbouring village. 'We can rest and eat there, though.'

Optimism lighted her heart. Hope gave way to joy, and then doubt sunk in. What if they hated her and resented helping an outsider?

Sensing her reluctance, Ayan smiled reassuringly, 'Don't worry. My wife's family live here. They'll help.'

'Your WIFE! You never said you were married! But we… we've… been…'

Ayan laughed, which sounded mocking and sinister to Crystal. 'You never asked, ' he said, continuing to walk.

It was true, she hadn't. Crystal ran and caught him up. 'But why did you not tell me? We should not have… you know… made love! Have you children?' Her voice was becoming hysterical, and she could feel the anger burning into her. They had shared beautiful moments, and they meant nothing to him. He had just been playing with her.

'No.' he answered flatly.

Now, she would be ousted from the people for having relations with a married man!

100

'I feel terrible. I thought… Well… You know. That we were a couple.'

His raucous laughter reminded her of Will. 'Don't be silly. There is no way we could ever be together.'

Crystal drew back her hand and slapped him as hard as she could across his face. Not satisfied, she did it again. 'How dare you laugh at me!' she screamed and went to slap him again.

Ayan caught her hand in his, fury clouding his eyes, which soon softened as he realised how much he must have misled her.

'I'm sorry. I thought we were friends, sharing and making the best of a situation. You've just lost your husband. There is no way I'd have imagined you were developing feelings for me. '

'You used me!' she cried.

Ayan smiled a little too sarcastically, 'I think you will find, it was you who used me!'

Crystal blushed, remembering she had requested their lovemaking on many occasions. 'But I thought you were single. I wouldn't have if you'd mentioned a wife.'

He had the grace to look ashamed. 'I'm sorry. I did not think… well, that you thought we could be together that way as husband and wife. Our worlds are so far apart. We would never get on or accept each other's ways. We are too different.'

'Don't flatter yourself,' she snapped. 'I certainly did not, or never would, want to marry you. You are a pig!'

She stomped off, leaving him standing for once. But tears of anger and hurt fell as she thought their souls had touched. It was weird to think that, but they felt so connected. They remained silent, the atmosphere between them angry. Crystal, tangling herself in brambles, lost her footing and fell, banging her leg badly on a rock. More tears escaped down her face as she clutched her leg until the pain subsided a little. Blood wetted her hand as it seeped from the wound. Ayan, seeing her fall, reached out his hand to her.

'Go away!' she cried and slapped his help away.

'You're bleeding,' his eyes were gentle and full of concern.

'Just leave me alone!' she shouted, pulling up her trousers to examine the damage. Ayan picked at a large leaf and bent down beside her, producing some string from his backpack.

'Please, let me help. I'm sorry I hurt you. I did not mean to.'

'You did not hurt me. I am angry you lied.'

Ignoring the comment, he pulled her hands away from the torn skin and wiped away some of the blood. Wrapping the leaf around the wound, he tied it as best he could. 'It'll help stop the blood. We'll rest for a while.'

Another hour later, they walked into the little village with its funny cube houses. Unlike the derelict deserted ones near the retreat, these were brightly painted and cheerful. Wall hangings decorated the outsides, hiding the dull grey walls. Wooden boxed chairs and tables were covered in cushions and throws. They looked comfortable and welcoming. Children ran around the streets, screaming and laughing with their made-up game. Women stood in little groups, weaving, preparing food, sewing and chatting. Everyone stopped as the little group walked into the village.

'Ayan... Ayan...!' A female voice screeched, throwing her arms around him.

She was an older lady who looked ancient, with her chiselled wrinkles and toothless mouth. An equally toothless older man limped over, leaning heavily on a stick. Other people appeared, and they began speaking all at once in their own language. They looked Crystal's way a few times and paused before speaking again in words that seemed made up, loud, with no break in between. She felt lost and awkward. Diesel and Puss stood at her feet, as scared as their mistress. A young, pretty woman walked forward, slightly older than Crystal and heavily pregnant.

'Come?' she smiled, taking her arm.

She was led inside one of the houses and offered a seat. No objection was made to the animals who scuttled along at her side. A cup was provided with some warm, sweet liquid; it tasted good. Water was put down for Diesel and Puss, and they lapped eagerly.

The room was bright, with blues, pinks, and yellows decorating the walls. Skilled wall art of paintings of animals and people were dotted around. More wall hangings warmed the area, and concrete cubes, covered in cushions and rugs, were dotted around for chairs and a table.

'You tired,' the woman said. Her face was full of empathy, and Crystal wanted to cry.

'You eat, then rest,' she handed her a plate with some sort of stew.

'Thank you so much,' she was grateful. 'Can my animals have some?' she cheekily asked.

The lady laughed and went off to get two more plates. Placing the food on the floor, the dog and cat finished the meal in moments. Diesel rudely whined for seconds, but no more was offered, and Crystal did not have the gall to ask.

After, she was led to a room where a large concrete bed dominated the area. It was also scattered in rugs and cushions.

'You rest with baby. You sleep,' the woman smiled, patting her own pregnant tummy with her hand.

Crystal's head snapped up, her eyes full of disbelief. 'How did you know? Did Ali tell you?'

'I woman. Children,' she held two fingers up and pointed to her bulging belly, indicating the third on its way.

She left the room, pulling a curtain across the doorway for privacy.

Diesel and Puss found their way to the bed and jumped on. The three of them were asleep in seconds.

It was dark when Crystal woke some hours later. She could hear talking from the other room. Stretching, she wondered if joining the group was OK. Ayan's voice could be heard amongst the jabbering noise. Amazingly, on the end of the bed were clothes, which she assumed were for her. There was a loose tunic top with long sleeves and cotton baggy trousers that tied at the waist to accommodate any size person. They were neatly pressed and looked new. Crystal gratefully swapped them for her raggy, torn clothes. Under the pile were some slippers with rubber soles. They all fitted perfectly and felt comfortable and cool.

The group stopped talking and stared as she pulled the curtain back. The same toothless older lady began shouting, pointing at the dog, who had followed.

'We don't allow animals in houses,' Ayan explained. 'It is bad luck. They need to be put outside,' he winked and slightly grinned.

Crystal picked up Puss, who was still asleep, from the bed. The cat moaned at the intrusion. Taking them both outside, she sat on one of the concrete chairs, thinking how beautiful the village looked in the darkness. Lights were burning on each house, the flames flickering, creating ghostly shadows and illuminating the colourful decor. It was magical and almost fairy-like; the war seemed to not exist. Men sat in little groups, talking and maybe putting the world to rights. They stared, their eyes curious. One of them said something, and they laughed, looking her way. Had Ayan told them they had been having sex? She blushed and fiddled with her shoe.

It was sometime before Ayan appeared. He handed her some water, which she relished, not realising how thirsty she was.

'The clothes suit you,' he told her.

Thank you. Who left them?' she asked, grateful for the thoughtfulness.

'The same lady who fed you, my wife's twin sister... We leave in the morning,' he told her.

'Are they identical twins?'

Ayan smiled, 'No, but both are very pretty. I could never decide which I wanted from the two,' he laughed, his eyes twinkling with mischief.

'You make it sound like a shop!' she snapped, not finding the joke funny after his betrayal. 'Who are these people, your wife's family?'

'No, the two sisters don't have many blood relatives, just a grandmother. They are mostly my family - Aunts and cousins. They are frightened. I've told them we need to leave. But they're refusing. This is their home. They want to take their chances. But I fear they will die, as have the other villagers. The soldiers have not yet reached here, except to recruit men and boys at the beginning of the war.'

Crystal felt miserable thinking of the little village's fate. 'But what about your wife's sister? Will she not come with her children?'

'She wants to. But is afraid for the people left behind. She has chosen to stay with them.'

Crystal fell quiet with her own desolate thoughts. Maybe they'll be safe, she hoped.

Seeing her sadness, Ayan added, more to himself than to Crystal, 'I'll return for them once my wife is safe.'

She felt better; there was still some hope for the people. After seeing the burned-out villages, time was running out. The young woman appeared out of the house. Her name turned out to be Mira, as Ayan introduced them properly. A small child about two or three years old was hanging on her skirt, and another, slightly older, peered around the door, fascinated by the stranger.

'I bought for animals,' Mira waved a plate full of goodies that both Diesel and Puss's noses twitched at. 'Older people traditional. Not like dogs and cats inside. She laid the bowls of scraps on the floor, and Puss and Diesel gobbled the contents.

'Thank you,' Crystal smiled. 'You are very kind and I'm so grateful for the clothes. My others were ready to fall off.'

Mira did not understand but smiled anyway. 'I, and sister, England once. School trip. Charity paid. To give women chance to see world before joining and babies. We go London, Paris. I want to travel.'

Crystal imagined it was an arranged marriage but did not like to ask. Ayan was standing with them and would probably not approve of her objections.,

'Did you meet your husband at the sacred ground?' she asked instead. Mentioning the place hurt her stomach, and she felt emotional tears well up.

Mira did not understand, so Ayan translated.

'Ah. We grow together and in love,' she answered.

'We force our women to marry between thirteen and fifteen. They need to look after men,' Ayan gave a cheeky grin and winked.

Crystal gasped; a look of horror crossing her features. She was unsure if he was joking or not.

His grin widened at her expression, assuring her he was.

The next day, before they prepared to leave, Crystal put her arms around Mira and thanked her. 'Please come with us? It's not safe here.

We've seen what they have done to the villages. Your children will die if you stay.'

Sadness and fear clouded Mira's eyes. 'I cannot leave people.'

A heavy weight hung in Crystal's stomach as they left. She could see Mira watching until she was just a speck in the distance.

'Can't we do something?' she asked Ayan. 'We can't just leave them.'

He assured her again he would return.

The next part of the journey was reasonably flat as they weaved around the valley at the side of a large stream. Ayan explained the river led to the sea and his village, which was three miles away. Crystal's pace was more rapid with the new shoes. But the journey was still slow as they avoided the main pathways and roads for fear of soldiers. Thankfully, they spotted none.

Ayan's home village, apart from being larger, was almost identical to the village they had left. Similar bright rugs hung from the walls, and wooden and concrete structures were used for outside seating and tables. People gathered in groups, fear on their faces, as they saw a soldier approaching. All too soon, a young woman ran from one of the houses and fell into Ayan's arms, sobbing. Crystal felt slightly jealous; he was no longer hers, as the two were clearly very much in love. After the long romantic meeting, Ayan introduced his young wife, Maya. She was friendly and as beautiful as her sister, but as he had told her, not identical. Her glossy black hair shone like a raven, and her penetrating brown eyes were kind and gentle.

The young woman linked her arm in Crystals. 'Welcome to village,' she pulled away, smiling, which made the beautiful eyes sparkle with warmth and made Crystal feel even worse about having sex with her husband.

An older lady, clutching a child, walked forward. Lowering the little boy to the ground, she gave Crystal a scathing look before throwing her arms around Ayan. Everyone began speaking at once, and the noise alerted more people, who ventured from their houses. A crowd began to form, as it had in the other village. Crystal tried to shrink into the background, wanting to be part of the stone. Puss and Diesel obviously felt the same, as they had already skulked away, hiding amongst the shadows of a nearby house.

The older lady, who she assumed was his mum, let Ayan go. She curled her lip in distaste and looked like she was going to spit at Crystal as she looked her up and down before snorting and turning her back on her.

'Take no notice,' Maya smiled reassuringly. The same with me once.'

She took Crystal's hand and led her into one of the little houses. Puss and Diesel, seeing their mistress move, quickly followed, finding a corner to squash into.

'This is me and Ayan's home. You welcome here.'

The little house was styled like the other. Beautiful scenes were expertly painted onto the inside plaster walls. The stone chairs were awash with cushions and throws. A wooden bowl was brought to her, filled with rice, some sort of sauce, and vegetables. It was lovely food, and she ate greedily, apologising for her haste.

'I'm so hungry,' she told Maya. 'Could my dog and cat have something too?'

Maya looked around, surprised to see the cat and dog just as a little boy, who had followed them in, was about to hit Diesel on the head with a stick.

'NO!' they both shouted.

The boy stopped. Maya took his hand and pulled him to a chair. 'This Kenji, cousin's boy,' she told her while placing food on the floor for the animals.

'Hello, Kenji,' Crystal smiled at the small boy, who eyed her suspiciously.

'When due, baby?' Maya asked as she went to fill two bowls with food for the animals.

'I'm only about eleven or twelve weeks. I've lost track of time. How did you know?' Everyone seemed to know she was expecting; there was not even a bulge yet.

'Ayan.' It his baby?'

Crystal was shocked at the bluntness, but Maya was still smiling. There was no spite in her eyes, only sadness, which wrenched at Crystal's heart. Her face reddened so much that she could feel the heat in her feet. She lowered her eyes to the floor and fidgeted with her slipper to avoid the penetrating gaze.

'No! No… it's my husband's. He was killed by soldiers.'

After laying down the food, Maya returned with a little pot with steaming liquid. She poured Crystal a cup and sat down next to her.

'Ayan said we leave, soldiers come. Worried about sister.'

Crystal was glad about the diversion from her pregnancy. 'Your sister wanted too, but the older people won't leave. They must, though. The soldiers have destroyed all the villages we passed. You need to get off the island before it's too late.'

Maya nodded slowly, her eyes sad and tearful. 'Many dead. I pack.' She walked away, needing time with her grief.

'I'll help.'

When Ayan came in, a large pile of belongings was already on the floor and concrete table, including the chair cushions and throws. He spoke to his wife in his own language, seeming to forget Crystal was present.

'Husband rude,' Maya apologised.

Ayan grinned and began speaking in English. 'We leave as soon as we can. But we need to travel a bit lighter,' he turned to his wife and then pulled a face at the heap of goods.

'I not leave!' she protested, waving her arms at the pile and going off into a rant in her own language, which caused both Ayan and Crystal to cringe.

The stubbornness reminded Crystal of Pat, the older lady from the retreat. She felt terrible remembering how kind she had been to Crystal, who had snubbed her, thinking her boring. How she regretted it knowing the terrible death Pat had faced.

'Could I get a lift to the mainland?' Crystal asked. 'I mean, after the move?'

'There's no way! It's too far!' Ayan snapped, still reeling from the ear bashing.

'Airport bombed. Sorry,' Maya told her.

'Well, I guess I'm just grateful to be alive,' Crystal smiled sadly. She would never get home.

Ayan managed to convince some of the people to leave. The elder ones, as obstinate as the other villagers, refused. This was their home; they would fight and die in it. They would not let the enemy have their land and destroy their houses. Ayan was firm, telling them they would be leaving; if they refused, they would be carried.

Within the next four hours, a small crowd gathered, holding as many belongings as possible. The hangings had been removed from the houses, and the benches were no longer decorated with throws. The village looked as dull and lifeless as the other cube houses Crystal had passed. A few donkeys and some chickens, plus a goat, were amongst the crowd.

'The other animals need to be let loose,' she said to Maya, finding her more accessible to approach than Ayan and thinking about the farm she had passed.

'Yes. Ayan, come back. Bring more.'

Goods were loaded onto the donkeys, and people carried what they could. The children, old enough to walk, were herded into an orderly line, and babies were carried in slings of cloth attached to some of the women's chests, who also had squawking chickens under their arms. Crystal loaded Puss onto her shoulder and carried what bundles she could manage. They were ready to leave after a few disasters with the protesting goat.

Ayan's mother and another ancient lady were among the people. She was apparently the grandmother, a wise village elder, and a healer.

'We figured if Sanskrit came, others would follow,' Ayan whispered. 'She took some persuading, though.'

Ayan's mother, who was called Veda, still had not warmed to Crystal. She threw sideways looks of hatred at each opportunity, making her uncomfortable. She particularly hated Puss and Diesel, making a big fuss that they should not come with them. At least, that is what Crystal assumed, the way she waved her arms and shouted angrily.

They were off, and the little party followed the river towards the sea. Ayan held his nephew's hand for a while before scooping him up in his arms to fasten the pace.

'Is it far to walk?' Crystal asked Myra, feeling she was her only friend. The elderly people and the youngsters were even slower than her.

'No,' she reassured, helping Sanskrit while clutching a child's hand. 'Faster without children and older people.'

The journey was gruelling and painfully slow; they rested every few minutes as some young children and older people struggled with the distance. Then, the goat chewed through the rope that secured her. She ran, bucking, into the trees and undergrowth to make an escape.

The children squealed with giggles as Ayan had to chase her. He was not pleased when it leaped from behind a rock and butted him in his man parts. He doubled over, rolling on the floor in agony. He was even more perturbed when everyone began to laugh. Crystal had tears streaming when Ayan's red face returned, with the goat trotting primly behind him. She giggled for the rest of the journey. Ayan sent her caustic stares, which made her laugh even more.

'Karma!' she said, once close enough for him to hear.

Chapter Ten

A few hours later, Maya pointed to a small cove where eight boats bobbled on the ocean.

'How far's the island?' Crystal asked Ayan.

'It's pretty close, about three-quarters of an hour. It's far enough from the war, though. Once everyone's gone, I'm staying to try and persuade more people to come.'

'I'll stay too!' she suggested eagerly, not wanting to be left alone with the strangers.

'NO!' He objected.

Crystal felt fear for Ayan but soon dismissed this. It was not her concern. He was different now he was back with his own people, mostly ignoring her. Likewise, she did him.

The donkeys were let loose; they were too large to take with them. They stood dolefully watching for a few moments before wandering off, back the way they had come. It was difficult to load the goat and chickens, who clucked around in objection and kept hopping onto the boat's edge. One fell into the sea and had to be retrieved before it drowned. Puss and Diesel did not want to get on either. Puss wriggled and scratched as Crystal held her firm, calling Diesel across the plank. The dog took a cautious step forward and then ran onto the beach, barking and bouncing on the sand.

'Leave it!' Ayan shouted. 'It'll survive.'

Crystal jumped from the boat. 'I'm not going without Diesel!' she said, near tears, calling him in panic.

'Leave her too,' Ayan's mum said, surprisingly speaking English. 'She useless as animals.'

'NO!' Sanskrit defended, which surprised Crystal.

Ayan was angry but managed to calm himself. Crouching low on the sand, he called gently to the dog. Diesel hunkered and crawled on his belly to him. Scooping the dog in his arms, much to Crystal's relief, he plopped Diesel onto the boat, tying a rope around his neck so he could not jump off.

Four of the boats, loaded with baggage, people and animals, rumbled into life and began to move. Ayan watched them sail away before turning back the way they had come. The boats, driven by older men, too ancient to be taken by soldiers, headed towards the open sea. Crystal was fearful they would bump into military ships; she watched constantly but saw nothing, not even an island in the distance.

Puss flopped onto the seat next to Veda, much to the woman's disgust. Crystal stifled her giggles as the cat lifted her back leg and began vigorously washing her bottom, not noticing the scornful looks, which worsened at the uncouth cat. Diesel barked at the water with his front legs on the side of the boat. Eventually, with a worn-out voice, he twisted three times and flopped on the deck, exhaling a huge sigh. Curling into a circle, sticking his nose next to his bottom, the dog closed his eyes.

Crystal smiled at Sanskrit, who was studying her intently. The old lady, whose fingers were twisted and gnarled, surprisingly, gave a wide toothless grin back, causing her wrinkled face to screw and her watery eyes to sparkle, giving a glimpse of a lost youth.

'Ayan's?' Sanskrit indicated a pregnant belly as she shouted over the chicken's chatter and the engine noise.

Crystal was mortified that everyone seemed to think this. No wonder his mother did not like her.

'No!' she shook her head vigorously. 'Husband died,' she indicated a gun with her hands. 'Soldiers shot.'

Sanskrit looked sad and nodded slowly. She turned her attention to the sea, and her eyes distanced to somewhere far away.

A speck could be seen on the horizon, and someone pointed and shouted.

'Island,' Maya told Crystal, 'safe!'

'What's it called?' she asked.

'No name, no people. We call Gozho.'

Crystal vaguely remembered Will telling her that uninhabited islands did not always have names, so she guessed that was what Maya was trying to say to her. As they drew closer, she observed that it did look like a lovely island. It was plush with greenery, and there seemed to be a small cluster of woods. Cliffs dominated one side, and a long sandy beach lay before them.

The boats were anchored a small distance from shore, so they had to paddle the rest. Crystal lifted Puss onto her shoulders and heaved Diesel into her arms. After placing them on the sand, she returned to help the older people retrieve belongings from the boat. The chickens were a challenge as they ran around, giving chase. Finally, catching one, it pecked her nose and cheek, flapping its wings so fast that she yelled and dropped it.

'Bugger!' she shouted, looking around to see everyone had stopped just to watch; a roar of laughter erupted.

'It's not funny!' she snapped.

'Karma!' Sanskrit was laughing too.

Crystal was shocked. Had the older lady heard her say that? Those wise, old eyes seemed to have poked into her soul, blurting out the whole story of her infidelity with Ayan.

An older man scooped up two chickens, tucked one under each of his arms, and went off, chuckling to the shore. She felt silly but copied. After a few more disasters, she had chicken catching, off to an art. The goat was far more challenging, as it would not go into the water. It took a great deal of pushing and pulling by three of the older men until it budged.

Diesel did not help as he danced around barking at the goat, who was so startled, broke free of the rope, and dashed off up the beach. The elderly men were furious, and Crystal received a telling off as angry voices and cross expressions were directed her way. One of the men flicked his hand, indicating she retrieved the goat. After seeing what it did to Ayan, the goat was scary, with its beady eyes. As she reached it, it lowered its head and ran at her. Crystal sprinted away, terrified. Tripping over a log, she went flying and lay sprawled on the sand. Many of the group burst into fits of giggles, much to her distress. Maya came over, tears running down her face, and reached out her hand to help her up.

'Funny,' she giggled.

'Very!' Crystal was not amused.

While the men unloaded the boats, the women grabbed bundles of items and walked away from the beach through the trees. Crystal copied and followed, calling Puss and Diesel after her. The trees opened into a clearing with seven little huts clustered around. She wondered why they would have such a thing on an uninhabited island but shrugged, grateful there was some shelter.

Separate groups of people began carrying belongings into chosen huts. Crystal wondered where she should go. Two were yet to be taken, so she pulled open the rattan door of one. She coughed at the dust and sand that invaded her lungs. There was not much inside. A bed made from wood, with a dried grass mattress, filled most of the space. A familiar wooden bench and a small table were inside, too. It was cosy and cute.

'OUT!' it was the elderly man who had grabbed the chickens again. He stood at the door, looking annoyed.

'I'm sorry… I didn't mean to… intrude.'

'OUT!' he shouted again, pointing her way out the door. He slapped her hand as she passed.

Everyone was busy bustling about. She tried to help but began to feel in the way and excluded. Returning to the beach, she saw two more fishing boats on their way to the shore. Mira and some of the older people were on board one of them. Ayan was not among them.

'You came?' Crystal smiled at Mira as she waded out to meet them.

Judging by the elder's faces, it had taken some persuading. Crystal grabbed at some of the bundles and began carrying them to shore. Dumping everything in a heap, she returned to retrieve more.

Mira was still on the boat, doubled in pain, as she cried out.

'Not the baby? Surely,' she asked, thinking, what bad timing.

A lady shouted something in her own language to Crystal, forgetting she could not understand. Once the contraction subsided, Mira translated it into - towels, water, and Sanskrit. Without hesitation, she waded back to where the group was sorting through the piles at the huts.

'Sanskrit!' she called, who soon appeared.

'Baby!' Crystal rocked her arms and pointed back at the boat, 'Baby,' she repeated.

Sanskrit understood as she disappeared in the boat's direction, as hastily as her legs allowed. Crystal began sorting through the pile of belongings until the same man smacked her hand.

'No!' he shouted.

'You don't understand. We need towels and water.' She demonstrated by cradling a make-believe baby in her arms before pretending to gulp at a bottle.

The man's features relaxed as he nodded. Sorting through the pile, he pulled out some cotton sheets and a bottle of alcohol.

'No!' she shook her head and returned it to him.

One of the other ladies spoke; he sniggered, digging deep in the pile, and producing some water. Maya popped out from one of the huts, covered in dust.

'Miras on the boat. The baby's coming!' Crystal called.

She ran back to the boat with Maya and the goods. Mira had her garments lifted and trousers removed; sweat was pouring from her face. Crystal cringed, not wanting to face the same fate but knowing there was little choice when her time came. She took Mira's son in her arms and grabbed the hand of the other young boy. Both were crying with fear. Carrying him to the shore, the younger of the two became hysterical, kicking and screaming. Another lady came forward and took both children from her.

Little else was left to do after carrying the bundles to the camp. The village people busied themselves, creating a home and unpacking. The boats had now left again to gather more supplies from Panchaea. She hoped Ayan would come to the island this time and be safe.

On each visit to the shore, she heard Mira scream as the baby ripped her insides. The thought of her turn filled her with horror, and she wondered why childbirth was so painful when it was supposed to be natural. It seemed to Crystal that women suffer so much compared to men.

No one wanted her help at the camp; they mostly snubbed her by turning their back. Mr Slap, as she thought of him, again slapped her when she tried to help one lady carry some bundles into her chosen hut. Nothing left to do, she walked to the edge of the camp. Finding a fallen tree, she sank down. Diesel skulked over, having finished cocking his leg around various points. He looked up with big, sombre eyes.

'At least you're my friend,' she patted his coat and smiled.

Not to be outdone, Puss jumped onto the bough next to her and climbed onto her lap. How Crystal wished it was just her and Ayan again. Or she should have stayed at the villa; at least she had comfort and a shop. After a while, feeling really fed up and with nothing better to do, she headed off to explore the island. No one seemed to notice as she walked away, calling the dog and cat after her.

The woods, with an abundance of trees, were surprisingly larger than had appeared from the sea. The island was a haven for birds of all colours, like parrots. Their wings flapped, showing gleaming blues and greens as they squawked and took off in protest of her intrusion, or rather Pusses, who was extremely interested in them.

The trees were sparse in parts, and the sun magically beamed through onto large patches of grass and wild plants. A wide freshwater stream weaved through the island, trickling down from the cliffs and spanning into the sea. At the furthest point was a smaller sandy area hidden by a rocky border, which was hard to clamber over to reach. To one side, the land graduated to the cliffs, where nature had carved a few shallow caves. It was a gentle climb through the trees to the top. Finding a clearing, Crystal found a rock where she could look out to sea. Unlike the beachside, this was a sheer drop into the ocean. The water was choppy, and white froth from the waves crashed into the rocks, offering no mercy to anyone falling in.

'I don't think anyone wants us here, Diesel,' she put her arm around the dog, who sat next to her, also looking dejected and sorrowful.

Her mind drifted to the tranquillity of the sacred ground and Ayan's body. Crystal had no idea how long she sat daydreaming and playing with her thoughts. Diesel barking scared her half to death, as she jumped up, seeing a young man approaching.

'I thought I'd find you here; don't ask me why. I hear you had an altercation with a goat.' His English was perfect. Without an invite, he sat on the rock Crystal had vacated. 'My name is Cristiano, but you can call me Chris; most people do. And you must be Crystal.'

His expression was so cheeky she began to laugh. 'Very funny! I don't remember seeing you on the boat,' she responded, sitting beside him and shaking his outstretched hand.

He was a good-looking young man, not too much younger than Crystal.

'I've just arrived. More of the island people have come. Ayan told me about you. He said you may feel a little ostracised, so I thought I'd come and meet you.' He bent forward and patted Diesel, who had calmed down and seemed to like him.

Puss, who was sitting stick straight, with an aloof expression on her face, ignored Chris's coaxing. Not being able to resist some attention, her features relaxed, and she sauntered over. They both seemed to like him, as did Crystal, grateful for someone who seemed to accept her and, hopefully, for a friend.

'Are you Ali's friend?' she asked, curious.

'We're cousins, although I like to think we're mates too,' he smirked.

'How come you escaped the army?' Crystal asked.

Chris grinned, 'I'm a slippery devil.'

She laughed, instantly liking him with his easy-to-get-along-with attitude and his laughing eyes.

'I was born in England,' he went on to explain. 'My father's English. We visited the island every year for holidays to see my mother's family. I was working on the mainland for a year, work experience. I was visiting my family when war broke out, and I couldn't return to the mainland.' His voice grew serious, 'I'm stuck here now, as you are. Apart from Ali, I'm treated as an outsider too. Considered neither Panchaean nor English.'

'Why do the people resent me?' Crystal asked.

'They're afraid of you, as they are me. They think we'll corrupt the younger people with loose Western ways and their culture will be soiled. The elders don't like change. They'll get used to you,' he reassured.

Crystal looked a little shocked but did not answer. She found it odd that Chris was not included either, but felt better having an ally.

'Ali's returned to Panchaea to try and gather more people. Fuel's low, so it'll be the last time. Only one boat's gone... Come,' he stood and reached for her hand. 'Dinner'll be soon, and there's the new baby to look forward to. Judging by the screams, I don't think it's here yet.'

He grabbed her arm to lead her through some dense bushes. A meal had somehow been produced when they arrived back at the huts. A fire blazed in the centre of the camp. A large pot was on top, bubbling away. People sat around on the hut benches, which had been bought out. There was not enough for everyone. Coloured throws had been draped on them, and blankets for the younger members were on the floor. The people stared as they entered; one of the older ladies offered them plates of food, which they gratefully accepted. The same lady handed two plates to Puss and Diesel, which Crystal could not believe. Chris bought them wooden cups of the same sweet drink she had before. They sat on one of the vacant blankets and chatted easily while they ate.

'The people look so sad,' Crystal observed.

Chris looked around and nodded. 'They've lost everything. Most of their families have been killed or have been taken to fight. They don't know if they'll ever see them again. So many are dead already. Their homes and way of life have all gone, and no one knows what'll happen or if this will ever be over.'

Crystal nodded in understanding.

Another hour later, Sanskrit came from the beach, holding the newborn baby in her arms. Mira's mother was supporting her, followed by Maya. The people cooed and clapped, and despite her exhaustion, Mira smiled proudly, before the little group disappeared into one of the huts.

'A little girl,' Chris smiled.

Ayan returned with more people a few hours later, only five this time. Crystal felt a prang of jealousy as he ignored her, disappearing into the hut to join his family.

As night fell with its usual deep blackness, candles in lamps were placed around the area. With nowhere to sleep, the youngest lay around the fire on the blankets. Puss and Diesel curled with Crystal. The cat gave her a customary wash on her face, causing her to moan at the roughness of her tongue before they drifted.

In the early hours, thunderous rain visited them, falling in the usual bucket loads. The fire hissed and died in seconds. The sleeping people squealed or yelled as they jumped up and ran to find protection. Children squashed into their parents' huts, and the older ones ran for trees, scooping up blankets to keep them dry. The foliage offered no protection, as its leaves and boughs bulged under the weight of water, eventually releasing their load on the sheltering victims.

'I hate this bloody rain!' Crystal shouted to Chris over the thundering bounces and rustles.

'It is rather disconcerting,' he shouted back, making her laugh despite her distress.

Over the next few days, the men began working to build more huts, benches, and beds. Crystal collected wood for the fire, dried grass, and useful leaves to create shade or umbrellas. She also collected water from the stream, which was bursting its banks since the rain. Many of the older ladies needed help to carry the full vessels. She worked hard, wanting to earn approval and pay for her, Diesels, and Puss's keep.

After a few days, she was invited to visit the new baby. Not knowing it was customary to take a small gift, she arrived empty-handed.

'She's beautiful,' Crystal cooed, and Mira glowed with pride as she held the tiny infant to her breast. She had never really taken notice of babies before.

'You next,' Mira smiled. 'Divina.'

Crystal took that to be the name. 'It's lovely.'

She bent over the suckling child, gently stroking its head, wondering what it would be like to be responsible for a tiny, vulnerable human. 'Hello, Divina. Welcome to Earth. You're gorgeous.'

Chris began learning a new trade, hut building, with Mr. Slap, which he wasn't very pleased about. He received many a slapped hand when he got something wrong, which made Crystal smirk. They began to compare slap stories by the fire at night. They would both be in fits of giggles, causing the elders to look on disapprovingly and even Ayan to stare coldly.

If one of the children was disobedient, refusing to collect eggs, Crystal went with them. She invented egg stories to amuse the youngsters, where giant eggs were chasing them through the trees, and they had to hide. She also made a big game of pretending not to see eggs and jumping in surprise when one was discovered. The children would be full of giggles, and egg hunting and giant egg hiding became great fun for them.

Chapter Eleven

Puss was intrigued by the chickens. She never went into the coop, considering the birds too large to hunt. They were scary, with enormous flapping wings and pecking beaks. But the cat liked to run around the coop, pretending to catch one. She would lay in the grass watching them. If one was close to the edge, Puss stuck her bottom in the air, wiggled it a few times, and pounced, startling the victim, who took off around the coop squawking and flapping, causing the rest to do the same. The elders were not too pleased, but the children found it hilarious. Watching Puss became another favourite pastime amongst young people. The cat became very popular, receiving much attention and tasty morsels.

Puss was not the only one fascinated by the chickens. Crystal giggled until she cried when she discovered they slept clamped by their large claws on a stick. She could not understand why they did not snuggle in the straw.

'All birds sleep this way,' Ayan explained, confused about why she found this funny.

'Do they?' Crystal could not get over it. 'It's all so cute.'

Ayan shook his head and went off, leaving her with her amusement. She spent hours examining their behind. In the end, she asked, 'Have they only one… you know… hole, to do everything with? I mean the poo, which they seem to do every few seconds, and the egg comes out of the same place. I always thought it fell out of their middle. And where does their wee come from?'

Ayan burst into hearty laughter, much to her annoyance.

Soon, the whole camp had been told of Crystal's fascination with chickens. Every time she was near, Mr Slap made clucking noises, which everyone seemed to find amusing.

'It was a perfectly reasonable question!' Crystal defended, annoyed that they found it funny. She raised her eyes in disgust and turned her back on them.

After this, Crystal refused to eat the eggs for a while or the chickens. Even more so when one of the birds, she'd named Jemima, was slaughtered for a stew.

They mostly ate fish, which a few men went out in the boats to catch. This never became boring, as different spices, herbs, and vegetables were used to create a delicious meal each day. Everyone adopted chores; even the people too old or sick to help much sat making things from wood, weaving twigs to make baskets, or preparing food.

Crystal learned many new skills and survival techniques. Two of her most detested jobs were washing clothes at the stream. Which involved crouching by the water's edge and rubbing the material together until it was clean. The women chattered amongst themselves, glancing her way, which was uncomfortable.

The second most hated job, and worse, was retrieving the waste from the allocated latrines. These were holes dug a short walk from the camp. The waste was used as fertiliser to grow vegetables, which horrified Crystal. Fish guts, heads, and tails were also used. They were buried beneath the seeds, which were always saved from organic produce. At first, she heaved, and often got sick when assigned this chore. But after a while, the duty was accepted as part of their life.

Once in a routine, time began to pass quickly.

Despite the waste of precious fuel, needed for fishing, it became too dangerous to sail to Panchaea. The last journey, Ayan reported, soldiers had now taken control of the whole Island. It had become their main base. There was no news of survivors, which devastated everyone. A depression had descended, and the constant rainfall made the place even more gloomy.

There were fifty-three of them, fifteen were children and baby, Divina. Except for Ayan and Chris, all the men were elderly.

'We need to get the population going,' Chris suggested.

'What do you mean?' Crystal puzzled.

'Well, with only me and a to impregnate the women, I think we need to get working, sod hut building, there's more important things.'

Despite the gloomy atmosphere, Crystal burst out laughing.

Most people, attempting to pull themselves from the depression, consoled themselves with the thought that survivors may be hiding in the Panchaea hills. This thought appeased them slightly. Many older people had complete families missing sons, grandsons, and even daughters and granddaughters. Many a tear fell on those dark days. Taking responsibility as their leader, Ayan did his best to keep morale up with parties, songs and storytelling.

After four weeks of island life, Crystal returned to camp one afternoon after collecting wood; unusually, to find everyone was grinning her way.

'What's wrong?' she gushed in a panic to Chris, who was also grinning.

Ayan stood by the fire, which was never allowed to go out unless the rain came, which seemed to be increasingly often. He gave a cough, and everyone hushed.

'I would like to say, Crystal, you are an outsider to our people. However, you have proved that you work hard and join in with any horrible task. So, we would like to present you with your own home. Where you can bring your child up.'

Crystal was overwhelmed as Mira and Maya grabbed her hands leading her to one of the newly built huts. They pulled open the rattan door and even though the inside was as all the others, she whooped with excitement bouncing on the bed and sitting on the wooden bench, running her fingers over the small table.

Everyone was smiling when she returned outside. 'Thank you so much,' her eyes were wet with tears at the kindness.

Even Ayan's mother, Veda, was smiling; now she had warmed to Crystal.

'Tonight, we have a party,' Ayan shouted, and the camp became a buzz of lively, excited chatter.

They never seemed to need much excuse for one. What could be better, at that moment, than Crystal's new home? It kept spirits up to dance and sing. So, preparations began.

The women magically produced excellent buffet food out of seemingly not much. Eggs were placed into cooking pots to boil. Once hard, their yolks scooped into a bowl and mashed with herbs before being pushed back into their case again. A large root was cut into slices and roasted in the ash embers. This was called Yam, which Crystal had heard of but, until that time, had never tried. Bath Gasa, which grew on trees in huge bulbs, was chopped and used as rice and made into sausage shapes; they had a sweet taste. Mixed with herbs and other vegetables, they were lovely. There was also Brinjal, which was so versatile that the skilled women produced many dishes from it. Crystal had had this one before and knew it as an eggplant. Each dish that was made from it tasted so different. Her favourite was a dessert made from what they called Tamarind, which, after preparation, was presented back in its shell and tasted delicious.

'These people are so skilled. It is amazing how they survive,' she marvelled to Chris, sneaking a sweet as they readied for the party. 'I've even got to like that grey Binnie stuff we have for breakfast.'

'Bint!' he corrected. 'It's made from

 a bean. It's nutritious. They have lived off the land for hundreds of years. Knowledge passed down from generations, they're amazing people.'

Crystal nodded in agreement. How little she knew about the world, never giving it a thought before. Ayan was right western people lived in such ignorant poverty.

By her fourth month of pregnancy, Crystal's belly had a slight bulge. Luckily, the trousers Mira had given her were easy to let out with their tie waist. A few people had also taken pity and offered more garments, so at least she had a few changes.

Communication became slightly easier when Chris was not around to translate. People were learning some English words, and Crystal, a few of theirs, was now able to understand and make herself understood, even though spoken words were mostly a mixture of the two.

'You no lift!' Sanskrit waved a finger at her.

How she began to love this lady, who was a wise grandmother to everyone, whom they turned to with health or emotional problems.

'You get grass and eggs,' Sanskrit continued.

This was one of Crystal's and the children's favourite chores. Even the adults began to love the chicken games and played along. So, egg collecting was extremely popular, and many wanted to join in. Crystal began to invent more games to help the youngsters with chores. She felt sorry when they received a hard smack from elders for misbehaving or not doing as they were told. She did not understand this harshness. As a child, she had never been hit, so it did not seem right they were chastised this way.

'Children must learn!' Ayan told her when she complained about a little boy put over someone's knee and his bottom smacked. The youngster screamed and cried. He hid for ages, feeling humiliated.

'But it's wrong,' Crystal snapped. 'Children should not be hit! There are other ways.'

'Yes! Western ways. And look at your unruly children, rude, ungrateful, and very naughty, growing up into equally bad young people!'

'That's not true! Not all youngsters in England are bad. When parents talk and explain, some lovely young people develop. Your way is wrong!'

'Just keep out of it,' he warned. 'It is not your concern.'

'No wonder you haven't had children,' she snapped back.

This hit a sore point. Ayan eyes darkened with hurt and anger. Crystal was a little alarmed, so she quickly stomped off, deciding she really did not like him after all.

Villagers were not pleased when she sought out a crying child and cuddled the tears away, rubbing the hurt area. This annoyed them even more, as did her objections. They felt she had no right to interfere. So, Crystal invented games to settle the arguments and avoid future smacks. If a child had to do something they did not want to do, they found Crystal. She thought up a game and did the chore with them, making things fun instead of gruelling. It was difficult to keep thinking of ideas, so most of the time, they had competitions such as: Who could collect the most washing from the line? Or who could peg the most out? The prize was a cuddle and a big wet kiss on the cheek, which the children ran from giggling and screaming.

Crystal complained to Chris about her row with Ayan.

'It is their way. I received many a smacked arse when I was a kid from my mum. But I never did it again.'

'But it doesn't make it right! There are other ways.'

'I don't think you should interfere. Their ways are sometimes harsh, but it is for a reason. Life for them is difficult. They are not bad people.'

'I'm not saying that they are bad…'

'Just different,' he interrupted.

'Well… yes, I guess.'

'Don't interfere,' he advised. 'You'll upset them, and it'll isolate you more. You've only just been accepted. Don't make life difficult for yourself.'

It was a while before she spoke to Ayan again, feeling angry for some time. He equally avoided her, not even meeting her eyes if they passed. She wondered why he and Myra did not have children; she could not imagine they used birth control; judging by her sister's three, it wasn't a thing recognised yet.

Sanskrit, who still gave her toothless grins whenever their eyes met, took her under her wing. She began to teach Crystal about what plants could be eaten and which were poisonous, making her an apprentice. The older lady struggled to collect herbs with her gnarled fingers. As Crystal was keen to learn, the arrangement suited them both.

'Malabar grass!' Sanskrit shouted as though she was deaf. 'Malabar grass!'

It just looked like a clump of grass. But Crystal knew it was used in cooking. Also, she had seen it used for anti-inflammatory medicine. It was some time before she could tell the difference between tall and regular grass.

'Sanupushpam!' Sanskrit said. She was excited when she found this. It was a pretty blue flower they used in salads, but also it was dried and tucked into a magic bag in the medicine box. Crystal did not know what it was used for until Sanskrit began hissing, weaving her arm in the air, and nipping her skin to interpret a snake bite. Crystal giggled, and the old lady gave a big smile. Tamarind, she found it easy to identify. It looked like big monkey nuts growing from willowy trees. The woman showed her how to use it as deodorant, which she was grateful for. She found the times foraging fun. However, Sanskrit always warned she was never to take too much from the land. Chris explained that the islanders believed the gods provided enough for them to eat or heal. Still, they should never be greedy, or the gifts would be taken away. Although she found this strange, Crystal carefully followed the rules and only took what was needed. Listening intently to Sanskrit, she became intrigued by plants, struggling with their names because of the language barrier. At times, if she couldn't sleep, she lay in bed going over and over the pronunciation to impress the older woman. Very soon, she began to advance to what herbs and roots to collect, too. And the names of medicines and foods.

Sometimes, she got it wrong and picked a similar-looking plant, receiving a slapped hand from Mr Slap. It was never hard. Instead of being offended, Crystal laughed and began calling him Mr. Slap to his face; sometimes, she slapped him back, causing the elderly man to look a little shocked. Women never hit men! In the end, he gave her a big gummy grin. When she got it right, he would shout, good lady, good! And her shoulders would puff with pride.

Crystal began to love these people and their peculiar ways; apart from the slapping of children, they were good, kind people. She no longer missed the internet, her phone, or the television. They were a distant memory. Even the war seemed far away.

It was most weeks now that they had regular parties. Everyone looked forward to these nights, which sometimes went on for a few days. Somehow, alcohol was brewed, which amazed her at how it was made. Music was played on peculiar instruments. Many of the elders sang strange, haunting songs, which Chris or Ayan explained the story of once they began talking again. These were usually tales of old legends. About the gods, Heroes of ancestors, who fought mystical creatures that had once lived, or people who fell in love. Most of the love was forbidden, and the pair died tragically by jumping into the sea or being pushed from the cliff.

One song made Crystal cry and played in her mind when Chris explained the words. Two separate rival tribes, the young people of each fell in love. They were caught, and after being tied, they were buried alive under stones until their ribs caved and they died. They met in the afterlife and were never parted again.

'Is it a true story?' she asked Chris.

He shrugged, 'Dunno.'

So she went to Ayan, 'Is it true?'

'Is what true?' he puzzled.

'Did they crush those youngsters to death cos they fell in love?'

He laughed, 'How do I know? It's just a song.'

'But why sing it if it wasn't true?'

'Crystal!' he put his arms on her shoulders and met her eyes. 'It's just a sad song!'

The electricity that passed through her body was disturbing as she shook him off.

'It's not just a song. They killed those poor people for loving each other!' she shrieked, stomping into her hut.

'You're too sensitive!' he called after her. 'Women. I'll never understand them,' he muttered.

Crystal did not think about the young people anymore, but Ayan's hands on her arms and the sparks that shot through her body.

Most of the parties were exciting and something to look forward to. After a few sombre songs were played, the lively music would start. Crystal often joined in the dancing with Chris, who would swing her around until they were both dizzy. At times, she sang with them, slowly grasping even more words of their language, with Chris's help. Communication was becoming even more manageable.

Crystal managed to forage a few pretty shells and stones to use for ornaments inside the hut. Then, she made a bead curtain from large seed pods, threading them onto grasses to keep out flies and mosquitoes. The camp women smiled at her cleverness and the offer of curtain-making lessons. Instead of feeling patronised, she glowed with pride, having never been good at anything before.

'Don't suppose you fancy getting married?' Chris asked one day.

'What!' Crystal gasped.

Ayan stood within earshot and gave a harsh, dark scowl.

'I could be a dad to your baby. You need a husband to take care of you,' his chest puffed, his shoulders pulled back, and his expression serious.

'We don't love each other. At least not in that way,' Crystal answered, not really knowing what to say. 'Besides, you're younger than me.'

It was true; Chris was only eighteen, soon to be nineteen, as he reminded everyone often.

'I'm fond of you. We get on well; what more do you want?'

Crystal laughed, kissed him on the cheek, and nudged him with her shoulder. 'You're like my brother. I think the world of you. But I don't think either of us are ready for marriage.'

Ayan's features relaxed as he walked away. Was it because he had feelings for her? Or was it because he thought Crystal was not suitable for his cousin, she wondered. Chris looked hurt.

'Come on, let's go for a swim,' she said, grabbing his hand and dragging him to the beach.

Forgetting his rejection, Chris stripped off his tunic and trousers and ran into the warm sea.

Crystal, not stripping away her clothes, ran after him and splashed him, giggling. Ayan watched from the trees for a while before walking back to the camp.

It was a few months later when Ayan began fretted terribly that there may still be people waiting for rescue on Panchaea. Fuel was now needed for fishing; there was none spare to make the journey.

'It was also too dangerous now the military had full control of the Island,' Chris translated to Crystal as the group talked.

'One more journey,' Ayan said.

'NO!' Maya objected, 'I need my husband; we need a man here to help us. It is suicide to go again.'

'I cannot live with myself if I don't try, just once more.'

'Then I must go in your place.' It was one of the older men, Koa, who was speaking. 'I am old and not much use. But I can sail a boat. Maya is right; this Island needs a fit man to help them.'

It was decided that Koa and another of the men were to leave at first light. Ayan was not pleased, knowing they were at significant risk, but there was no choice; he would be too valuable to lose.

The atmosphere was heavy and tense as everyone awaited their return the next day. The children were quiet, attending chores without objection and playing without much sound. Much to everyone's relief, the boat returned four hours later, bringing three survivors. Two of them, women, daughters to one of the older ladies, who cried and sobbed in each other's arms, thankfully reunited. The other was a white foreigner, possibly English. It was a man, half-starved and delirious from fever. He had made it into the hills, where people were hiding, as they had suspected. They could not help him, so they took him to the shore, hoping the boat would come.

A few men carried the man to the fire. Sanskrit attended to him with her magic bag of medicines. The man was about thirty, blond, and very good-looking. He reminded Crystal of Stuart; her heart flipped when she saw him. He was semi-conscious, rambling words that did not make much sense.

'I wonder how he escaped?' Ayan said, not really looking pleased at his rescue. 'We have so many mouths to feed now,' he complained.

'But it was your idea to rescue more people,' Maya pointed out.

He huffed, making Crystal wonder why he objected to this man being helped. Was he jealous? She crouched beside him, which was difficult, with her now bulging stomach. The baby had recently been kicking inside of her, which was a peculiar sensation. It kicked now, protesting at the squashing.

'It's OK, you're safe,' she told the man, who mumbled and groaned. Sweat ran from his face and body as he was near to death.

'Will he make it?' she asked as the group stared at him.

'He young and strong,' Mira pointed out. 'He has a chance.'

Crystal sat all night, mopping his brow with cool water and willing him to pull through. Ayan was not pleased when he found her curled in a ball, asleep the next day.

'You should not be here! You need rest. The man may be contagious!' he snapped.

'I was just looking after him,' she defended. 'In case he woke.'

'You need to be responsible. You have a baby to think of… And animals,' he added as an afterthought.

Crystal looked around. Diesel and Puss were curled beside her. Making her suspicious as to why Ayan cared so much. But it was true; she should take more care. Her time was getting nearer; she needed to get rid of the bulk, which made getting around difficult.

Chapter Twelve

'What you call baby?' Maya asked.

'I've no idea. How come you've not had children?' Crystal blurted and instantly regretted as her friend's eyes clouded with sadness, and she looked away.

'Not blessed,' she shrugged and making an excuse, left.

Crystal felt dreadful; she had seen tears in Maya's eyes. She could not get it out of her mind, so in the end, she sought out Mira to ask. Mira looked sad, too, when she asked why her sister had no children. Her hands were full with the new baby and her two unruly youngsters.

'She longs for baby. I feel bad for her.'

'But why then?'

'She cannot have them.'

Crystal was mortified, 'Oh no! I feel so bad asking her and guilty being pregnant.'

'Me too. It unfortunate. Ayan would make good father,' Mira responded feeling sad for her sister.

'I'm not sure about that,' Crystal bristled, looking surprised that Mira thought so. 'He can be so harsh,' she added.

Mira grinned knowingly, 'You like him lot? He handsome man.'

'I don't. And I certainly don't think he is handsome,' Crystal lied, gushing the words a little too quickly.

Mira laughed and raised her eyebrows.

'I don't. But I got a bit fond of him on our travels. But he is annoying, and we have different opinions. Plus a few arguments.'

'But that, like all men! I want to slap my one when here. I miss him much. He does not even know about baby.'

'What's he like?'

'Very handsome, hence having three children.'

They both laughed.

'He is Ayan's brother, Masa. A year younger than him.'

'I didn't know. Ayan is not very forthcoming with information, and no one said. Everyone seems to be related. I need clarification about who belongs to whom.'

'It true. We mostly related. The four of us grew up together. The sisters are married to cousins. We went school together on mainland.'

'Where are their sisters?'

'They live Buranda. More work. They used to visit regularly.'

'Did you and Maya marry at thirteen?'

'No!' she laughed. 'We both seventeen. My baby came straight away, too close to ceremony. Their punishment for not being joined when baby come,' she giggled. 'I just made it. Sanskrit covered me and pretended baby early.'

After a few days, the unconscious man came too, a little. He turned out to be German. Luckily, he spoke reasonable English, which Crystal was grateful for. She did not fancy learning another language. He was still poorly, so she insisted he be moved to her hut.

'No way!' Ayan objected. 'It's not right to put a stranger in there. It's for you and your baby!'

'But he can't be left here, laying on a blanket. He needs privacy.'

'NO!' Ayan's jawline was set firm, and his eyes blazed, indicating no negotiation.

'But...'

'But nothing... NO!' he stomped off, leaving Crystal with her mouth open with unspoken words.

'God, that man!' she raved, and Maya, standing close by, grimaced.

'You cannot let a stranger in your hut. He could be dangerous,' she agreed with Ayan.

'He's right,' Chris stated, joining them, after having made a hasty retreat when he heard the row raging.

'He hardly looks dangerous,' she huffed.

Later that day, when Ayan and Chris were fishing, Crystal asked two of the elders to help move the man to her hut. They had not heard Ayan's objections, so she told them he had agreed.

Maya was distraught when she saw. 'There will trouble!'

'I don't care. It's not right.'

'What if contagious, could harm baby. Ayan harsh, but he thinking of you.'

Crystal hadn't thought of that. 'I'll sleep by the fire. A sick man should not be out here.'

Ayan was furious when he came back and found Crystal had disobeyed him. His eyes bulged with rage, and most people, knowing there would be an almighty row, disappeared.

'How dare you!' he yelled.

'You can't tell me what to do!' she shouted, equally angry.

Ayan grabbed hold of her wrist, dragged her kicking and screaming to a bench, pulled her over his lap, and began smacking her bottom. Diesel jumped about barking, snapping at his ankles. Ayan kicked him away. Crystal screamed for help, but no one stopped him; they just stared, knowing her actions would cause repercussions.

'You want to act like a naughty child; you'll be treated like one!' he barked between each whack.

The smacks were not hard, but she wriggled and hit any part of him she could reach with her fists.

'Let me go. How dare you!' she raved.

He lifted her to her feet, his eyes still blazing with temper.

She went to slap his face, but he caught her hand in mid-flow. 'I bet you got off on that!' she screamed, running into the woods, Diesel close at her heels. Tears of humiliation streamed down her face.

'You're no longer a Princess who always gets her own way! And no, I didn't get pleasure from it!' he shouted after her.

'I hate you. YOU ARE A PIG!' she screamed back.

Crystal thought she would never go back to the camp again, guessing everyone would be laughing at her. The sun began to die, and the dense blackness fell like snow. She was hungry but still would not return and face the people. Her name was called a few times, recognising Chris, Maya, Mira, and even Sanskrit.

Then, surprisingly, Ayan came to look for her. 'I've left you some food here!' he shouted. 'There's some for Diesel too…. I've fed Puss.'

She listened to the sound of rustling becoming more distant, as he walked away. Hunger rumbling in her stomach, Crystal grabbed the dish and ran back to her hideaway. Ayan had gone too far this time; she vowed never to speak to him again as long as she lived. Even if it meant a horrible death of starvation.

It was an uncomfortable night with her stomach bulging, there was not a good position to sleep. She dozed fitfully, listening to the night creatures, reminding her of those months when she slept alone in Panchaea.

The next day, Chris found her sitting on the cliff edge, looking out to sea. He plopped down and put his arm around her. Crystal burst into floods of tears on his shoulder.

'You do get into some scrapes!'

'He is a pig!' she sobbed.

Chris laughed, 'He's a good man. He's a lot of responsibility, keeping everyone safe and fed.'

'He is still a pig!'

'Come back to the camp. It is not safe alone, not with lump.' Which was the pet name for her tummy.

'I can't,' she sobbed miserably. 'Everyone must be laughing at me.'

'Everyone's sorry. They think Ali went too far. It was wrong. Maya gave him such a telling-off and whacked him with a broom. His face was red for an hour.'

Crystal laughed at the image.

'Sanskrit threw tamarind pods at him, and one hit him in the eye. And Mr Slap slapped him four times on his arse.'

Knowing it wasn't true, she laughed again. Chris always managed to cheer her up.

'Puss is missing you. She keeps yowling.'

Crystal sniffed a few times, wiping the tears with her hand. 'OK. I'll come back. But I'm never talking to that creep again.'

'Well, you don't have to. He's gone fishing, so isn't even there.'

Maya ran to her as they entered the camp, 'Are you OK? I am so sorry; Ayan went too far.'

'He's a pig!' she cried, trying to control the tears from bursting out again.

Several of the ladies came and hugged her. Sanskrit hobbled over, with Veda.

'You too much spirit,' she said, but her eyes were sympathetic.

'I got dunked in the sea once, naked, for misbehaving. Everyone saw,' Veda, unusually kind to Crystal, confessed.

'Oh, how horrible,' she empathised as an image of the naked woman trying to cover her dignity popped into her head.

The German man had been moved back to the fire. His condition worsened, and he became delirious once again. Crystal and Ayan did not speak for a while after that. She sent him looks of hatred if they met, and he looked away.

'It's cruel! The poor man needs to be in a bed!' Crystal raved to Chris each time she was sure Ayan was close enough to hear.

Chris did not answer as he looked away, embarrassed.

One week after the German man came to the Island, some of the children began to develop sore throats, swollen glands and fever.

Mira was beside herself when both her boys became sick. A few days after, the new baby, too.

'What is it?' Crystal worried for her friend.

'We do not know. Sanskrit is mixing potions, but it is not helping,' Maya told her.

The older woman, as if hearing her name, wobbled over and began speaking with Ayan, both looking Crystal's way.

'You need to leave the camp!' he said.

Despite his serious expression, she thought he looked smug. Or did she imagine it?

'Your baby is at risk. The German man has spread something,' he continued.

'You cannot be sure of that!' she snapped, not wanting to admit he may have been right to chastise her. 'Children are always getting sick!

'You leave! You cannot risk baby,' Sanskrit added.

'It's probably just a cold! Besides, where will I go?'

Ayan paused while he thought, speaking to Sanskrit again. Then, a decision was made.

'We'll create a makeshift camp. Food can be left daily. But you must go.'

'Yes. Leave. No argue. GO!' Sanskrit pointed a finger out of the camp.

Upset, Crystal stomped to her hut and packed some of her belongings. A few able men built her a canopy with large leaves in the wood. Ayan and Chris carried the bed, bench, and table from her hut. Once finished, it was very cozy. That night, lying on her bed, Crystal felt lonely. The woods were creepy on her own. If it was not for Diesel's company, she would have taken herself back to the camp.

Chris came to see her the next day, bringing food. He sat on a log, a safe distance away. 'Things are not good,' he told her.

'What's happened?' she fretted.

'Mira's baby is worse. Sanskrit thinks Divina might die. She's working flat out trying to help, as the children are also worse, and some of the elders are ill now, too.'

'That's terrible!'

The next day, Ayan bought her food and carried an objecting Puss under his arm. Keeping a safe distance away, he plopped the cat on the ground. She, most disgruntled at being evicted from the camp, washed her paw with vigour before jumping on the bed. Turning her back on them, she sat bolt upright, staring in the other direction.

'She's a stubborn, spoilt Princess too!' Ayan laughed.

Crystal huffed but did not take offense. He lingered for a while, not knowing what more to say, made towards the camp.

'Sorry!' she shouted.

Ayan stopped and turned; his face full of surprise.

'I'm sorry for taking the man into my hut. I know you were only looking out for me.'

Without answering, he nodded and left.

Boredom taking its toll, Crystal gathered herbs, thinking they might help Sanskrit. Not really sure what was needed, she picked what she thought.

When Chris came later with food, his face looked grave. 'The baby died; her throat closed… she suffocated. Mira is beside herself with grief.' His voice was choked.

Crystal burst into tears. 'Oh, poor Mira. What a terrible death for that beautiful baby,' she sobbed.

'That's not all. The German died late last night. Me and Ali are taking his body out to sea later. We don't even know his name. More of the children and a few of the elders are ill. It's not looking good. We've no medicine.'

'But what is it?'

'Sanskrit says it's Diphtheria. She saw much of it as a youngster.'

'I don't know what that is,' Crystal said. 'Will everyone get it?'

'Apparently, it affects mostly young and old. But it could spread to anyone. Ali has a sore throat and skin ulcers. He is using your hut to keep away from Maya. We need antibiotics, but of course, that's impossible. All Sanskrit has is marshmallow root.'

'I can gather that for her,' Crystal wanted to do something.

'It's not enough. It only helps a bit. It's criminal to see the poor children suffering so much. Ali is talking about returning to Panchaea to see what he can find. We need medicine, or more children will die.'

'But it's too dangerous!' Crystal's heart leapt at the thought of Ayan being shot.'

'What's the alternative? We need Penicillin. Ali knows ways onto the Island that no one else does.'

'But surely soldiers guard the coastlines, and even when there, where will he find antibiotics?'

'The surgery, of course.'

It had never occurred to her that such a thing existed on the Island.

Chris laughed at her surprise. 'So, you thought they lived in caves, dragged women around by their hair, and hunted woolly mammoths?'

Her face flooded with embarrassment. 'Well... I... I don't know what I thought. I just did not imagine a doctor's surgery or hospital on the island.'

It was almost dark when Crystal went to the coast and watched the fishing boat leave with Ayan on board. She began to pray for his safe return. With Diesel, they sat on a rock to wait for him. Maya, keeping a safe distance, appeared and sat on the sand. She pulled her knees up and rested her chin on them. Her eyes were red, and her face was swollen from crying over the loss of baby Divina.

'She beautiful. Terrible. Die before live.'

'How is Mira?' Crystal asked.

'She cries. I not know what to do. The boys bit better. Mira has sore throat. Ayan sick. He should not go, but no choice.'

They stared out to sea, no more words spoken. The situation was desperate; would any of them survive?

Crystal heard the rumbling in her sleep. She could not work out what it was. Diesel began to bark, startling her into consciousness. It was the boat on its way back. 'Thank god,' she breathed.

Maya was already at the edge of the sand, eagerly waiting for Ayan. Diesel was bouncing up and down beside her, with his tail wagging. Ayan greeted the dog with a pat on his coat and an ear tickle. 'The surgery had been raided. Nothing much was left inside. I managed to find twenty tablets.'

'Not enough!' Maya shook her head despondently, looking tragic.

'Well, some are better than none,' he smiled weakly, but his eyes were full of worry and concern. 'We must use what we have for the children.'

Crystal and Diesel left them, going back to the small camp.

Over the next few days, three elderly people died, including the mother, only just reunited with her two daughters. Two more of the children had passed away by the evening. The camp was crushed and grief-stricken. Many tears fell for the loss.

Ayan and Chris sailed the boat to sea with the bodies of the dead, including baby Divina. Sanskrit held a funeral for them. The villagers, who were well enough, gathered around, burning precious candles, while she spoke words of comfort to put the souls to rest as they watched the boat leave the shore. Mira was apparently too ill to attend. Maya feared for her sister's life.

Although she did not understand all the spoken words, Crystal stood a distance away, her head bowed and tears flowing, as did they all, for the loss. Even more for the children, who did not deserve to have their lives cut so short. One little girl had only been two years old. Her mother sobbed hysterically as she fell to her knees on the sand.

'I thought there were more inhabited islands around here?' Crystal asked Chris on his next visit.

'Apparently,' he answered. 'But I think the people on them are mostly hermits. They don't mix with plebs like us.'

'But maybe they will have medicines to help.'

'God knows. Ali's already thought of that. But it's too dangerous as they may have been invaded.'

'Guess so!' Crystal said gloomily.

Their situation was hopeless. More people had become ill, although Ayan was apparently fine now. The ulcers had cleared, and his throat was OK. Crystal still gathered dry grass and wood each day, leaving it at the edge of the camp for the fire in a small effort to help.

'Mira's getting worse. Ali won't let Maya visit her for fear she'll catch the illness. There's been a few rows between them,' Chris told her, a few days later. So far, he had been fine and not infected by illness. 'Four more of the elderly died last night. That's seven adults now, not including the children. The antibiotics Ali managed to find have been eked out amongst the sick children.'

155

Each day, either Maya, Ayan or Chris visited. They brought more shocking news of sickness and two more deaths amongst the older people. Crystal cried for each of them, wishing she could grieve with the rest of the group.

Three weeks after the illness broke out, Sanskrit made an unexpected visit, bringing her food for the day.

'Oh god!' Crystal cried; seeing the older lady could only mean dreadful news. 'Is everyone ill now?'

Despite the heavy cloud looming over the camp, the old lady laughed at her. 'No, better. People, improve.'

'Thank goodness,' she breathed, a small weightlifting.

'I come, see if, OK. Baby getting closer.'

'Apart from the huge lump on my belly, I'm OK.'

Sanskrit smiled, but her eyes looked weary and sad. 'Good, Good.'

She did not stay long, needing to get back to her patients.

Over the next few weeks, every visitor thankfully brought brighter news. They were coming out of the other side of a very dark storm. The people were pulling through. Thankfully, there had been no more deaths. The only person not showing signs of improvement was Mira.

'She does not want to live after losing baby,' Maya told Crystal, bulbous tears weighing heavily in her eyes. There were few words that could be given in comfort.

'She must live. For her two sons and her husband.' Crystal said, feeling despondent and hopeless as Maya, that she could do nothing.

'Children are staying with me and Ayan. She not see them. Not eat. Just stare or sleep.'

'Can Sanskrit not give something for depression?'

'She try. Nothing helps.'

After one more week in quarantine, Crystal was allowed to return to her hut.

Mira did live. She had to for her two boys, Sanskrit, and her sister and husband, who may one day return. But after losing her baby girl, her eyes looked soulless; there was no longer a spark or zest for life in their depth.

Chapter Thirteen

Crystal had four more weeks of pregnancy to endure. Her tummy was uncomfortable, and her internal organs felt squeezed and trampolined on, she told Chris.

He grimaced, shuddered. The information was far too much for his head to cope with. 'I prefer to think of female organs like the holy grail. Not battered cod.'

'Even the tie-string trousers were stretched to the limit. And I constantly need to pee, as my bladder is flat!' she continued, ignoring his wrinkled nose and look of distaste.

He stuck his fingers in his ears and began an out-of-tune 'LaLa,' to blot out the images. 'I may never have sex again!'

'You mean you have?' she laughed.

He puffed his chest and looked affronted. 'Course I have. Women flock to me for nuptials. I'm known as super-stud in England! I'd offer to prove it. But I've suddenly gone off you and have post-traumatic stress disorder about your innards. Especially as I now have to imagine that huge lump coming out of your Tootie.'

In many ways, Crystal could not wait to be rid of the lump. But on the other hand, she was frightened. Often, in the early hours, she lay worrying about the birth. There was no protection of a hospital, doctors, midwife, or pain assistance. What would happen if the baby or her was in trouble? Mira tried her best to reassure Crystal. Sanskrit had apparently delivered hundreds of babies. It did not comfort her, though; she was scared.

That morning, mild cramping pains woke her early. She had them a few times before, but Mira had convinced her this was sometimes normal. To distract herself from it, she called Diesel and went to leave for a stroll and wash at the stream.

'I don't suppose you're coming?' Crystal said to Puss.

The cat had become lazy these days, preferring to snooze on the bed.

'You'll get fat,' she told her. But Puss just raised one eye, sighed, mashed her lips, and fell asleep again.

'I wish I could sleep that fast!'

It was early; most villagers were still asleep, and even the sun was just beginning to rise. Leaving Puss to snooze, Crystal called Diesel and headed to the stream. One of the things she missed about home was a warm shower and hair conditioner. There was no Zingiber flower, that her and Ayan used at the Sacred ground. But there was at least a type of soap, as Sanskrit had shown her a leaf, which they all used to bathe. It did not pollute, so was safe to water and sea life. This was really important to the people, as they protected nature where they could.

She was surprised to find Ayan and Maya were already at the stream. Crystal hung back, not wanting to intrude; she watched from behind a rock. They were giggling at some private joke, splashing each other like children. A great knot of emotion flooded her body, settling in her stomach. The two were so close. Ayan wrapped his arms around his wife, kissing her head. Maya snuggled into his chest and looked up at him, eyes full of devotion and passion.

'Oh, to be that much in love! It's sickening,' she said to Diesel, who did not understand, but he wagged his tail anyway.

Crystal patted his coat and turned back to the camp before she saw any more of their private time. Chris was just leaving to bathe when she got back.

159

'I'd wait if I were you,' she told him. 'Ali and Maya are having a moment.'

He looked puzzled before realisation hit. He winked and grinned. Causing the mixture of emotions to weigh even heavier. She needed time to process and assess her head.

'Come on! Why don't we go for a swim in the sea?' Chris suggested.

Mr Slap, hearing them, objected. 'No! No! storm coming.'

'But the sky is sparkling,' Crystal laughed.

'Silly old codger. Come on,' he grabbed her hand, ignoring the older man, they left for the sea. 'A swim might help ease your whingeing about lump!'

'I do not whinge!' she looked affronted.

'No! No!' Mr Slap called after them, really agitated.

They pretended not to hear and carried on to the beach. There was no storm, and Chris was right. The swim did ease the burden of lump a little. When they returned to shore, Ayan was waiting for them on the sand with Diesel. His eyes blazed with fury.

'What the hell are you doing!' he shouted.

Chris looked surprised, 'Easy, old chap, we only went for a swim.'

'You know full well you were told not too!'

Crystal was surprised by his anger; she became defensive and annoyed. 'You can't tell us what to do! We went for a swim, like usual. What's the big deal?'

'I think you'll find I can tell you what to do. And you were told not to go! There is a storm coming, anything could have happened!'

'Absolute rubbish, there's no storm. How dare you dictate!' Crystal stomped off into the camp, furious.

Ayan followed, still raving behind her. 'You're a spoilt, stubborn brat, woman! You need to listen to wiser people than you!'

She turned to him, fists clenched. 'What do you mean, a man? You are kidding! You do not control me. You are a pig!' With that, she picked up a fish from a nearby basket and threw it at him, hitting Ayan on the forehead.

Following them, Chris put his hand over his mouth and tried not to laugh. 'You've been kippered, mate.'

It was not the right time for the joke because it worsened the situation. Ayan was so angry that he rushed at Crystal and grabbed her wrist. She screamed and kicked him in the shin, hurting her toe. It gave her enough time to run. Fear of another smacked bottom drove her into the woods, with Diesel close behind her. She tried to walk off the anger, stomping to her favourite place at the cliff top. The ocean always seemed to ease her head. After the anger melted away, Crystal began to giggle, and once she started, could not stop. Mentally, seeing Ayan's shocked face when the fish hit him. Becoming almost hysterical with laughter, so much so that her muscles began to object. Crystal decided to call him Fish Face from now on, whenever the arrogant pig annoyed her. Or even Kipper Chops, which was silly, but in that giggly moment added to the amusement, as tears streamed down her face. She clenched her stomach against the ache. Then, more so, at Diesel's confused face. The dog twisted his head to one side, then the other. He thumped his tail slowly, unsure if he should or not. Was his mistress angry or happy? He could not decide.

'Oh, Diesel, you're so funny.'

A flood of water seeped down her legs, wetting her trousers. At first, Crystal thought she'd had an accident, laughing too much. Then, as reality hit, a pain shot through her, which felt like being scraped from the insides with a sharp knife. Diesel, seeing her face screw as she hugged her stomach, began to bark, and whine. His eyes were full of unease as Crystal cried out in shock. Another cramping pain shot through her.

The sun snubbed out at that moment, and huge, thick clouds swept across the ocean in seconds. The rain fell in enormous glops; their power stung her skin, soaking her in moments.

'Great!' she gasped, 'Right on time… Get help, Diesel!' she shouted through the thunderous roar. Despite the icy water, sweat ran down her face as she doubled in pain.

Diesel cowered and began to whine as water fell from his ears and coat. He did not want to leave her.

The sea had become choppy as a great hurling wind swept across the ocean, like the jaws of a monster, coming to swallow them up. Within minutes, the waves crashed violently against the rocks, almost reaching where Crystal was doubled over. The noise of screaming wind was horrific as it slapped into trees, bending their trunks and branches, which bowed under the strain. Bits of wood and debris whirled into the air, dancing before crashing into random targets. Leaves whirled, and rocks splashed, punching into the sea.

'Go, please, Diesel. Get help!'

The dog cowered, petrified, whimpering. The sound was whisked away, along with Crystal's cries, with the noise of the wind, which whistled, screamed, rustled and howled around them. She clung to the grass and a rock against the force, which almost lifted her into the ocean, as she fought with panic and pain.

'Diesel, please, go!'

Dutifully, he stood, taking one last look at her, and with his big sad eyes, he ran towards the camp. The tree crashed to the ground, unable to fight any more against the onslaught. Diesel's pitiful yelp - silenced.

'NOOOOO!' she screamed, 'Not my baby! Not my lovely dog!'

Afraid of the storm, Puss had long since vacated the bed. She was now hunched behind a tree bough. She heard the heartbreaking yelp of her friend with her acute hearing. Her ears perked up, and she looked towards the cliff.

The roofs of huts tore from their homes, sweeping into the air and twisting before hitting the ground and brushing along the sand. The campfire had long since been snubbed by the rain. Ash and charcoal pirouetted around the floor and air, bashing into people's eyes. They were terrified, not knowing where to run for cover. Some were trying to secure what they could with ropes. All were drenched, with hair plastered to heads, like helmets, and soggy clothes, transparent.

Taking her chances, Puss, ran to Ayan, her slight body battling the gusts. He did not see the cat as he tried to hunker down what was left of the camp. Her fur blew, and her ears flattened, by the force of wind. She let out a huge yowl and stuck her claws into his leg.

He swore, shaking Puss away, and shouted to Chris over the noise. 'We need to check the boats!'

Chris nodded, and they made their way towards the beach, bent double against the force of the wind. Not to be put off, Puss ran to Ayan again, meowing loudly, but he could not hear over the noise. So, she stuck in her claws again, before darting toward the cliffs.

'Bloody cat!' he shouted, then realised: Where was Crystal? He had not seen her for ages. Amazingly, the cat was trying to tell him.

'You check the boats!' he yelled to Chris.

Ayan sped off, as best he could with the force of wind, in pursuit of the cat, who ran into the woods, turning often to check he was following. She stopped by the fallen tree, letting out a huge meow.

'Is she under there, Puss?' Ayan asked. He spotted Diesel's body through the branches. 'Crystal!' he called. Pulling away what debris he could.

Then, a short distance away, he heard her cry in a wind lull. Running to the cliff edge, he weightlessly scooped her up in his arms and tried to carry her to the camp.

'Diesel!' she cried.

'I know. I'm sorry.'

The wind was too strong, so he put her back on the ground again. She had hold of his ear when a contraction caused her to scream out, ripping at his flesh.

'Jesus, woman!' he cursed as blood began to trickle down his face.

Another tree creaked precariously near them; it crashed to the ground a short distance away, blocking the entrance.

'I'm not delivering a baby!' he shouted, the words just about heard over the orchestra of untuned noise.

Scooping her up again, he negotiated a route around the tree, back to the village.

'Sanskrit!' he called urgently.' Sanskrit!'

164

The old woman came hobbling over, blown by the wind; she almost fell. Ayan went into what was left of Crystal's hut and laid her carefully on the bed just as another contraction surged through her. Sanskrit came in and unceremoniously evicted Puss, who had followed them.

Maya and Mira appeared, along with Veda, who surprisingly held Crystal's hand, wiped her brow, and whispered words of encouragement as she cried out.

'It's too early,' she wept after one gripping contraction.

'It is fine,' Sanskrit reassured. Baby, quick. You lucky. You're near.'

As Crystal cried out, Ayan did his best to secure the side walls for privacy.

Two hours later, a tiny, six-pound male miniature of herself was born. As Crystal held him to her, counting the tiny digits of fingers and toes, a rush of love saturated her heart, like nothing ever felt before. Then guilt, that she ever considered having an abortion. Her tears fell, wetting the baby's head for her beloved Diesel, who she would miss so much.

As the wind began to die down, the villages tried to repair what they could of the damage to the camp. Mr Slap, not holding a grudge, waved from the roof as he secured it back. Crystal quickly hid her breast as he peeped over the edge. They made it a priority as a new mum.

'Good lady,' he called, grinning to show his almost toothless gums.

The next day, everything was calm, and the sun shone. If it wasn't for the disarray, it would be like the storm never happened.

People visited between repair work, bringing lovely gifts. Amongst them were an expertly sewn baby outfit, fruit, nuts, homemade incense, a kipper, which she giggled at, and two brightly coloured throws for her bench and bed. They were all so precious. Crystal kissed each person, thanking them for their kindness. She was one of them, and they were looking after her.

Ayan came into her hut later that day, 'Truce?' he waved a package, like a white flag, but his eyes were wary, unsure of her reaction.

Crystal smiled, remembering how he had risked his life for her. 'You're still a pig…I'm sorry about your ear, though.'

'He's a very handsome boy. What will you call him?' Ayan asked.

Each visitor had asked the same. She had no idea. Up until that time, Crystal's Lump was just a bump. Then, the strange dream at the sacred ground came flooding back.

'Billy Blake. It has a ring to it.'

Ayan laughed. 'It's a big name for such a little bundle.'

Crystal opened the package he had bought. It held fish heads and tails. She cringed at the bloody mass but laughed and thanked him.

'For Puss?' sadness flooded her face, thinking how Diesel would have loved the tasty meal.

'Ah! Hang on,' Ayan went to the doorway and called.

Crystal began to sob as Chris came in, carrying a wiggling Diesel in his arms. With a bandaged leg on one side and paw on the other, the dog struggled to reach her. Chris laid him on the bed, and he washed her face repeatedly while she sobbed into his fur.

'A bit of concussion, but Sanskrit says he'll be fine,' Chris told her.

'Well, they're not bad animals. Although Puss is a very upper-class Princess, like her owner,' Ayan grinned mischievously.

She gasped but laughed, 'I'm not an upper-class Princess!'

Ayan winked, making his eyes twinkle.

Much to Crystal's distress, a bed was made up in her hut, and Veda moved in.

'To help with baby. Till you get strong,' Myra explained, chuckling at her friend's dismay. 'First one, need rest.'

'First and last,' she vowed.

Her biggest marvel was when baby Billy wrapped his tiny lips around her nipple and sucked, snuffling and snorting like a piglet.

'It's so cute,' she told Maya.

Her friend smiled, but her eyes looked sad, and Crystal felt such sympathy for her, knowing how she longed for a baby.

She was sure all mums thought their babies beautiful, but to her, Billy was the most stunning infant on earth. Even though his face was crinkled, and he looked like a little Buddha, it made him more endearing.

Puss hated the new arrival. She sat in the corner and gave Billy harsh glares whenever he cried, which was often. Diesel was more maternal, guarding the cot made by Mr. Slap. His leg was still bandaged, and he limped badly as he tried to follow Crystal everywhere.

When she finally ventured from the hut, the camp was fully restored. There was no evidence left of the vicious storm.

Crystal was sitting at the cliff's edge, looking out to sea, one day, with Billy, Diesel, and for once Puss, when Chris lumbered through the rocks and plonked down beside her.

'What are you thinking?' he asked, seeing her faraway look.

She smiled. 'You mean apart from how my breasts have gone from puppies to fat bulldogs!'

'OH!' he grinned cheekily, 'I hadn't noticed.'

'I was thinking how contented I am. When I came here it was on holiday with my husband. I never realised how meaningless my life was at that time. It was all so shallow. But looking back, I really was miserable. It's extraordinary that something good can come out of something bad. Ali once told me that people like me were poor. I didn't understand. I never realised how happy life can be with nothing. What will it be like when I finally return to England? It'll be so hard to settle into life again.'

'That's too deep and meaningful for me,' Chris laughed. 'I want to see the world, have a fast car, a big house and lots of money. That's what would make me happy. Or winning the lottery. Or even just going home.'

Crystal smiled at him. 'Well, I would have said the same at one time.'

Motherhood proved to be arduous work, as Billy never seemed to stop crying, night and day. Crystal was exhausted but glad Veda was there to help. They became very close as the woman was like a mother, showing Crystal how to bathe him in the stream and create nappies from large leaves and a cotton-typed plant. Once soiled, they were put into a heap to rot as compost and fertiliser. Clothes were a problem, so he was usually placed on a throw, in the shade, naked, apart from his nappy. Some women donated clothes their own children had grown out of.

Many of the Islanders helped with childcare, lightening the load. Chris and Ayan adored Baby Billy and gave him big cuddles whenever possible. Maya often cared for him while Crystal went herb picking for a break. Mira tended to stay away, as the baby's presence caused too much pain.

It was one of these days, while Veda was minding Billy and Crystal was herb picking with Sanskrit, that a few of the children followed them into the woods.

Sanskrit not pleased to have the youngsters around her, became snappy and impatient. Crystal began to tell them a story, miming and acting out words, making them and even the older lady laugh. When she did a growly bear, Diesel began to bark and wag his tail, delighting the children even more. Then she pretended to be a hunter, holding a big spear and being scared in case she met a tiger. Hiding in the grass, she jumped out at Diesel, who was the make-believe tiger.

'You teacher,' Sanskrit laughed. 'You teach. You good with children, teach.' She pointed her finger at her, which usually meant her word was final.

'What, me? No way. I don't know anything,' she laughed, a little shocked. 'Besides who would mind Billy?'

When they returned to the camp, Sanskrit began ordering some of the men around, pointing and instructing them to move things.

Mira came to Crystal. 'Sanskrit says you are now teacher for children. She setting up school for you.'

'Don't be silly; I couldn't teach. I don't know the first thing about it,' she protested.

169

'You good with youngsters. What Sanskrit says happens. She boss,' Mira chuckled. 'School starts tomorrow.'

'But what about Billy? He is a full-time job.'

'Grandmother caring for him... Veda,'

An area was cleared of leaves and brambles. Throws were laid onto the ground. Then, a bench for Crystal was brought over. Sand was carried from the beach so she and the children could write. And that was the school.

Crystal was terrified, but dutifully, the next day, the children sat cross-legged in front of her, ready and waiting to be taught.

'First...! We will learn English letters,' she began, drawing a big A into the sand.

The children gasped, and the elders, looking on, wooed and clapped. Ayan, standing by, had a huge grin on his face.

The school lasted four hours a day in the morning. It was too hot in the afternoon. However, if the rain thundered, the school was cancelled until it stopped, and the ground was dryer.

Chapter Fourteen

Crystal took her new teacher job seriously as she dug into her memory archives, trying to remember things she had learned at school. It wasn't much, as she had never paid attention. The older children were well-behaved and overseen by the elders who sat watching every day. Crystal separated some of her space into a nursery for the younger pupils. She encouraged some more youthful women, including Maya, to help. Mira, she didn't, figuring she needed a break from her two boys. Mr Slap found the school very amusing, as he seemed to most things. Whenever he passed, it was always with a long, continuous chuckle, which was annoying.

Crystal even managed to take the young people foraging for herbs and plants with Sanskrit, whom she nominated because she was the one who got her into this. Instead of being unruly this time, the children were well-behaved. They returned their gathered plants to school and learned how to hang them to dry. The next day, she fired herb questions at them as an exam.

The school was successful, and Crystal was proud. A new project had begun, and she took her role very seriously, each night, planning for the next day's lessons.

She made Ayan show the older children how to make a bench from wood. Hye, she borrowed for an hour to show them how to gut and prepare a fish ready for the pot, which Asako then demonstrated how to cook fish stew, with egg sauce. The children were in hysterics when Puss jumped up on the table and stole the fish, tearing off into the undergrowth, followed closely by Diesel, to share the prize.

One of the days, Sovann came to show the children how to weave a basket from twigs. They spent the day before collecting in readiness. And Mr Slap how to carve a toy from wood.

171

Crystal taught the younger children to swim; for this, she enrolled Mira and Maya so they were well supervised.

They played rounders on the beach using a wooden bat, she begged one of the older men to make. The ball was difficult, but Mr Slap came up with a solution. He used young branches that bent easily, then soaked them in glue made from boiling fish guts. The ball was wrapped in plant fibres before being glued again. This worked well. The children loved the game. Soon, she encouraged a tournament between the two sides and invited the villagers to watch. They clapped and cheered proudly as the children ran around the wooden posts. Even Puss and Diesel sat to watch, their heads synchronised as they followed the ball flying through the air.

Billy grew fast. He was all too soon crawling at speed and getting into mischief. Crystal had a challenging task keeping an eye on him. Lucky for her, everyone in the camp kept watch over all the mischievous youngsters. Billy, being the youngest, was spoilt with attention.

'I cannot believe Billy is almost a year old. It has gone so fast. But then again, so much has happened in that time. I left home almost a year and a half ago. It doesn't seem possible,' Crystal said to Maya while washing clothes by the river one hot morning.

It was unusually just the two of them. This was because Billy had thrown his breakfast over her, and Maya was helping to scrub the clothes clean. Washing was not Crystal's strongest skill. They always seemed to be as dirty as they were before she started.

Washing day was usually a Monday when all the women gathered for their gossip.

'I not believe Billy's first words were Al-Al,' her friend giggled. Then laughed louder at Crystal's unamused expression.

'Yeah, alright! Not funny,' she bristled.

172

It was true; young Billy adored Ayan, crawling to him whenever he could. Calling him, Al-Al, had amused everyone at the camp. Ayan, particularly, was elated as he scooped the baby into his arms, telling him how clever he was. It was not long after he began to say, "Ma-Ma," she pointed out, not finding her friend's humour funny. Now Billy knew her as Mamar, which Crystal found cute.

Maya changed the subject. 'Not believe Mira's children, five and seven. Go fast... You miss your home, Crystal?'

'I miss my mum. But nothing else. Except a bath. Oh, and Google, so I could look up herbs.'

'Who Google?' Maya looked puzzled.

Crystal laughed. 'It's a search on the internet. You can find out anything. I could beat Sanskrit at her herb knowledge.'

'I doubt. She's old. She knows everything....' Maya became serious, then looked hesitant. 'I have baby,' she blurted.

Crystal was momentarily stunned before throwing her arms around her friend, 'that's wonderful. I'm so pleased for you. But I thought you could not have children. It makes it so much more fantastic.'

'It secret. Please not tell Ayan. Or Maya. Or anyone.'

'But why, they'll be so pleased.'

'Wait! until further along.'

Crystal promised to keep the secret.

A few weeks after the conversation, Maya became ill. She was pale, withdrawn, and had lost weight. Ayan was beside himself with worry. Veda moved into their hut to care for her. Ayan slept outside alongside the fire, not wanting to disturb her sleep. Still, none of them knew she was pregnant. Crystal was worried, wondering if she should betray Maya's confidence.

Sanskrit fed her herbal drinks and potions to help. Two weeks later, Maya appeared from the hut looking better, much to everyone's relief. She blossomed, her skin was radiant, and she no longer had the sadness deep in her eyes.

'Oh, Maya, thank God. You look so well,' Crystal said while trying to retrieve a worm from Billy's mouth.

Her friend smiled, but her eyes looked serious. 'We talk. Come, walk.'

Veda took Billy from her, and the two headed for the stream. Puss unusually followed, nudging at Diesel playfully as they strolled.

'You to promise me something.' Maya began, 'if something happens, look after Ayan.'

'Don't be silly; nothing will happen to you.'

'Promise Crystal.'

'No way,' she laughed. 'He is a pig.'

'You not know him. He gentle. Cares about everyone. He much responsibility.'

'Mmmmm,' Crystal responded. 'Nothing is going to happen. If I can give birth in the middle of a storm, then anyone can.'

Maya stopped walking, grabbed Crystal's hand tightly, and stared sincerely into her eyes, 'Promise!'

'OK, I'll keep an eye on him,' she shrugged feeling disturbed by Maya's urgency.

Veda gladly handed over a screaming Billy when they returned to the camp. These days, both Diesel and Puss hid from the naughty toddler. His energy was relentless. As much as Crystal adored him, she swore never to have another.

Mira had been looking worried for a while lately. She was snappy and no longer cheerful. Crystal repeatedly asked what was wrong but always received a curt reply, so she stopped asking. Then, one day, Mira screamed at her over something so silly that Crystal raged.

'I've had enough of this! You tell me what's wrong, or I'll get Ali to smack your bottom too.'

Mira started to laugh, her anger dispersing. 'I'm sorry. I worried about sister.'

'But why? She seems OK. Has something happened to her and Ali?'

'No. She baby coming.'

'But she wanted a baby. Surely, it is good news after being unable to have them.'

'It not that she couldn't have them. She must not have them.'

'I don't understand.'

'Heart not good. Bad to have baby.'

Crystal went quiet while she thought about this; she was upset to believe her friend was in danger.

'Told when small, not live long life. Baby could kill her. But want so badly.'

'And Ayan still join with her? I didn't think a man like him, would.'

'A man like him?' Mira wrinkled her brow in confusion.' He loves her. Always close.'

That knot of emotion tugged inside Crystal's stomach again. She hated herself for feeling this way about her beloved friend, but hearing how much love Ayan and Maya shared caused her stomach to flip.

'But how did she… you know… not get pregnant?'

'Sanskrit give herbs to stop baby. But she not take. And heart medication, stop baby coming. Now here, cannot get medication.'

'But surely it is dangerous to not have her heart medication.'

'Yes. Sanskrit giving herbs. But not enough. Everyone be upset when find baby coming.'

As the enormity of the conversation with Mira sunk in, the blood drained from her face. Surely Maya was not going to die?

Later that morning, Crystal was playing rounders on the beach with the children when a thunderous sound of planes approaching could be heard.

'Run!' she screamed, terrifying the younger children. Most froze, bursting into petrified sobs and squeals at the alien noise and the urgency in Crystal's voice. Hearing the rumble, the older children ran towards the village as she screamed at them again.

As the planes became visible, she knew there was no chance of getting them to safety fast enough, so she shouted again, 'Get down!'

She threw herself on the ground, dragging a terrified boy and covering a hysterical Billy. Maya, also on the beach, had already dragged two toddlers under the tree's canopy.

Ayan and Chris ran to the beach just as the planes flew over. The noise was deafening, but no bombs were dropped. There were eight flying in an arrow shape.

'They're American!' Ayan shouted over the noise.

Crystal looked up, surprised, watching them leave.

'What does that mean?' she asked, picking herself up and trying to calm the youngsters.

'I don't know. Maybe they've stepped into the war. They've not flown from America, it's too far.'

The planes flew back an hour later, and Ayan explained they were heading towards the mainland.

'I wonder if Chris and me should sail to Buranda and find out what's happening.'

'It's too dangerous,' Maya panicked. 'What if there are enemy boats along the way?'

'The mainland is only twenty minutes from here, we'll be OK. This could mean you can get home, back to your people,' he said to Crystal.

'Yes,' she answered flatly.

But her heart bounced with mixed feelings. This could mean the end of the war, which was fantastic. But she was happy and contented on the island. She loved her job as a teacher, the children, and her adopted family. How could she leave Sanskrit, Mira, Maya, and Veda? What would happen to Puss and Diesel?

Ayan and Chris were outvoted to sail the next day. The island needed the young men, the older ones they could afford to lose, which Crystal thought sounded a bit callous. The discussion raged on into the night. Eventually, Mr Slap and another man called Rohan were nominated.

They left at dawn, and the rest waited eagerly all day for news of the war. They wondered if the two men, plus the boat, would be blown from the water and never seen again.

The little boat could be seen on the horizon in the late afternoon. It was painstakingly slow to reach the shore as everyone waited on the sand, eager for news. Chris translated to Crystal as voices all seemed to be shouting at once; she could not keep up.

'The US and UK became involved in the war near the start when Carbombya refused to allow holidaymakers to leave the islands. They have now managed to drive them from Buranda and take over the mainland. However, the islands are still invaded by Carbombya. Apparently, much of the mainland city is in piles of rubble, and many people killed. But there are still parts standing, a few houses and shops. The airport has been salvaged and is open. Although there are not many planes flying.' Chris clasped both her hands in his. 'We can soon go home!'

Crystal's face did not show pleasure as her heart sank.

'Chris looked puzzled, 'Aren't you pleased?'

'Well… I… I guess so.'

The two men came bearing gifts, apparently from aid workers. A station had been set up to help people who have lost homes. They hurled two huge sacks of potatoes, apples, and oranges from the boat, a first aid kit, several bolts of material, a few sewing kits, and a chalkboard, complete with chalk for the school. These were given after they explained about survivors on the island. Plus, they had managed to scrounge fuel for the boats; they unloaded several cans. These were precious items and so needed.

'But how?' Crystal asked, amazed at such treasures.

'Some they managed to forage amongst relatives who had been worried about news from the islands. Mostly it has been given by the aid team. People thought us all dead. This side of the waters is reasonably safe now. Carbombya mostly wanted control of Panchaea and the surrounding islands, so now there is a cease-fire while negotiations occur.'

That was not all. Mr Slap produced a large bundle of letters. There was apparently a huge memory board in the town. People who lost loved ones had pinned photos and letters hoping for news. They went and gathered letters for anyone on the island. As Rohan handed them out, there were cries of hysteria from both men and the women, receiving information from families.

There was a letter for Mira; her husband, like Ayan, had escaped the army and was living with his sisters on the mainland. She sobbed in Maya's arms when she read this. Even Ayan had tears falling, which he tried to hide. But his brother was safe, and his sisters, many other of his people and family were. Even Chris received a letter from his parents, which he took to a private place to read.

Lastly, Rohan, with a big grin on his face, handed Crystal a letter and a photo. Her jaw fell as she took the envelope. The image was one of her and Will when they became engaged. They looked so happy; she wore an expensive white dress, her hair tied in a bun. Will looked handsome, his blond hair neatly combed, and there was no big belly. He was grinning, and she was laughing. Her father had taken it; they had eaten at some posh hotel. Will, trying to impress her parents, had paid the extortionate bill. The envelope was addressed to Sarah

James, which confused her. Why had her mother done this? If Mr. Slap or Rohan had not recognised her photo, they would never have taken the letter. The handwriting was her mother's. Crystal tore it open and read the single sheet inside, tears running down her face.

My darling Crystal and Will,

We have been told to write to missing loved ones. Just in case they are still alive and probably to keep up our morale.

I do not know if you will ever receive this letter, and I write with tears streaming onto the paper. So much so that I have had to rewrite many times. I do not know what to say because I think you are both dead. I miss you so much. Things have been difficult here, but it is too much to explain.

I saw Layla and Janice, her mum, last month. They came to pay their respects. Layla told me you were pregnant, Crystal when you left. I could not believe it. Now I am grieving for a grandchild, too. I miss you terribly. There are many things I did not say to you when I could. I was a horrible mother. I do regret it so much.

I love you both. I pray each night for you.

All my love

MUM xxx

Her poor mother. Billy patted her nose, his thumb poked in his mouth and Diesel nudged at her hand. Even Puss jumped onto her lap and pushed her face into hers. She re-read the letter again and then again. Was it possible to get news back to her?

Chris was in such a good mood; he sang to himself and had a spring in his step.

'I just can't wait to go home,' he repeatedly said. 'You must feel the same, Crystal. But you don't seem happy?'

'Apart from my mum, there isn't anything there for me. Billy doesn't know England. He runs on the beach and is happy here. How will he cope with life there?'

'He's still a baby; he'll adapt,' he reassured.

'Ali and I are going to the mainland tomorrow to find out the flight situation. Also, he wants to see his sisters and brother.'

'Maybe I can come and find out if I can get news to my mum,' she said.

'I'd wait. Let's see what's going on first.'

They left as soon as the sun rose, taking Veda, anxious to see her daughters and son. Mira begged to go, too. Crystal and Maya promised to look after the children for her. A few of the older people went, wanting to reunite with their families.

As they waved the boat off from the shore, Crystal was sad. The island felt empty. Nothing would ever be the same again. She called the children into school to distract them and herself. They were unruly and unsettled - even Billy was fractious. They did not want to learn and could not concentrate. In the end, they played a game of rounders on the beach. It was also an excuse to watch for the boat.

It did not appear until the sun was almost setting. Remarkably, few people returned, preferring to stay with families on the mainland. Veda was not on board, either. After an emotional meeting with her daughters, she decided to stay with them.

They did bring Masahiko, known as Masa, Ayan's brother and Mira's husband. The two were inseparable, holding hands, not wanting to be parted ever again.

181

The people greeted Masa with affectionate cuddles and pats on his back, except for Diesel, who barked and ran away. He was like Ayan in many ways, his mannerisms and seriousness. They looked similar but not the same. Masa's eyes were as a soldier, dead and unresponsive.

'He's been through a bad time,' Chris whispered. 'He said soldiers are starving, there's not enough food. The killings and bombings have affected him badly. He's certainly not the same man.'

'It would, I guess,' Crystal nodded. 'Is Veda coming back, do you think? I really miss her?'

'Not sure. Ali said she was pretty made up to see her girls again. It's dire there. Bombed houses, people sleeping on the streets, with nowhere to go. There's rubble everywhere. My cousins live in the mountains, so Ali said their village is OK. But the poor people left with nothing is criminal. I spent hours at the aid centre and airport. '

'What about your flight?'

'You mean our flights?' he looked puzzled at her.

'Yes, of course. Our flights.'

'Not yet, in a few weeks, they reckon. But the aid workers arranged with the military to let me use a phone. I called my parents; my mum couldn't stop sobbing.'

'That's fantastic news. I mean that you could call your parents. I'm so pleased. If I go next time, maybe I can call my mum too.'

The group held a party that night to celebrate Masa's return to his family. It did not feel the same with so many missing. There were only thirty-seven of them, ten were children.

This time, they had jacket potatoes, which were a bit dry without butter. Some chopped herbs sprinkled over helped them go down well, though. The recently brewed alcohol was too strong, and many were wobbly as they sang and danced. The presence of the missing persons was noted in the atmosphere. It had spoilt the dynamics of the close group.

Chris was very clingy with Crystal, which caused many of the elders to glare disapprovingly. Ayan whispered something to him. He then skulked off to bed, not before begging Crystal to go with him.

She laughed and sent him on his way.

Chapter Fifteen

Masa was surly and did not interact with anyone. He preferred spending time alone on the cliff top or walking in the woods. When he was around, he constantly sniped at Mira or the children. She was often deep in her own thoughts, her eyes full of sadness, not able to cope with his mood swings. He also slapped the children for little reason, reducing them to tears.

Crystal or Maya tried hard to keep them occupied and out of the way.

'He's disgusting,' Crystal complained to Maya. 'Your poor sister, the man's a monster.'

Maya was worried sick, 'he not like this before. He like Chris, always laughing. It war.'

'War or not, he can't keep taking it out on other people.'

He was caught many times sneaking the party alcohol.

When Masa was in a particularly bad mood, Crystal went to Ayan.

'This has got to stop. You need to do something.'

'He's a grown man; what can I do?'

'It's not right how he treats Mira. She's afraid of him and so are the children.'

'I cannot interfere between a joined couple.'

'Maybe not. But you could at least have a word with him about his behaviour. It's not only Mira and the children who are afraid of him.'

Ayan did speak with his brother, but a row broke out, and Masa stormed off into the woods. After that, he was a bit quieter for a few days.

Maya could no longer hide her growing bulge as her stomach swelled. Crystal could not believe she still had not told Ayan or that he hadn't noticed. People at the camp eyed her suspiciously but did not say anything. However, it was soon after that Ayan did notice, as Maya could no longer disguise the swelling. An almighty row broke out, so bad that Sanskrit and Mira ran into the hut to break it up.

'What the hell's all that about?' Chris asked.

'I don't know,' Crystal flushed and looked away as she lied.

'Yes, you do. I can see by your face. What's going on?'

She figured it no longer mattered if Chris knew, as after tonight, everyone would. 'Maya's pregnant.'

'Oh,' Chris looked sad but said no more.

A brief time later, Maya came running out of the hut and fled for the woods, tears streaming down her face. The row inside continued to rage, Ayan's voice being the loudest.

Crystal left Billy with Chris and found Maya sobbing by the stream.

She put her arms around her, 'It might be alright, please don't cry,' she tried to comfort.

Her tragic eyes met Crystal's; they were full of despair. 'I want baby like other women. It unfair. Ayan says, must abort it. But cannot.'

'He's a brute and pig!' Crystal raved, defending her friend.

'You not understand,' Maya said. 'He afraid baby kill me.'

'But surely something can be done.'

'How? No hospital.'

'Promise, Crystal. If die. Look after Ayan? He in love with you.'

'That's rubbish. He doesn't love me. It's you he love.'

'That not true. You shared love. I know you did.'

Crystal blushed and looked mortified.

Maya laughed, despite her tears, 'It's OK. Understand. You alone. Share special time. Natural.'

'It's not natural. I'd just lost my husband. I didn't know he was married. I'm so sorry.'

Maya grabbed her hand. 'Stop! Inside, loves you. You him too. He need you, if die. Please?'

'I certainly don't love him. I strongly dislike him most of the time. But I promise, if I can, to look out for him.'

Maya did not really know what Crystal meant but accepted this.

When they returned to the camp. Ayan was waiting. Maya ran to him, and they fell into each other's arms. Crystal felt a prang of envy.

After that day, Maya flourished and glowed, although she was constantly tired. She was proud to be pregnant, showing off her bump like a trophy.

When Diesel yelped and whimpered, Crystal guessed Masa had kicked him as he stood close to the cowering dog, glaring hatefully at him. Anger exploding, she ran over and kicked Masa in the shins. It did not go down well, as he began shouting at her. She had no idea what he was saying but did not back down. Her fists were clenched, and her eyes blazed, daring that she would do it again if he came too near her or the dog.

A few days later, one of the children took an apple from the donation sacks, and Masa flew at the boy. He punched him around the head. Crystal lost her temper again. Drawing back her fist, punched Masa in the face. The man was stunned for a short time before he retaliated, bringing back his own fist and punching back at her. The thud sent Crystal flying to the floor. Not to be put off, she picked herself up and ran, kicking and screaming at him. Her nails clawed into his face, and her knee found the most precious place between his legs. He doubled, crying out in agony. Crystal, despite Billy screaming and crying, not satisfied, threw herself onto him and began punching at any part of his body she could reach. Masa's fist flew out and knocked her away.

Ayan, just coming in with his daily fish catch with Chris, heard the commotion. He ran into the camp just in time to see his brother hit out at Crystal. Many ladies were screaming in horror, and the men were shouting. He grabbed Masa and punched him in the face. The two began to fight, one on top of the other, blood splashing from cut skin, as they turned over and over on the floor.

Both Maya and Mira were screaming for them to stop. Chris ran to Crystal and helped her up. Her face and eyes were swollen.

'What the hell!' he shouted.

The fight ended when Sanskrit hobbled over and threw water on the brothers. Then, hit the top one with the pot. Stunned, they stopped.

Still unsure what happened, Ayan shouted at his brother, 'You need to leave. NOW!'

He stormed into his hut. To everyone's astonishment, Masa began to sob uncontrollably. The blood mixed with tears smeared across his face. Mira threw her arms around him as he cried into her shoulder.

Ayan came out again, blood smeared across his own face. He did not know what to do as he stood awkwardly, watching.

'I'm sorry,' Masa sobbed. 'I'm sorry. I kill so many people. I kill our people, innocent people. I can't live with it.'

No one spoke; they did not know what to say. Masa pulled away and ran from the camp. Maya went to her sister and put her arms around her, leading her away from the staring eyes into her hut.

As Ayan left to find his brother, Chris took Crystal back to her hut. Sanskrit came in with an ointment and tenderly applied it to her swollen eye. 'You silly,' she said. 'Too much hot blood.'

'You certainly have a temper,' Chris laughed, his arm around her shoulder. 'Ali's going to take me to the mainland tomorrow to see if we can arrange our flights home,' Chris told her.

Crystal's heart sank. The feeling was clear on her face.

'Do you still not want to go home?' he asked gently.

'I don't feel ready for it yet.'

'You'll be fine once you're there and decompressed. You've got your lovely big house, friends and your mum. I can come and stay with you.'

Crystal gave a small smile that did not reach her eyes. 'Yeah, I guess so. Maybe Ali will let me come too; I might be able to call my mum. It'll do me good to leave here for a while.'

Ayan didn't appear until the evening. Masa did not come back with him. He went to Crystal's Hut,

'How's your eye?' he asked.

'How's yours,' she laughed, his equally as swollen.

'You shouldn't have punched him. He's ill. It has taken its toll, the bloodshed. He suffers guilt.'

'He deserved it. The man's a worm. I understand. What he has been through is shocking. But he takes it out on vulnerable children, women, and poor Diesel.'

'At least he isn't a pig like his brother,' Ayan gave a weak smile, his eyes full of concern.

'NO! he's far worse. He's a snake!' she returned an equally weak grin. 'If I come to the mainland tomorrow, do you think could I phone my mum?'

Ayan thought for a while, 'They allowed Chris. The aid workers are helpful. I'm sure if you speak to them, they'll arrange something. The Americans are trying to get people who survived home.'

That evening, Masa appeared. Ayan agreed he could stay as long as he behaved himself. He did not speak to anyone but stayed in his hut.

The next day, they set off, and Mr. Slap came, too. Crystal left Billy with Maya. He did not seem to mind at all. Diesel watched from the beach, whimpering and trying to limp into the water after the boat, making Crystal feel dreadful. He was frantic as he barked, whined, and shook with stress.

'I'll be back soon,' she shouted to the inconsolable dog.

They arrived at the port twenty minutes later. The site was gloomy and sooty. Many of the buildings were flattened. It was unrecognisable from the place it was when she and Will had arrived almost two years before. Rubble lay in heaps where houses and shops had once stood. The American military, holding guns, were everywhere. People slept in little camps at the edge of roads or on bombed sites, obviously where their homes had once stood.

While Mr. Slap left to see family, Chris, Ayan, and Crystal went to the remembrance board to see if there were more letters. There were thousands, some overlapping others. Crystal pointed to a photo and letter pinned underneath. It was of the German man who had been rescued.

'What shall we do?' she asked, unpinning it.

'I guess write back,' Chris said. 'Although I don't know any German.'

'Maybe we write in English, at least the family can have it translated,' she suggested.

After, Chris left for the airport to see if flights could be arranged. They agreed to meet back at the port in an hour. Ayan took Crystal to the aid base, where people queued for provisions and information. Some looked desperate and pathetic, their expressions desolate and hopeless, having lost so much.

'Ali, this is terrible,' she cried.

'We have been the fortunate ones, I think,' he frowned, 'it's heartbreaking.'

'I just want to get back to the island,' Crystal admitted, feeling bleak and depressed.

He nodded in agreement. 'We'll see if we can talk to the military about flights and I'll see if I can get provisions to take back. See you at the port.'

'Don't leave me. Please!' she begged.

He relented and waited in the queue with her.

'You're English?' the aid worker asked. She was young and looked worn out.

'Yes, I got stuck here when the war started.'

'I can get you passage home.'

'No. I don't want to go. I just want to get word to my mother that I'm alive.'

The woman looked surprised, as did Ayan, with his eyebrow raised in question.

'Come with me. I'm sure someone can help.'

She took Crystal and Ayan to a military officer, who led them into a building they had commandeered as a base. Crystal began to feel uneasy and wished she had just written a letter instead.

'Shall we go, Ali?' he again looked puzzled. 'I don't like it here,' she confessed.

'Can I have your name?' the officer asked after digging out a lengthy list.

'Crystal Blake. I have mine and my husband's passports,' she handed them to him. He looked at the photos inside and then at his list, then back at her again, scrutinizing her features closely.

'It's OK,' she said, making to take the passports back. I can just write a letter.'

'Stay here.' He walked away and began whispering to another officer, then calling to another. The three men came over.

'Can we ask where your husband is, Mrs Blake?' One of them asked, his face harsh and ungiving.

Her strange dream at the sacred ground suddenly flicked in her head. Will had told her he was sorry and had done something wrong, and she began to panic.

'My husband is dead. Why?'

'Mrs Crystal Blake, we arrest you for conspiracy to war profiteering under the War Profiteering Act of 2007. You have the right to remain silent. Anything you do say can and will be used against you in a court of law. You have the right to legal representation before questioning. However, during this war, it may take many months to arrange.'

Shocked, Crystal turned to run, terrified, and one of the officers grabbed her arm; they produced cuffs and clipped them around her wrists.

'You are in a lot of trouble!' He scowled.

'What the hell!' shouted Ayan, as confused as Crystal. 'Leave her alone!'

Crystal began to get hysterical as they led her away.

'What the hell do you mean, War profiteering? You've made a mistake! I haven't done anything! I have a son! You can't do this. I don't know what you're on about!'

They dragged her unceremoniously into a room.

'Crystal!' Ayan called; his voice was cut off as the door slammed, and her world caved around her feet.

Chapter Sixteen

The questions went on for hours. Fired, one after the other, by two military officers. It was not a case of good cop, bad cop, like the films. Both were horrible, unrelenting and cruel. Crystal was not given anything to drink, no break, even to go to the toilet. They did not believe Will had died; she was lying. He was not shot. Why did they come there on holiday? What were Will's meetings about? Where was he? How had she survived when other holidaymakers on the island were dead? Over and over, it went on and on. They told her she could be executed for her crimes. Crystal shook with fear each time one of them screamed into her face, the worst of the two, 'LIAR!' with his nose pressed against hers. They condemned her to hell for her part in killing so many innocent people. She was the scum of the earth. After hours with them, she felt it.

Eventually, Crystal was taken, stunned and shocked, to a prison and locked in a tiny, filthy cell by herself. The contents were sparse; a wooden bed was along one wall, with only a thin blanket and a pillow. A small sink was opposite, along with a toilet. At least, she assumed the wooden shelf with a hole and a bucket underneath was for that purpose. It had not been emptied for some time and smelt disgusting, as did the bed. The walls, maybe once white, had paint pealing, hanging in flakes. The last occupier had scratched nail marks into the plaster.

Crystal had never been so scared. The door closed, and she was left in semi-darkness. There was no window, only a tiny ceiling light that was more of a slight glow. She banged the door until her hands were bruised. Food was bought some hours later and passed through a little cubbyhole in the door. It looked disgusting and like some sort of grey lumpy porridge. No one came to help or see her. How could she believe that Will, who was always cheerful, kind, gentle, and would help anyone in trouble, could be guilty of War crimes? It did not make sense; there had to be a mistake.

There was nothing to do but think, cry, or scream, and she did all three. She wept so many tears that there were none left. None of the people who bought food spoke English; they looked coldly at her and were unresponsive when she begged to be let go.

On the fourth day, she was taken back to the military base, shaking with fear at the thought of facing the officers again. This time, it was a different one, slightly more amenable. He introduced himself as Lieutenant Warner.

'I'm sorry to have kept you so long,' he apologised. 'We are rather busy, as you can see.'

'Why am I here? My son has been left; he's only a year old. How could you do that?'

'I'm sorry. We can collect your son for you. I'm sure we can find someone to care for him.'

'What the hell do you mean? You need to let me go.'

'Mrs. Blake, I do not think you realise how serious these allegations are. If I hand you over to the authorities of Buranda, you will be shot for war crimes.'

Crystal gaped at him, shocked.

'You and your husband have been involved with selling arms to Carbombya. The penalty in this country is death!'

But... I don't know what you're on about.' Crystal's mouth had gone dry. 'I haven't been involved with anything. We came on holiday here. My husband was shot by Carbombya soldiers.'

'So you say! There is no proof of that. We know your husband and you came on holiday to secure arms deals.'

But… But…' she stammered.

'We have decided to transport you back to the States, where you will be tried and have a fair hearing. The option is far better than handing you over to this country. We will find your son and transport him back to….' he looked down at his notes. 'Ah, yes, your mother.'

'You are not to touch my son. You leave him there. How dare you. I've done nothing!'

'Mrs Blake, you are lucky your husband is dead, if he is, and we have decided to give you the benefit of the doubt. You will receive a fair hearing. In the meantime, you will be kept at the prison until transport can be arranged.'

She went to speak, but he held up his hand to stop her. He was no longer listening, his mind obviously on another matter, as he shuffled through papers. He called on another officer, who escorted her outside, where the two wardens took her back to the prison.

Crystal was kept in her cell, seeing no one for many days. She did not know how many, as it was difficult to know which was daytime or night. One of the wardens told her that two men had come to see her. But she was not allowed visitors. Crystal assumed it was Chris and Ayan. She was worried sick about Billy, Diesel, and Puss and she missed her friends terribly. Her weight plummeted as she could hardly stomach the muck they served. She guessed it was punishment for the alleged crimes against her. There was so much destruction; Crystal could not blame them if that was what they thought. There was no solicitor or any other defense for her. The country was not in a position as it was trying to crawl out of the war crisis.

Crystal had no idea how long she had been kept in the cell. It could be weeks or even months. Billy must have forgotten her by now, she reckoned. Maybe it would have been better to have been shot with the rest of the camp at the beginning of the war. Then, arguing with herself, if she had, there would be no Billy. There was still so much to be grateful for. This was just another of life's kippers. But her depression and feelings of hopelessness were so deep in her insides. Only her thoughts of Billy kept her wanting to live.

Over and over, Crystal mentally relived the journey to the mainland, seeing Diesel, in her mind, crying on the beach. Then, Ayan's face, confused and upset, when she was arrested. Did he believe she was guilty?

Crystal no longer banged at the door; she stared at the gloomy wall. But it wasn't the wall she saw; it was the sea, the cliffs, and her time at the sacred site with Ayan. She saw Billy growing into a little man. Puss washing her bottom next to Veda on the boat. Then at school when she ran away with the fish. Collecting herbs with Sanskrit. Sometimes, she laughed, thinking of the parties on the island, watching the dancing and singing. There were times when the music played in her head, and she danced around the tiny space, humming to herself.

The cell door opened one day, and an English-speaking lady came in.

'Mrs Blake? My name is Lucy; I'm one of the aid workers. I studied law in England. I took a year's break to come to Buranda and help the people. I cannot help much, as I'm not qualified.' She held out her hand, and Crystal shied away, startled to be spoken to.

Lucy looked around and swore, 'How long have you been here?'

'I don't know,' she answered, grateful for an ally.

'Your mother asked me to see you. It was a hard job. You're not allowed visitors.'

'My mother? Is she here?'

Lucy smiled regretfully, 'No. I'm sorry.'

'I've done nothing wrong. You've got to believe me. Please, you've got to help me.'

Doubt clouded Lucy's face. 'They believe you and your husband were investing in an illegal company that was supplying arms to Carbombya. It's a serious crime. You have been all over the news in the UK and the US.'

'But why would they think I was involved? I knew nothing about it.'

'You were on the payroll of your husband's business. So, it's believed you were conspiring with him.'

Crystal's jaw dropped, 'But... But... I've never had a wage. I've never worked. Surely, if they look at my bank account, they'll see that.'

'They've looked at your account. A wage was being drawn and spent.'

'Our joint account?' Crystal's heart sank further. She never got involved with money; she just spent it. She never even looked at bank statements; that was Will's job. There was no way of proving her innocence.

'They also believe you were spared from being shot on Panchaea because of your involvement.'

'But why did the soldiers kill my husband then?'

'It's not believed he's dead. He's with your son, and that is why you are refusing for your child to be taken to your mother. There's no other explanation.'

'But I've been living with island people for almost two years. It's all my son knows. They love and will care for him and my animals.'

'Your animals?'

'Yes, I've a cat and dog, I rescued them.'

It was clear, by Lucy's matter-of-fact tone, she did not believe Crystal.

'The British Government wants you to be transported to the UK. The Americans want you sent there for trial. Buranda wants you to be shot for the crimes against their country. So, there is a hold-up while they all argue. You are lucky you are here. At least you are safe. I'm sorry, there's no better news. But we can at least get you out of this room. Keeping you here is barbaric.' Lucy looked around at the grey, gloomy walls before continuing. 'If what you say is true and your son is stuck somewhere with these people, he needs to be found and taken to your family. It is not practical to leave him here, is it? You are facing a life in prison. Possibly, if taken to the States, you could be executed, so you need to plan for his future.'

Crystal stared at her, not believing what she was hearing.

'I'm innocent!' was all she could muster.

Lucy made to leave, 'Have you a message for your mother? I can get it to her.'

'Tell her... I love her.'

The door closed, and Crystal was again left with the miserable wall. Shocked and desperate, her stomach twirled in turmoil. There was no way out of this. What was worse, life in prison or death? She could not decide. Either way, she would never see Billy again.

Later that day, the door opened. Crystal was led out of the cell to a communal room. It was a huge, barred area, with beds dotted about and women sitting on each. The walls were brownie-grey and depressing. She was allocated a space and sank onto it, staring with fear at her new roommates. Some looked fierce and aggressive as they glared back in her direction.

Soon after, the barred door was opened. The women were led to a huge courtyard. At least Crystal had some air. It was fantastic to see the sun again, even though the brightness caused her to squint and gave her a headache after the cell's darkness.

A young lady ambled over and sat on the wall beside her; she only looked about seventeen or eighteen. Crystal wondered why such a young person would be in prison.

'Name, Kaipo. You English?'

'Yes, I'm Crystal.'

'You cause war and kill people?' she asked.

Her heart fell further; everyone must hate her. No one spoke to her after that, but they did not beat her up either. The fierce-looking women stayed away. She was too afraid to sleep in case they attacked her.

Crystal was unsure which day it was, but one of them, visitors came. They were not allowed into the prison but could gather by a fence to speak for one hour. The guards paced up and down to ensure no one touched hands and order was kept.

Many weeks later, Ayan appeared, and Crystal ran to the wire, with tears of joy, to see a friendly face.

'Is Billy ok? Are Diesel and Puss all right? How's Maya? And Sanskrit?' she gushed through her sobbing.

'They're fine. Billy is living with Maya and me. We're taking good care of him. Chris moved into your hut so he could look after Puss and Diesel. Well, at least that's what he tells us. Maya is glowing, and her belly is huge. What the hell, Crystal!' he looked confused and concerned.

She spilled out the sorry story, including that she may be executed. 'No one believes I'm innocent,' she finished.

'I do!' he gave a sad, hopeless smile. 'I don't know what to do to help you.'

'I don't either,' she said, equally as despondent. 'They think Will's alive and I'm lying and that my son's with him.'

'I can tell them he isn't, and your son is with me and Maya.'

'I'm afraid they'll come and take him though. I don't want him to go to England. He doesn't know my mum. She's not young enough to care for him. She won't cope. If something happens to her, Billy will be put in an orphanage.'

Ayan went quiet; he was thinking. Crystal knew the signs by the expression on his face.

'We've no choice but to tell them. Could your mum also tell them you did not work for your husband?'

'I guess, being as she's my mum, they won't believe her. No one is going to believe it, are they?'

'You had no idea what your husband did?'

When she admitted she didn't, Crystal looked at the floor, not wanting to sound stupid.

'Does Maya always know what you get up to?' she looked up, meeting his gaze.

'She knows about us,' he said, but Maya doesn't know everything about me. So, I understand what you're saying.'

All too soon, the hour was over. Ayan left with a promise to come back the following week.

'Ali!' she called as an afterthought. How long have I been here?'

'Two months!' he called back.

As promised, Ayan came to see Crystal when he could. It was not weekly, though. At one point, he had not come for a month, and Crystal was worried.

Lieutenant Warner called for her once again.

'You've got to believe I'm innocent! I had no idea Will was claiming a wage for me.' She knew it sounded pathetic that she never checked bank accounts or asked about his work. No one was ever going to believe her.

'My husband took care of everything. I was only eighteen when we married and more interested in having a fun time. Will was so much older. He took care of me.'

'I'm sure he did! Mr Ayan Sahal has clarified that your husband died on Panchaea. That he met you when you were in hiding from soldiers. I admire you for managing to stay alive. So far, we believe everyone on the island to be dead. That is almost eight thousand people due to arms being sold to Carbombya. Not a pretty picture, is it?'

Crystal looked stricken, 'All those people! But surely, with Will dead and me running to hide, it shows I'm innocent.'

'Not at all. How do we know your husband is not protected by the military and you ran from the situation? Mr Sahal did not see him shot. He only went on what you told him.'

'But that does not make sense. Why would I run if I was safe there?

'You don't understand, Mrs Blake. Whether I believe you or not is irrelevant. These people have lost everything, including families, they want someone to be held accountable. So, unless we find your husband, that's you.'

'You've got to believe me,' her eyes were wide with bulbous tears, accentuating the depth of sincerity.

'Do you know what, Mrs Blake? I almost do believe you. The trouble is, no one else is going to.' His smile almost held some warmth. Although it was a small victory, it did make her feel slightly better.

'What is going to happen to me?'

'There are still negotiations with the UK where you will be tried. Your mother is fighting the government for this to be done in England. But the US wants you there. I'm sorry, but they want you to face the death penalty for war crimes. As I say, what I think is irrelevant. My opinion does not count. The most important voice is that of the people. They need to direct blame somewhere, and at the moment, they only have you.'

'So, what you are saying is, if I am innocent or not, it makes no difference. As long as there is someone to point a gun at?'

'I'm sorry.' His eyes unusually flashed with warmth and sadness.

'So how many innocent people have been blamed for things they did not do?'

'Your young age is showing, Mrs. Blake. Sadly, this is life.'

'What the hell does that patronising comment mean!'

He smiled dryly, 'It means you have not yet lived long enough to see this is what happens in life. People's minds are put to rest once a gun has been fired. As long as the firer shines, it does not matter who it is at.' He was speaking metaphorically, of course.

When Ayan finally did arrive, he brought Billy, who had grown so much. Crystal ran to the fence and put her hands through the wire, receiving a tap on her back from a guard.

'Mamar!' the little boy cried. He held up a small animal carved from wood.

Crystal choked back tears, not wanting him to see her upset. 'My, haven't you grown? You're a big boy now. Are you being good for Aunty Maya and Grandma Susu?' which was what Billy called Sanskrit.

He nodded and reached out his arms towards her.

She told Ayan what the officer had said, thanking him for his input.

Ayan looked as stricken as her. 'So, you can never be found innocent?'

Crystal shook her head, unable to find words for what was happening to her. At that moment, she hated Will.

'The only solution is if they find your husband's body,' Ayan said. 'If it helps, everyone at our camp believes you.'

'It does help, thank you. But even if they find Will's body, they will still need someone to blame.'

Tears fell when an hour later, they left. Crystal went to her bed space and sobbed into the straw mattress. Someone put their hand on her back and rubbed gently to comfort her.

'I saw little boy. So handsome.'

Crystal looked up to see Kaipo, the young lady who spoke to her in the yard.

'You not look like war criminal,' her voice was so gentle, more tears fell for the show of sympathy.

'I'm not,' she sobbed. 'I did not know anything about my husband's business. But no one believes me.'

'Well, I believe you, if want.'

Crystal couldn't help laughing. 'Thank you. Why are you here?'

'I kill husband.'

'Why?'

'I young. Thirteen, when marry. Beat me every day. Wait till sleep and stab him. I Twenty-one. Here eight years.'

'You look so young. I thought you were about seventeen! If my husband beat me that much, I would have stabbed him too. How long have you to stay in prison?'

'All life, forever. Old ladies here. All hurt husbands. Here, since young woman. Two girls. taught English. They here drug smuggling.'

'What happened to them?'

'They sent to England prison.'

'How long did that take?'

'Five years.'

Crystal was shocked. How long would she have to wait before a decision is made?

Kaipo continued, 'The War been bad. Much prison ruined. We kept here now. Move to another prison in different part of the country. But take long time. Too much other important things at moment.'

Crystal felt panicky. If they moved her, she would never see Ayan or Billy again. She would be forgotten until the war was over.

Chapter Seventeen

After Kaipo had spoken to her, the other women did, too. They were not fierce and aggressive, after all. In fact, most were very gentle and kind. Crystal's heart went out at the injustice, as they eagerly wanted to share their stories of why they were in prison. From their own experience, she guessed why they did not judge her. They knew England did not treat women so harshly, so they felt Crystal would have much empathy for what had happened to them.

There were quite a few forced into marriage at a young age. The stories of abuse by husbands, old enough to be fathers and grandfathers, were shocking. After finally retaliating, they were locked in that gloomy hell hole for the rest of their days. It was all so cruel. They loved to hear about life in England. Crystal dutifully answered the many questions. She used body language and play-acting to make herself understood, reminding her of the children on the Island when they laughed, delighted. Some could speak good English, although Kaipo translated for the ones that could not.

They had never heard of a computer, and it took some explaining to make them understand what one was. When they finally got it, they arred and oooed, eyes wide, amazed by such magic. The explanation of a mobile phone was equally fascinating to them.

Lucy came to see her once more, bringing a letter from her mother. She handed over a pen and paper and promised to return after a week so she could write back. Again, the letter was addressed to Sarah James; now she knew why. Her mother was worried it would be destroyed if her used name was written. Finding a private place in the outside yard, she tore open the envelope.

My darling Crystal,

I hope this letter finds you well and you are safe.

I cried when I heard you were alive. I could not believe it. My prayers came true. Is Will OK? They said he wasn't with you and they have not found him yet.

I'm doing everything I can to get you home to England, but it is not much as no one will listen. They do not believe me when I tell them you are innocent.

The house and all the belongings were taken, and all the assets were frozen until the trial could be heard.

There is no money. I managed to hide some of your jewellery and a few other bits.

They found me somewhere with old people, in sheltered housing. Me! In an old people's place! I'm not that old! But I had no choice; there was nowhere to go. It's alright. I have friends here and have built a life for myself. It took some time, as people scorned me at first.

I have seen Layla; she has given birth to a little girl called Jade. She seems incredibly happy and sends her love. She will stand as a witness at your trial, as she knows you are innocent, too.

I miss you so much.

Love you, always,

Mum.

It was a difficult letter to read. Crystal did not think she would ever see her mother again. Her house and belongings had gone. Strangely, they no longer mattered. But there was no money to hire a solicitor if she ever went to trial. It all looked even more dismal. She re-read the letter over and over. There was so much Crystal wanted to write back, going over and over the words in her head, then forgetting once she put her pen to the paper. There was just too much to say and so little paper. So, she put off writing until the right words did come.

Crystal's days in prison improved with the new friends she had made. To pass the time, she began arranging exercise classes each morning. From her gym days in England, she was an expert. Her own muscles ached after two years of not doing them herself.

Then, they played charades. They used quite simple things, like trees, sky, and animals. They had to repeat answers in both languages. Some of the actions had them all in peals of laughter.

The women at the prison came to adore Crystal. She brightened their lives and made the gloomy days less dull. Each morning, one or another would shout,

'What we do today, Crystal?' There was silence until she came up with the day's program, including times. One of the ladies produced some chalk. The agenda was written daily on the wall. However, with the lack of space and facilities, activities were limited, and each day was the same. They still loved to ask, though. So, each morning, Crystal obediently wrote the day's agenda. Each one formed a line to look at it. Even though none could read the English words.

This amused and saddened Crystal; she understood they had never had anything much happen in their lives before, and no one had ever shown them any attention.

9 am: breakfast

10 am: exercise

11 am: walk around the yard

Midday: Lunch

1 pm: free time

3 pm: games

5 pm: dinner

7 pm, party.

At party time, one person was chosen to perform. This could be singing, dancing, acting out a part or even telling a story. This would have them in peals of laughter long after the gloomy light was switched off at 9 o'clock. Sometimes, the story would reduce them to tears, as it was a true-life account of what the person had been through.

Her favourite person, who became a close friend, was Kaipo. She was so warm and loving. This surprised Crystal after all her years spent in prison. Kaipo cared for every one of them, even the wardens. She was there with a big cuddle and a warm, sympathetic smile if anyone was upset. She sometimes cried with the person, rubbing their back as their tears fell. Even if a row broke out, which it did often, Kaipo would somehow settle the argument and disperse the anger in minutes. There were never any hidden agendas or gains for her. Crystal had so much admiration for the lovely, kind, selfless lady. In another time and place, she imagined her to be a nun, serving God or some sort of spiritual guru, with so much sincerity. The woman was unbelievable. She never felt sorry for herself, never had any animosity, and always saw the good in everyone, never any bad.

Eventually, Crystal wrote the letter home with a few crossing-outs; she had no choice, as Lucy was due the next day.

Dear Mum,

It was so fantastic to hear from you. I miss you so much, too. You are never far from my thoughts. I am sorry you were ousted from the house. It must have been terrible and such a shock, as it was for me.

As you know, I'm alive and well. Prison is not so bad, I guess. I have made friends and got used to the terrible food. Because of the war, it's pretty grim.

Sadly, Will was shot at the retreat just as the war started. All the people in our holiday group were. I was not with them at the time. So was able to hide, hence escaping. This is the cut version, as it is too much to explain, and it's a long story. I hid in the hills and even adopted a cat named Puss and a dog named Diesel. They kept me sane on those long, dark nights. Eventually, I met a man called Ayan. He was hiding, too. He helped me escape, and I have lived amongst his people since.

You are right; I was pregnant with Will's baby. You have a one-year-old grandson named Billy. He is wonderful, clever, and such a good boy. I have told him about his grandma, Mary, and about Daddy. He is living with Ayan's lovely people, so he is safe. They are taking good care of him.

I am so sorry you had to move and begin a new life. Thank goodness you are OK there.

My paper is running out. So, I cannot write anymore.

I did not know Will was involved with arms and was horrified to find out. I am so glad you believe me.

I love you and miss you, Mum.

Crystal

Xxx

Even writing the letter made her cry, as she sealed the envelope and kissed the flap. Would she ever see her mum again?

As promised, Lucy came the following day, assuring her the letter would reach her mother.

'After all, it's not your mum's fault,' she pointed out.

'What do you mean? That her daughter is a criminal!' Crystal glared at her.

Lucy's face flushed, 'I… didn't mean…'

'It's OK,' she relented. After all, she needed Lucy's help, it was all she had.

'When an Aid worker comes from England, if they can get through, I'll pass it to one I trust,' she promised, trying to make amends.

'Is there still no news about when I'll be moved? Or where I'll be going?' Crystal asked.

'I'm sorry, there are so many issues being dealt with. There are gas and water leaks in the city now. The war is still raging over the islands. It'll take years to put things right even when it's over.'

'I guess,' she agreed. 'With all that going on, I'm the last priority!'

'NO! You're a top priority. People want justice for the war.'

Crystal glared at her again. 'Guilty before proven innocent. Hung drawn and quartered! I thought it was meant to be the other way around?'

'Sorry!' Lucy stammered, 'that was very judgemental of me.'

Ayan appeared the next visiting day, which Crystal now knew was a Sunday.

'Fuel's low. I'll struggle to return for a while,' he told her. 'As you know, we need all our reserves for fishing. I'm sorry,' his eyes looked sad.

Crystal was devastated; all she had to look forward to were his visits. But she bravely smiled and told him she understood, not wanting to seem selfish.

'How come Chris hasn't come to see me?' she asked, trying to distract herself.

'He comes, but each time goes to the airport to battle for a flight. He sends his love though and promises to visit before he leaves.' Ayan looked down at his hands; his face had an awkward expression as if he did not know how to begin his next words. 'You know… Crystal… I just want to say. It was the best time of my life when we were at the sacred ground. I hurt you badly; I'm sorry. But I did and do have feelings for you.'

'It's OK, Ali, I understand. Maya is so lovely. I still feel terrible about it all. Anyway, I've no feelings for you. You're a pig!' She grinned naughtily, trying to lighten the heavy moment.

Ayan grinned, too, but did not want to let things go; now his words were out. 'It was my fault. I should've told you. But you were so beautiful and sexy. I couldn't resist. I was cruel because I was covering my guilt. But it's something I've had to live with. Ever since, I've not liked myself much.'

Crystal blushed, 'You were so beautiful, gentle, and sexy too. In another lifetime maybe, ah?'

He touched her fingers through the fence, and she felt a shockwave shoot up her arm, sizzle through her body, and settle into her stomach. Quickly pulling her hand away, she asked how Maya was. 'She must be close now.'

'Yes. Another few weeks. She's blooming. I've never seen her so happy and well. Sometimes, very tired though.'

'You'll make a good father, Ali. Will you promise that you and Maya will always look after Billy if I never get out? Will you tell him about me...?' She stopped then because tears were choking in her throat. But there was so much more she wanted to say.

'I promise, Crystal. He'll be a brother to my child. I'll always treat them the same. Even though he is a white baby.'

She smiled, knowing he was saying that to make her laugh.

As he left, she shouted, 'You're a good man, Ali. You're kind and wise, and I love you for who you are…. You're still a pig, though.'

As he looked back, she could swear he had tears in his eyes. She knew then he would never return and had been trying to tell her. She went to her bed space and sobbed for her broken heart.

'What we do, Crystal?' one of the ladies called.

Taking a big breath to pull herself together, she choked back the tears and stopped crying. Looking up, several pairs of eyes stared intently at her, eagerly waiting for the afternoon's activities.

'OK,' she smiled, 'Yoga?'

'Who Yogi? Not know Yogi.'

Crystal burst out laughing, suddenly realising for the last two years, she had begun to laugh easily. It did not matter how hard life was; if she could find a smile, things always looked better. Crystal not only laughed easily, but she cried easily, too.

214

Once they got used to her, the prison guards were not so bad. They often smuggled in cigarettes for the women if they could, maybe feeling sorry that they were locked up because of the injustice towards some of them. At least, this is what Crystal assumed. Sometimes, they smuggled in some chocolate or a cake, only a morsel each once shared. A few times, even alcohol. They did not ask for any payment, which may confirm Crystal's theory.

Recently, a bottle of spirit was given to them, and they were so excited. They spent the day whispering and conspiring for a party after lights out, knowing there would only be two wardens on duty, who tended to sleep the night in one of the cells. One of the ladies had two candles hidden so they could see slightly.

'It's a shame we've no food, too,' Crystal said, getting into the mood of breaking prison rules and remembering the parties on the Island.

As they all did, she knew the guards would turn a blind eye. But it made it more fun to think they were being naughty.

The bottle was pulled out from under a mattress when the lights dimmed that night, and the last check was done. The candles were lit before they passed around the bottle, all taking a large swig and cringing at the vile taste.

'What the hell is this stuff? It's gross!' Crystal gagged. Causing the women to giggle at her screwed-up face and curled top lip.

Four swigs later, they were all tipsy.

'Dance,' Kaipo stood up and began to wiggle her bottom.

There was a lot of laughter as they joined in, wiggling their behinds.

'Keep the noise down!' the warden shouted but never came to check.

They continued dancing around the room, bouncing on beds and sniggering behind their hands to keep as quiet as possible.

None noticed one of the candles fall onto a straw mattress, which, with its combustible innards, became a blaze in seconds. Smoke and flames soon bellowed out as the fire consumed one bed after another. The noise became deafening, the scene a mass of bewilderment as bodies flew around the space in a frenzied panic, not knowing where to run for safety. The flames crackled, and smoke flowed and swirled. Flakes could be seen through the thickness as they danced on the ceiling above the inferno. Clothes began to catch fire, the screams harrowing and agonising, as others ran to the burning people, frantically patting the bodies to kill the torture. Flailing arms hitting out could just be seen through the blackness.

It was hopeless as the blaze spread from one to the other, eating clothes and the flesh underneath that melted like wax, leaving skeletons with hollowed burning eye sockets before crumpling. Everyone was choking and gagging on fumes as more of them began to burn; the room was too crammed with bodies and straw not to.

A warden ran shouting into the corridor beyond the bars. Her hands shook as she fought with the keys to find the correct one to unlock the barred gate. The door was pulled open, and the ones left burst out, gasping, with clogged, smoke-filled lungs.

Crystal pulled Kaipo to the farthest point of the corridor to get away. Staring back at the ladies with horror, at the piercing screams of their cellmates. Through the thick blackness, they could just make out shapes of crumpled bodies, no longer conscious or dead. The second warden appeared, carrying a bucket of water, hopeless in fighting the furnace. The first warden had run and opened another barred door that led to another corridor. Ladies were screaming from inside of cells, banging frantically, to be free from the death they faced. An alarm was shrieking, adding to the already ear-piercing noise.

Crystal dragged a hysterical Kaipo and another lady, Dara, into the next corridor to the farthest point near the main entrance. A small grid in the thick wooden door offered little air as they spluttered. The lock was being turned to make way for the fire brigade. As the door swung open, the force of air hurled the flames that burst throughout the rest of the building. The explosion was violent, as the fire found gas. The prison erupted into indescribable pieces, hitting great heights before it rained down to form a non-descript pile of rubble that left thick dust in its wake. The prison bars, insultingly, still stood proudly around what was once rooms.

Crystal was in a dark place of nothingness. It was peaceful and a long way from reality. She was roughly shaken, and someone was calling her. But she did not want to return; the place was serene and safe.

'Crystal! Crystal!'

She opened her eyes, and Kaipo was across from her, beneath the prison outside door.

'What happened?' she mentally checked her body. A few bits ached, but everything seemed to be in order.

'Dara dead,' Kaipo's eyes were tragic with shock as the woman's body lay across her.

Patches of the white face showed despite the black soot.

Crystal pushed to free herself, but the door was too heavy.

It was being lifted from them, and she could wiggle free and pull herself to a crawling position; her eyes stung and were gritty as she began to clamber over debris.

Someone grabbed her arm and began pulling. It was a man trying to rescue anyone he could. She could see nothing in front of her or behind but dust and smoke as she scrabbled and fought with the bumpy ground that dug into her knees and caused her to cry out. Debris was scattered everywhere, and people were shouting urgently, shocked at what had happened. Once free, the man pulled Dara from Kaipo.

'Run girls! While there is so much mayhem,' he said once they both lay crumpled in the street.

He was an American, possibly a soldier. But neither gave it much thought. Gasping and spluttering, desperately trying to free their clogged lungs of the gunk and force air into them.

'Thank you,' Kaipo managed through gasps, as both did precisely that, as much as their smoke-filled lungs would allow. They did not get far, as neither could breathe, but it was far enough. They sank to their knees, coughing, a few streets away.

'We're free!' Crystal gasped, barely a whisper, as she put her arm around Kaipo and squeezed her. 'We're free!'

She froze, reliving the loss of lives at the prison. The women burning to death. The horror. What a price their freedom had cost. No one left there could possibly be alive. They were only spared because they were at the front.

'Maybe they free too,' Kaipo gasped profoundly. 'They my friends,' tears ran down her sooty face, smearing more dirt.

'Try not to think,' Crystal said, grabbing her hand and pulling her away.

'Where we go?'

'Back to the island, of course,' Crystal said, her eyes full of the same trauma as Kaipo's. 'I'll see Billy, Puss, and Diesel. We'll be safe. No one will ever look for us because they will believe we died in the fire.'

'I not know what free is,' Kaipo said, a wistful, confused look in her eyes, 'But how we get there?'

'Ali'll come. He'll take us back.'

'But you said he not be back!'

Crystal realised it was true, and her heart sank. They were stuck on the miserable, crumpled mainland.

Chapter Eighteen

Freedom was not easy after being locked away for so long. It was far worse for Kaipo after eight years behind prison walls. They camped in derelict shop doorways, on the streets, or crawled into fallen buildings, huddled together for comfort in sleep. After the initial adrenaline rush, when they escaped, both now suffered from trauma. Bursting into tears for no reason or screaming out when they dreamt.

Kaipo struggled mentally without the control of an institution to govern her life. She wanted to hand herself in and be locked away again. Crystal spent hours talking her out of it. Convincing her she just needed time to settle down and adapt.

Food and water were difficult to find. People, assuming they were war victims, kindly shared what they had. They managed to wash in the sea early each morning when no one was around. But their clothes were filthy, with burn holes, and their hair was singed, suggesting they had escaped from the prison. Both were terrified of being caught and locked up again, especially Crystal, whose future looked bleak if she was.

'Maybe you could go to the aid station,' she suggested to Kaipo, in desperation, three days after freedom.

'But I be recognised.'

'You won't. There are too many people, and you've been locked away for years. There's no way I can go. Being English, I'll stand out. Tell them you've a family to feed. You need clothing, food, and water; oh, and you have a sister, similar size.'

They walked near the station, keeping a safe distance away. Kaipo looked dubious and hesitant as Crystal pushed her forward, shooing her with her hand as she watched from behind a building nearby. The queue was long and relentlessly slow-moving. Kaipo was nervous, constantly looking over her shoulder.

It was almost two hours before she came back with a huge bundle.

'Well done!' Crystal hugged her, elated.

'I not, like lying,' Kaipo grumbled.

They headed back to their latest camp, in the remains of a tumbled building, before looking at their gifts. Food was the priority as both were hungry, having not eaten since the day before. And what they did have was tiny. The food given by aid workers was sealed packets containing ready-cooked rice and sauce. There were seven each, so it would last a while if they were careful. Neither bothered with the provided food bowls as they scooped from the packet with their fingers, not even worrying that their hands were filthy. After food and much-needed water, they examined the rest of the goodies. There were two vacuumed-packed sleeping bags, pillows and blankets. They expanded once the wrapper was removed. This absolutely amazed Kaipo, which caused Crystal to giggle at her friend's expression of disbelief.

'Wow! Luxury!' Crystal breathed as she examined the contents of the rest of the bundle.

Kaipo held up a pair of baggy tie-string trousers and a tunic top, running her fingers over the fabric like it was silk.

The rest consisted of two head scarves, a six-pack of bottled water, more clothes for the supposed children, and a few small toys. Both felt bad for the lie, maybe depriving others. But then again, Crystal justified that if they got to the Island, there were deserving children there, too.

That night, they slept in relative comfort in the remains of the building that moaned and groaned around them.

'This is the life,' Crystal laughed.

She was so grateful to be free; she did not care. Anything was better than life in prison or execution, reasoning that things could always be worse, however lousy life got. How many times had Crystal longed to be back on the Island? Now there was a chance, but they could not find a way of getting there. She could not wait to see Billy and give him a huge cuddle, not to mention Diesel and Puss, Ayan, and everyone who was now her family.

Kaipo felt different; at various times, she had a faraway look in her eye. Crystal knew what was coming.

'I go back prison,' she said.

'No! You'll adjust. Give it time. It'll be OK. I was the same when I got caught here as the war started. But now I don't want to go home.'

This seemed to pacify her until the look came into her eyes again. It got to the stage where Crystal would lose patience and snap at Kaipo whenever it did.

'You're not going back! End of! They think we're dead. Let's leave it there.'

'I not thinking that' Kaipo defended, her lip almost stuck out in a sulk. 'I think about baby.'

Crystal was shocked. 'What baby! You never said you had a child!'

'Yes, girl. She be...' Kaipo held up eight fingers. 'I think, every day.'

'Who has her?'

'I not know. I never saw. Once here. No one told me. Could be dead.'

Crystal went quiet. She reached for her friend's hand and held it, unable to find words of comfort.

Each day, for something to do, they weaved around the bombed-out streets. Feeling sickened by the people sleeping, as they were, on pavements or in clearings of rubble.

One day, they went back to the prison. Both were in tears as they stared at the burned-out heap, once their home. The metal gates and some of the bars still stood at precarious angles. The entrance to the outside yard was still intact, a reminder of what the building once was. Charcoaled wood, ash and blackened bricks littered the site. Amazingly, one bed had escaped the flames. It sat lonely and isolated, surrounded by the charred remains that told a horrific story.

'I wonder if anyone came out alive?' Crystal said.

A lady wandering past stopped beside them, sadly shaking her head. Kaipo began speaking to her. She then turned to her friend and wept, burying her face into her shoulder.

'What did she say?' Crystal asked once the sobs subsided slightly.

'All gone. None got out. Even wardens. That was my family. All dead. Remains gone to a mass grave.'

'Come on,' Crystal grabbed her arm and gently pulled her friend away from the ugliness.

Kaipo shook her off. 'Need to go grave.'

'Do you think it's a good idea?'

'Go grave,' Kaipo jutted her jaw in determination.

223

Giving in, they walked to the edge of the town. They saw the mass graves in the distance—long, dark pits dug so the war dead could be buried quickly. This was necessary because of the hot sun and to prevent disease. There were ditches still open, unused, and others freshly covered.

They went to the one that appeared to be the newest. Kaipo put her hands together and began to say words. Crystal lowered her head and closed her eyes, seeing the burning bodies in her mind again. They both cried fresh tears for the ladies whose lives had been stamped out in such a vicious, cruel way.

Afterward, they went to the port, watching the boats and military vessels bobbling on the gentle waves to ease their anxiety. They sat on a wall and had more rice and sauce for lunch.

'Ride on another boat, maybe?' Kaipo asked.

'We could try, but the Island has no name. I've no idea where it is, and we have no money to offer.'

Crystal began to tell her about the people she had lived with, even Mr Slap.

'You love Ali?' Kaipo blurted in midsentence.

She stopped and looked at her friend. 'Why would you say that?'

'Because eyes light when talk of him. They alive and spark.'

'I don't love him. He's married and loves his wife. She's like a sister to me.'

Kaipo looked sad. 'I'm sorry,' her eyes were full of understanding.

Crystal shrugged and looked away. 'It's OK. I have as much of him as I can hope for. I'm grateful for that. Besides, we would never get on.'

'You wise.'

'What, me? Don't be silly; I'm the most stupid person I know.'

They giggled and left for the ruined building, now their home. Their few belongings were hidden as they left each day. That night, they slept with their bodies close, feeling comfort, just to know the other was there. In the early hours, Crystal was woken by Kaipo's gentle crying. She reached for her friend's hand and held it to let her know she was not alone.

Once the food ran out, Kaipo queued at the station again. They were lucky to be given another set of clothes. These were the usual string trousers and tunics, but it was fantastic to have a clean outfit. Each day, they headed for the port in case a boat from the Island came.

'What if any of them find out the jail has burned down? They'll think I'm dead,' Crystal fretted. 'I might never see Billy again.'

'One day, see someone, come for supplies.' Kaipo reassured, not really knowing what else to say.

After a month, street living became a way of life. They were starting to be well known, making friends amongst some of the war victims, waving and greeting people as they passed. Families had lost so many children, sons, fathers, and mothers; everywhere you looked were tragic circumstances. Often, they helped people dig through the debris of someone's home to find belongings not destroyed by the war. Sometimes, they found the rotting remains of a body or body parts. It was heart-rending, and Kaipo always cuddled the person, who, until that time, still had a tiny hope of finding life beneath the rubble. She cried tears with them, trying her best to comfort their grief, which would live with them for the rest of their life.

225

It was exciting when they recovered a few intact belongings for the person or family. It was never much, as little ever survived bombs. But the odd ornament, toy, or item of clothing meant so much to the person. They were reminders of how their lives once were.

Slowly, machines began to clear rubble, allowing new buildings to take their place.

Neither of them ventured onto the streets at night as bitterness and injustice rippled among unpleasant gangs who pillaged, mugged, and raided shops still standing.

It was in their second month when they spotted an English television crew. It was an ideal opportunity for Crystal to get word to her mum. However, it was risky that they might recognise her from the news story. Especially if they heard her speak English, it would raise suspicion. Crystal's hair was now wrapped in the scarf, and her face was tanned by the sun; she could easily pass as local. But it did not make her confident, even though she longed to let her mum know all was well.

Kaipo came up with a solution: 'I tell the man, family in England. Ask if he sends word.'

'But we have no paper or a pen.'

'We try.'

So, she approached the team, watched by Crystal, biting her lip in anticipation.

Kaipo coughed behind one of the men. He didn't hear, so she pulled at his jacket. He turned around, looking surprised.

'Family in England,' she began. 'You post letter? So, they know, I safe.'

The man smiled, 'of course. But what is it worth? Can we interview you?'

'No interview. Pen and paper.'

He laughed, 'You're cheeky.' He turned to his colleague and asked, 'Have we such thing as a pen, paper and envelopes, Ed?'

The other man fiddled inside his case of goods, handing out a pad and envelope, smiling,' No pen, though.'

Ed handed over the small bundle, including his own pen.

'Come on, love, do us a favour, just a quick interview!'

'No, love!' Kaipo grabbed the goods and scuttled off to where Crystal waited, laughing.

'The reporter was taken back. But also laughed, shouting after her. 'You've about half an hour before we leave!'

Finding a small wall, Crystal sat and quickly began to write, addressing the letter to Layla's mum.

Dear Janice, hope everything is OK. Give my love to Layla and congratulate her on the birth of Jade. Please can you give the enclosed letter to my mum?

Sarah James. Xx

She decided it was best to use her old name, just in case. On another sheet, she wrote to Mary.

Dear Mum,

I am sending this to Janice in hopes she can get it to you. I cannot send it directly for fear the authorities will get hold of it.

I want you to know I am safe, well, and alive. I am no longer in prison.

I can't go into any detail. I want you to know I am happy. Please do not worry about me. Never let anyone know I have written, or I will be at risk of being caught. I will get word to you when I can.

All my love,

Crystal. xxx

It was enough for now. At least her mum would know she was safe. She addressed the envelope, and Kaipo returned it to the reporter. After handing it over, she scurried away again.

By now, they had been free for three months; time flew, as they always found something to occupy themselves.

Early one afternoon, when they made their way to the port, Crystal spotted one of the Island's fishing boats. She could not contain her excitement as she bounced up and down before grabbing Kaipo's hand and dragging her towards it.

'Well! Mrs Crystal Blake!' A man's voice said from behind them.

Sickness rose in her stomach, threatening to spill as she turned to see, first, a gun and then Lieutenant Warner's finger on the trigger.

'It's good to see you. We thought you had perished in the flames!' An ironic grin spread across his face, which she wanted to claw off with her nails.

'Please, Crystal begged, 'You believed I was innocent. I know you did. Just let me go.'

'He lowered his gun slightly. 'Why would I do that?'

Because you're a good, kind man? And it's unfair to pay for something I didn't do.'

Out of the corner of her eye, she saw Mr. Slap and Rohan loading goods onto the boat. The engine was ignited and rumbled into action. They were about to leave.

'You're going to have to shoot me. I'm not going back to prison. I would rather be dead!' Crystal's voice was full of conviction. 'You know, as well as I do, it's unfair. I had no idea what my husband had done. So, please. Let us go!'

Lieutenant Warner relaxed the gun slightly, seeing her eyes frantically flicking from him to the boat sailing away from the port.

He waved the gun barrel, 'Go! One day, Mrs Blake, we will come for you when the war ends. But for now, I've not seen you.' He turned and made to walk away.

Grabbing Kaipo's arm again, they ran as fast as possible towards the boat, shouting.

'In fact, Mrs Blake, maybe you did die in the fire,' he hollowed after them. He would never be sure if she heard, but he had more important things to attend to for now.

As they reached the shore, Crystal and Kaipo began jumping and screaming, as loud as they could, 'Mr Slap! Rohan!'

Neither heard her over the rumbling engine. Kaipo grabbed a stone and threw it as hard and as far as possible. It hit the side of the boat. Mr Slap, hearing the thud, turned, startled. He saw the two women calling and waving their arms on the shore but did not recognise them. He continued his journey, thinking they were strangers, cadging a ride. Kaipo grabbed another stone and threw it. This time, it hit him in the back. He was not too pleased as he shook his fist, shouting angrily.

Crystal pulled off her head scarf and screamed, 'It's me, Mr Slap!'

Recognition flooded the old man's face as he swung the boat around and returned to the shore. The two women were ecstatic as they fell into each other's arms, crying and laughing simultaneously.

'You dead! You dead!' Mr. Slap shouted as he reached the coastline, skilfully parking the little boat between two larger ones.

Crystal threw her arms around him, kissing the wrinkly, weather-beaten cheek. She did the same to Rohan, who looked clumsy and embarrassed at the show of emotion.

'You dead!' Mr Slap repeated.

Lieutenant Warner watched the scene from a distance. 'Well,' he said out loud, 'I guess those people believe you. Even if no one else does.' He gave a small laugh as he left, heading towards the base.

Crystal made them wait while she ran to the building where their belongings were safely hidden. Inside were the toys she wanted Billy and the other children to have, plus the few clothes they had been given. She vowed never to visit the mainland again.

Returning to the boat, she found Kaipo looking awkward and guilty.

'What's wrong!' Crystal began to panic, thinking Lieutenant Warner had come back, changing his mind.

'I not come. I go back to prison,'

'You've got to be kidding!'

'I not do this,' Kaipo was near to tears. 'Please. Not make this hard for me. I not free, in heart.'

Crystal grabbed her friend, who struggled, pushing her roughly onto the deck.

'Drive!'

Mr. Slap was confused but obeyed. Although Kaipo was not pleased, she had no choice but to go with them.

Crystal began to feel apprehensive. After being away for seven months, would she be accepted back on the Island? But then justified in her head, that Billy, her son, was there; of course, she would be.

Once Kaipo forgave Crystal, she began speaking to Mr. Slap, translating the conversation.

'Ayan had taken Maya to the hospital on the mainland to give birth because of her heart. She was kept in for two weeks and hated it.'

So, Crystal thought Ali had been to the mainland and had not been to see her. How selfish she felt to expect he would when his wife was in danger and giving birth. Crystal began to dislike herself strongly for her thoughts, especially as a knot tightened in her stomach at the mention of his name. Kaipo seemed to sense this; she gave a slight, knowing smile. Causing her friend to look away and stare out to sea, not wanting sympathy for her sin of feeling.

'Maya had given birth to a little girl; they called her Tiare. She was elated and took to motherhood like a flame to paper. Ayan was a proud father, strutting around like a peacock. He doted on his daughter. Everyone was mortified to think Crystal had perished in a fire in prison. Chris had taken her death badly. He was full of guilt for not visiting and offering more support. The children missed school, and Crystal, they all did.'

231

'Tonight, big party,' Rohan grinned. 'And welcome pretty Kaipo to our little home.' The young lady blushed and lowered her head.

Crystal could not contain herself when she spotted the Island in the distance. People were waiting for the return of the boat on the beach. She could see their silhouettes as the sun dazzled behind them. Diesel was bouncing up and down at the water's edge. Amazingly, next to him was Puss.

'They know! How incredible is that?' she told the others.

Tears wetted her cheeks; as they drew closer, she spotted Billy in Ayan's arms, his thumb stuck in his mouth. The boat had barely stopped as Crystal jumped off and waded through the water. Diesel ran into the sea to greet her, his tail spinning like a helicopter blade. He was yelping and barking all at once. She threw her arms around the dog's neck, kissing his head. Not minding that his pink tongue licked inside her mouth. Puss was clawing her way, painfully, up Crystal's back to launch over her shoulder and into her arms. The cat rubbed her wet nose on hers. Ayan had put down wiggling Billy, who was running to her.

'Mamar, Mamar,' he shouted, tripping a few times in his haste. Lowering Puss, Crystal scooped up her son, spinning him around, before raining kisses onto his sweet-smelling hair.

As she lowered the little boy onto the sand, Chris threw his arms around her.

'Oh my god. I thought you were dead. I've cried so many man tears.'

'How come you've not yet caught a flight home?' She asked him.

'I just couldn't leave. Not without you,' he whispered into her ear.

'Ali,' Crystal said tearfully, holding out her hand.

He took it, pulling her into his arms and wrapping her around his chest. He kissed her hair openly. Maya looked on, but there was no malice, as she also had big tears.

She grabbed Crystal's hands, her grin wide and happy. 'We missed so much.'

Crystal was shocked at how ill Maya looked. She appeared so much older and had lost weight. Her eyes were circled with black, and her lips seemed to have a tinge of blue.

Kaipo stood at the water's edge while Crystal greeted everyone, looking lost and conspicuous.

Maya, seeing the young woman's awkwardness, held out her hand. 'Welcome to our home,' she smiled.

The tension melted from Kaipo's shoulders as she smiled warmly back.

Billy was delighted with his rubber dinosaur, toy car and Lego given by the aid workers.

'They must be shared with the other children,' Crystal told him.

'NO!' he objected, running off into Maya and Ayan's hut.

'Oh, what a beautiful baby,' Crystal raved as she cuddled Tiare.

Maya glowed with pride. 'She marry Billy, when grow.' They both laughed.

Chris was evicted from her hut, and Kaipo was moved in.

'Are you..., You know..., having relations? Only, if you are, I could help out here and there,' Chris suggested as they sat on a blanket by the fire a little later that day.

'You men always see things as a threat to your Winkie,' Crystal laughed.

'I see that as Winkie persecution and discrimination,' Chris objected.

They giggled like children. It was so good to be home.

Chapter Nineteen

Late in the afternoon, a buffet, which had been prepared by the ladies of the camp, was laid out and a welcome home party began. The food was fantastic, especially after what Crystal and Kaipo had been eating at the prison and on the streets.

Crystal was overwhelmed with the love and attention everyone showed, happy to have her home where she belonged. They all, except the children, drank alcohol. Lively music was played and the people who were able, joined in the singing and dancing.

Sanskrit wobbled over to where Crystal sat with Chris.

She put an arm around her shoulder, 'Granddaughter.'

'I missed you so much, Sanskrit,' Crystal leaned towards her and kissed the older lady's cheek. 'I missed everyone. It's so wonderful to be home.'

By the evening, most of the people had drunk too much. Chris and Crystal wept with laughter as Mr. Slap jigged around the fire out of sequence to the music and Sanskrit was dancing with Rohan as best she could with her rheumatic limbs.

'Do you think there's a budding romance blossoming?' Chris winked, a wicked glint in his eye.

'I reckon, by her age, she's sick of winkies,' Crystal grinned.

'God, I've missed you,' Chris said, his voice intense, as he draped his arm loosely over her shoulder. 'This place was not the same without you.'

235

'I missed everyone so much,' she replied, feeling emotional and happy. 'I thought I was never coming back. I certainly won't ever leave again.'

'You surely don't mean that?'

'I do. I've no passport and the authorities will be looking for me. They still need their gun to fire at someone, and apparently, I have the target on me.'

Chris looked puzzled, but after drinking too much, he let the comment wave over him and pulled at her hand to dance instead.

'So, you're an illegal immigrant,' he whispered in her ear.

'OH! I never thought of that. But, yes, I guess I am.'

'Do you think your mate would fancy a date sometime?' Chris asked, changing the subject and staring in Kaipo's direction.

'Where would you take her?' she giggled.

'I could manage a romantic meal on the beach. Although candles may be a problem.'

'Mmmm, maybe. Stone chairs and sand in the sarnies doesn't sound gripping.'

Kaipo sat at the edge of the group despite Crystal and Chris's encouragement to join in. She was having problems adjusting. She had heard about the islands but had never visited them. These people were so different from her own. Unlike her culture's strict, regimented upbringing, they were free and light-hearted.

'Go talk to her, Chris,' Crystal whispered. 'She feels lost. Make her feel welcome. Like you did me when I first arrived.'

He nodded and went off to sit next to Kaipo. It was not long before her face lightened, and she was laughing.

For the next few weeks, Kaipo mostly remained in the hut. At times, she disappeared into the woods, preferring her own company. This surprised Crystal; she thought her friend would be happy once on the Island. But Kaipo was still finding freedom difficult.

'It's understandable; she's been locked up from fourteen until adulthood,' Chris reasoned when Crystal confided her concerns. 'Maybe I could try and befriend her.'

'She may find it difficult. The last man she was around, she stabbed.'

For Crystal, it was as though she had never been away. School started a few days after her return. In the afternoons, she collected grass and eggs, for the camp. Some days Sanskrit went with her to gather herbs. There was still so much to learn, as she was reminded frequently by the older lady. In the mornings, before school, she swam in the sea with Chris and sometimes even Ayan joined them.

Billy did not adapt to his mother's return easily. He refused to come back to the hut to live, screaming if she tried to force him, wanting to stay with Maya and Ayan. Crystal was hurt.

'This natural,' Mira consoled. 'Confused. He not understand.'

'I guess. I've been away a long time. He thinks they are his parents now. But what should I do? Leave him, or force him to come home?'

'Not sure.' Mira shrugged, not knowing what to advise. 'Leave him. Let him get to know you again.'

Maya, overhearing the conversation, wandered over. 'Mira right. He confused. Ayan and me, treat like son as thought you dead. Made a big fuss of him. He thinks Ayan daddy.'

237

This depressed Crystal even more as she realised that her son missed having a father. She wondered then what Will would have been like as a parent. She guessed he would have spoilt Billy terribly, as he did her, doting on the little boy as Ayan did his little girl. Mira was right; she should leave her son to adapt and not force him home.

'It's just another one of life's kippers,' she said.

The sisters looked at her, their expressions screwed in puzzlement.

'Not understand.'

To Crystal, it seemed no one had noticed how unwell Maya looked. She was concerned for her but worried about drawing too much attention. No one had mentioned it, so was it that they had not noticed the difference, seeing her every day?

'Just when you think everything is OK, Life has a big kipper to slap you around the chops!' Crystal continued, giggling at the bewilderment on their faces. They still looked confused, so she changed the subject. 'How's Masa? I've not seen him much.'

Mira looked sad and anxious at the mention of her husband's name. 'Told him to go live at sisters, on the mainland. Cannot do it anymore. He is angry. Not speak to me. Not speak nobody. Not even Ayan.'

Crystal had hoped things had improved. How sad for her friend. There did not seem to be an answer. She had seen Masa skulking around a few times. But they avoided each other, their anger and dislike still ripe.

Since the party, Chris and Kaipo had begun spending a lot of time together. This caused gossip and speculation amongst the people about a budding romance. They were often seen walking in the woods or sitting on the cliff edge for hours talking. The two were fast becoming an item.

Crystal had not noticed until Mr. Slap nudged her and winked as the two sat lost in their own world, chatting by the fire. Kaipo laughed at something Chris had said; her eyes and face were sparkling. Crystal smiled, pleased the two were friends.

Leaving them to it, she went to gather some herbs, taking the opportunity while Billy was busy making a plane with Rohan. Delighted, Diesel appeared from nowhere and was at her side in seconds, ready for his long walk. It was pointless taking Puss; the cat still seemed to prefer the comfort of the bed almost all day. These were the times that Crystal loved most when she could be alone to gather her thoughts. Listening to the birds chattering and the trees rustling, with busy wildlife, was good for the soul, as Sanskrit often stated. After the prison, these moments were more precious than ever. It was strange, she thought, how so much happiness could be found in the simple things in life.

Hearing a louder rustling, Crystal turned just in time to see Masa dart behind a tree. He had been watching her, which was disturbing as she had just relieved herself, thinking no one was around. She suddenly became frightened, as a nightmare began in her head. Feeling very isolated, with only Diesel, who was not strong enough to protect her, Crystal ran toward the camp, almost knocking Ayan flying as he was heading to the river to wash.

'For god sake, woman, you scared me half to death!' he raved, retrieving his toiletries from the floor. 'What's wrong?' He eyed her suspiciously, seeing her frightened eyes and then his brother darting behind a tree again.

'Nothing. I… just got spooked,' she stammered.

'Did he touch you?' Ayan's voice was full of concern.

'No. he just creeped me out. But didn't do anything.'

After Crystal left, Masa ambled over, 'Must be handy having two on the go, brother. Especially now the wife is almost on her last legs. I heard you had been porking the English bit.'

Ayan's temper exploded as he flung his toiletries and punched Masa. He fell backward into brambles and began to laugh.

'Hit a sore point, have I?' he sneered, pleased to have such a reaction from his brother.

Ayan pulled Masa to his feet and went to hit him again. He then froze, with his fist drawn back. Sadness filled his eyes. 'What the hell happened to you? I miss my brother, the man he once was. Now Satan possesses his soul.' Ayan let go of him, turned his back, gathered his toiletries, and walked towards the stream to wash.

'I killed her husband!' Masa shouted after him. 'I shot him and all of them at the beginning of the war. If she hadn't hidden, I would have killed her too.'

Ayan stopped and turned to face him. 'How do you know it was her husband?'

'I heard the story; you were talking when the English bit was in prison. I remembered it. The camp. There was a pretty ginger girl. Felt sad about her; we should have kept her alive for a while longer. She could have been fun.'

He began to laugh again; it sounded evil and sinister as it rippled through Ayan's head. The laughter became louder and louder; he would not stop.

Ayan ran at him. His fists clenched, 'Stop it!' he shouted.

When Masa didn't, he began punching his face again, over and over, until blood splashed, and broken teeth crumbled and cracked. Someone was pulling at him; he could hear shouting and crying in distress. It was Maya begging him to stop. Then, her body crumbled, and she fell in a heap on the floor, dropping Tiare, who also began to wail in fear.

Ayan let go of Masa, who stumbled to the ground, his face a mass of blood. Turning to his wife, he fell on his knees beside her, gently stroking her hair from her face. He gathered her in his arms and carried her back to the hut, laying her carefully on the bed as though she was made of fragile eggshell.

Mira ran to Masa, who lay still, his breath coming in short gasps. Crystal carefully picked up Tiare. She seemed unhurt, but just in case, she took her to Sanskrit to check her over.

'Why?' Sanskrit asked once the baby was given the all-clear. Luckily, her fall was on soft grass, preventing any injury.

'I don't know,' Crystal said tearfully. 'Maya collapsed. Ali has taken her to their hut.'

Sanskrit nodded slowly; her eyes wide with worry. 'I go. You care, baby.'

She disappeared into the hut with Mira, who had left Masa in the woods. Crystal gently rocked the child, who had fallen asleep after all the drama.

Chris put his hand on her shoulder. 'What the hell?'

'I don't know what happened. Ali was by the stream, and I heard the argument. But I think it was my fault. Masa was hiding behind a tree in the woods. He scared me. I bumped into Ali on the way back. Then I heard them fighting. Maya looks so ill.'

'Yes, she has looked bad since the baby. I hope she's OK.'

No one emerged from the hut until late evening when everyone except Ayan filed out. Mira came to Crystal, who was having difficulty stopping Billy from running into the hut. He was screaming and kicking her in protest. Chris led the little boy away with a bribe to see the fishing boats. Seeing Kaipo go with them was sweet, holding Billy's hand as she spoke softly to the little boy.

Mira looked wretched, her face white and eyes large and traumatised. 'Maya, want to see you.'

Crystal was shocked when she went into the hut. Her friend's skin was grey. The bed seemed enormous, and Maya was so tiny as she lay on it. Ayan was sitting at the side, holding her hand, stroking her hair with his other. They were in a private world, staring into each other's eyes. Feeling like an intruder, Crystal made to back away, not wanting to break the spell. Maya turned, her eyes sunken; she looked to have aged so much. Whispering something to Ayan, he left, not even glancing at Crystal as he brushed past. She went to the bed, crouched, holding Maya's hand; it was still warm from Ayan's touch.

'I die, Crystal. Not long left. You promised care for Ayan. He needs and loves you. You mother to my beautiful daughter.'

'Please, Maya. You can't go. Everyone needs you.'

'I happy. Life been good. Now, time to go to the gods. But I not rest until I know you care for them. Please!'

Crystal could hold no more tears; they fell in glops onto the tiny hand as her head lowered, and she felt ashamed to let Maya see her so upset when she was so brave.

'I promise.'

Maya died in the early hours of the following day. No one was asleep as they waited around the fire. The silence almost buzzed, as even the night creatures were still. Some of the group prayed to their gods that Maya would arrive safely in the afterlife, be at peace, and find happiness.

Ayan and Mira were inconsolable as they wept in each other's arms. Chris held Crystal to his shoulder as she cried. Kaipo reached out and put her hand on her friend's back to let her know she was there.

Anyone who wished to visit Maya once the sun rose could. When Crystal went, she was surprised at how young and beautiful Maya looked. Her body was swathed in pretty blue flowers. Her hair shone like a glowing halo around her lovely face. A small smile was on her lips, as though she had now found peace.

'Rest well, my beautiful friend. I'll always love you. I'll never forget you.' She kissed her forehead before turning to leave.

Because of the heat, the funeral was held later that day. A grave was dug a short distance from the beach. Masa stood away from them, his bruised face bowed, as though he too was praying, and through his concrete heart, something still human ran.

Sanskrit, who led the service, found words hard to say. She was burying her granddaughter, whom she never expected to outlive and whom she had been a mother to. There was not one dry eye amongst them as Maya was lowered into the ground, swathed in white cotton cloth.

Later that day, Crystal found Ayan on the clifftop, staring out to sea. She sat and reached for his hand. There they stayed until the sun set and darkness fell, without words, watching the swish of waves crashing against the rocks below. Diesel sat on the other side, resting his head on Ayan's arm as though trying to comfort the broken man.

The next day, Ayan went to Masa who was sitting on a fallen tree at the edge of the camp.

He looked up, 'How you doing, bruv?' he grinned smugly through swollen lips, showing broken teeth. 'Now you're free for the English bit.'

Ayan's eyes were full of loathing as his temper exploded. 'You leave, now!' he spat as he grabbed his brother's tunic, pulling him to his feet and dragging him to the beach.

'Steady on,' Masa chuckled.

Ayan shouted for some of the men, 'Get him away from here before I kill him.'

He threw his brother onto the sand, where he lay sprawled.

Everyone followed, worried about what Ayan might do.

Masa looked towards Crystal. 'Did Ayan tell you I killed your husband? And all those Brits who were on their luxury holiday. Our people waiting on them like slaves. Even that cute redhead. We could have had some fun with her. I bet she would have squealed. Shame we never found you. We would have had some good times, but sadly, my brother got there first.' He began to laugh, a deep, cruel, sinister sound that threw a spear into her soul.

Crystal remained frozen as she stared back at him, 'I don't believe you.' Although she had never mentioned Sonya to anyone. He wouldn't have known about her unless he was there. 'I don't believe you killed Will.'

'Really? Fat bloke. Grizzled about his wife and unborn baby. Yeah, was definitely him? But then again, he and you sold us all, didn't you? Became rich for the price of our lives. It is not me who needs to pay for the bloodshed. It's you, isn't it? You and your fat husband did this. How much was the wealth from our blood?' Masa's eyes were wide and full of repulsion as he jabbed his finger and words towards her with conviction. 'It's you who should pay with your life.'

The attention was no longer on Masa but on Crystal, as everyone's eyes burned into her.

'I didn't know what Will did,' she defended. 'I knew nothing about his business. I promise you all.' Her voice was almost hysterical; no one spoke as time seemed to stop.

'You destroyed me, our homes, and our people, all for your fancy life. I hope you rot in hell, Crystal Blake!'

Ayan's eyes, full of accusation, cut into her. The pain of his glare and hatred shot into her heart.

Kaipo broke the spell; she stepped forward and put her hand on Ayan's arm. 'You know in your heart this has nothing to do with Crystal. That thing is not your brother. He died in the war and was recreated into what you see before you. His soul is dead. This monster is all that is left. He wants someone to take the pain from him by having another to blame.'

Ayan turned his eyes away and looked to the sand as though trying to digest her words. His mind was to exploded with grief to fit more inside at that moment.

Masa stared at Kaipo, his eyes seeming to see the young woman for the first time. He picked himself up, ran into the sea, and onto one of the boats. Two men ran after him and sparked the engine into action; they sped away.

Ayan looked into Mira's eyes, which were full of unshed tears. He put his hand on her shoulder and they returned to the camp.

Kaipo grabbed Crystal's arm. 'I'm sorry. Everyone knows it is not true. These people love and trust you. Do not let his words wash away all that is good for you. You are as innocent in this as we are. Everyone knows that.'

'But those words can never be taken back, can they? Deep in people's hearts, they'll never really believe I was not part of the cause of war?'

'He is damaged and angry. He needs to blame someone because he cannot live with what he has done. Of course, it is not his fault. But he wants to point that gun of blame at you. Do not be bitter and angry at Masa. Forgive him, as he will never forgive himself for what he did. He is damaged beyond repair.'

Kaipo, like everyone else, had spoken in their own language. Crystal suddenly realised she had understood every word. She sank onto the sand, pulling her knees under her chin.

'I cannot bear Ali hating me.'

'He doesn't. He is grieving badly and confused.'

'Will Masa ever be the person he once was?' Crystal asked.

Her friend smiled sadly,' I do not think so. That person is dead, the same as the Crystal of old.'

'True.'

Billy was confused and fretful after Maya's death. He constantly called for MayMay, running into the empty hut to see if she had come back. Crystal had no choice but to force him to live with her. This caused more disruption to the young boy who cried himself to sleep most nights. Even in his dreams, he called out for MayMay. It did not help that Ayan ignored him, along with his baby daughter, whom he seemed to be blaming for his wife's death.

Everyone tried to comfort the young boy, but he was inconsolable, having lost so many in his short life, first his mother and now Maya and Ayan. The worst thing happened: he stopped talking. Crystal was beside herself with worry, not knowing what to do.

Kaipo helped as much as she could by spending hours talking and playing with the little boy, trying to distract him from his grief.

Mira took charge of Tiara, whom she moved into her hut. This slightly consoled her and eased some of the pain from her sister's death.

At school, Crystal missed Maya dreadfully. She had taken care of the younger members. The two of them had planned lessons together and chatted about the progress of their individual pupils. Eventually, she convinced Kaipo to take Maya's place. She did and soon found a niche in the group. Along with her friendship with Chris, Kaipo began to settle into Island life.

Slowly, everyone began to accept Maya was no longer among them, except Ayan. He no longer went fishing, took charge of the camp, or interacted with anyone except when necessary. He slept beside the fire or in the woods, no longer wanting to go into the hut he shared with his wife. His gaze was always distant and far away, full of sadness and deep wounds.

Sanskrit also struggled terribly with the loss of her granddaughter. In quiet moments, the older lady shed many tears. She looked very depleted and tired. Her limbs seemed more painful and twisted as she hunched on a stool beside the fire, staring into the flames each day. A huge dark cloud had once again settled over the camp. There were no more parties to keep up morale, no laughter, or even just light-hearted chatter.

Chapter Twenty

Two months after Maya's death, Chris made a surprising announcement, 'We're going to look for Kaipo's daughter.'

Crystal was astounded. It had never occurred to her that this was possible. After all, Kaipo had no idea where her little girl was. 'But how, and what if she gets caught?'

'I still need to iron out the creases. But we're going to try, with Ali's permission.'

Crystal raised her eyebrows, 'Why Ali's permission?'

'We need to borrow a boat.'

'Oh, course. Can I come?'

Chris looked doubtful, 'But you swore never to go to the mainland again. Plus, we might be gone for a few days. What about Billy?'

'He can come to. It could help with bonding. And looking for the child is a different reason for returning to the mainland. It would be amazing if Kaipo found her daughter.'

Chris was still unconvinced, 'Do you think it's a good idea to drag a toddler all that way? We might need to sleep rough.'

'It'll be an adventure for him. Besides, after Masa, being away from here will do me good. People are different towards me. They blame me for the war.'

'Rubbish. They're grieving. No one believes what Masa said. But if you're sure, it'll be good to have help.'

Ayan shrugged when Chris asked.

'I have money,' Crystal told them excitedly.

'Wow, how?' Chris was impressed. All his belongings had been lost when he had run from his lodgings at the beginning of the war.

'My husband hid emergency money when we came on holiday. The soldiers that raided the camp never found it. It's blood money, I guess, but at least it might be put to good use finding Kaipo's child. Where will we head?'

'To my hometown, Ukatira. It's where I grew up. Hopefully, my family's still there.' Kaipo looked apprehensive as well as nervous at the thought of returning.

'But didn't they disown you?' Crystal asked.

'They were forbidden to speak to me. I brought disgrace to the family. But my sister might help. Or even my mother, as long as my father is not around.'

Crystal said her goodbyes to Mira by giving her a big cuddle. She went to Sanskrit, who was in her usual place beside the fire. The day was scorching, and the older lady's face was red from the heat of the flames.

Crystal gripped the knarled hand, noting how stiff the fingers felt. 'I'll be back soon. Please look after yourself.'

Sanskrit smiled weakly and nodded. 'I lost too many now. I miss them so much. Do you think Maya will help with the school while you are gone?'

'You mean Mira?'

'I know what I mean. I am not stupid. Maya. As she already helps, she may take on all the children instead of just the youngsters.'

Crystal was taken aback. Was Sanskrit becoming confused? 'I'm sorry you feel so much pain. We all love you. Please remember that.'

Sanskrit's gaze returned to the fire and some faraway place where she now seemed to live.

They left with very few belongings except food for Billy. Crystal felt dreadful leaving Diesel, who sat on the beach looking panic-stricken. The last time she had left on a boat, she hadn't come back.

'I promise I will this time!' she shouted to the dog.

This did not pacify him as he whined and barked, running into the sea after her. In the end, she scooped him up and plopped him onto the boat.

'No way! You really are the limit, Crystal,' Chris huffed.

Kaipo giggled, and the little party was off as he cranked up the engine.

Billy was so excited about the boat ride that he wouldn't keep still and kept hanging over the edge to watch the water. Diesel, with a lulling tongue, stood on his back legs to watch with him. Crystal was so worried they would fall in that she eventually tied them around the waist so they couldn't.

Kaipo was quiet and withdrawn. This was a huge moment for her, and she had many memories to relive. Crystal grabbed her hand and squeezed it as Chris drove the boat.

'Was it an arranged marriage?' she asked.

'Yes, my people are farmers. My husband offered six cows for the match. He was a horrible man. Old, about 50. He had four children, and his wife had died. I had to be a mother to them; they were older than me. I begged my father not to allow the marriage. But women are not worth much, and six cows are much more.'

'How horrible. I can't even imagine how you felt, still a child and married to a man old enough to be your grandfather.'

'It was terrible, Crystal. I was desperately unhappy. I missed my family and friends terribly but was forbidden to even visit. Every night, I cried myself to sleep. My husband beat me for crying and regularly forced himself on me. I did not even know about sex. My periods had only just started, so when I was pregnant, I thought I was ill, being sick every morning, and my belly swelling. No one explained about babies. I figured death would be better than life with a monster.' Kaipo paused while she fought with her emotions.

'When I gave birth, I was so small that I tore down below. A few nights later, he was drunk and forced himself on me again. I cannot even tell you the agony. That's when I stabbed him, the same night. I waited for him to fall asleep and then did it. I remember thinking prison would be better than this hell. I was right; it was. I was happy being away from him. But not my baby. After I stabbed him, I scooped her up and ran home to my mum. My father dragged me back again. He said that it was for life once married, whatever the consequences. My mother and sister pleaded with him not to, but it did no good. I was screaming and begging, but my father took no notice. I hate him more than my husband.' She wiped away stray tears and sniffed. Recalling these times, which were still so raw, hurt so much.

'Oh Kaipo, your life has been awful.' Crystal was horrified but tried not to let this show.

'When I got back to the village, the police were there. They took my baby from me and I was taken to prison. That was the last time I saw her and my family. She will be eight now. At first, in prison, I was terrified. I screamed and cried for my mum and baby constantly. But after a while, I got used to it, and it was not so bad; it was better than being married. The older women looked after me. They became my family.' She lowered her head, 'until they burnt to death.'

'Did your husband die?'

'I do not know. I never heard what happened to him. My family would have been forbidden to ever see me again. My father would have seen it as a betrayal; he may have even had to return the cows.'

'This is all so wrong and twisted.' The story, Crystal thought, would haunt her forever. She was in disbelief that these things happened in this modern world. What a sheltered, ignorant life she had led.

'It is how things are. We learned about Western countries at school. I wanted so much to be free, too. You are a lucky woman.'

'Free?' But I'm not free.'

'You are Crystal. Your mind and life are your own. Mine is embroiled in cultural restrictions and duties.'

'Where's your village? And how do we get there?' Chris shouted over the engine noise. The moment was broken, and they were dragged back to reality.

'It is in the mountains. But there is a bus.'

'Thank God for that. It was bad enough facing the steep hills on Panchaea,' Crystal laughed, trying to lighten the moment. She squeezed Kaipo's hand again in understanding. Her own eyes glistened with tears for what this lovely woman had suffered.

The journey was not straightforward, especially with a dog and toddler with them. Once they arrived at the mainland, they caught a bus, which climbed up the mountain through the next three villages. Luckily, they had not been affected by war. Chris stood in the bus aisle, allowing the two women the only free seat. He was soon shimmied to the back as more people boarded.

The journey was slow and clunky. As the bus was old, it rattled, complaining along bumpy, steep roads that were alarmingly narrow. At times, the window view showed a sheer drop over the mountain edge. There was no protection along the perimeter to prevent a disaster. It was very disturbing and Crystal was glad when it finally headed inland, which, although still steep, was safer.

The bus stopped at random places, which appeared to be in the middle of nowhere, to allow people on and off. Some came aboard disguised behind goats or clucking chickens and geese. This delighted Billy, who wiggled and fought from Crystal's lap to stroke the goats. He then screamed and stamped when his request was refused. No amount of distraction seemed to pacify him. In the end, a kind passenger squeezed nearer to their seat so the goat's head could be patted.

Billy giggled delightedly and at last began to speak, 'Gogo.'

Diesel had squashed himself under the seat, feeling safer from being trampled on.

There never seemed to be any houses or dwellings from which the boarding people may have come. Seeing her confusion, Kaipo explained that people sometimes walked for a few hours to reach the bus route.

'But where are they going?' Crystal asked, amazed.

'To sell goats or chickens in other villages.

The bus driver stopped at an unexpected garage, which appeared from nowhere. He kindly bought every passenger a bottle of water, which was passed along the bus, as it was so crowded that no one could move along the aisle.

If someone wanted to get off, everyone standing did, to allow them room to move. The heat and stuffiness were stifling, not to mention the goat pooing little bunny droppings on the floor, which it then urinated on. The passengers groaned as the bus stopped. Once again, everyone vacated until the area was cleaned. Crystal had so much trouble encouraging Diesel out from under the seat that she had to leave him there.

'Think he's stuck,' she told the other two. Then visualised the bus driver having to call the fire brigade, if there was one, to cut him out.

It was good to have a bus break for a while. From the view at that moment, they could see the sea in the distance. Tiny white specks of boats dotted about the coastline. It reminded Crystal of the retreat, except this was more mountainous and they were higher up.

Finally, they arrived at the end of the route, which was more a village than a town. It had a few shops, though, and another garage, where the bus driver stopped to talk to the attendant.

'Everyone's so laid back,' Crystal laughed.

'Yes, a bit different from England,' Chris grinned.

Kaipo looked tense and worried. 'We should not have come.'

Chris made to hold her hand, 'It'll be fine, you'll see.'

Kaipo quickly shook him away, 'It is forbidden.'

'What is?'

'To show affection and for a man to touch you.'

'Where now?' Chris asked to hide his hurt.

'This is our local town. From here, it is about a three-kilometre walk.'

Both her friends grimaced. The journey had already taken most of the day.

'Is there nowhere we could stay the night?' Crystal asked, longing for a break and some food.

'That will be wasting time. If we get closer, a few unused farm buildings may still be vacant. We could stay in one for the night if we need to.'

'I can't let Billy sleep in a derelict building,' she protested.

'We have no hotels. Not in these poor parts of our country.'

'Guess not,' she winced, feeling silly for thinking there would be. 'I'm sure Billy won't mind.'

So far, since stroking the goat, the little boy had fallen quiet again.

Before the walk, they bought bread, cakes, cheese, and drinks. Chris had borrowed Ayan's backpack, so he carried the supplies. Crystal gave Billy a piggyback to save his legs and quicken the pace. Diesel ran ahead, sniffing at various rocks and clumps of greenery.

'It must be strange to grow up in the middle of nowhere,' Crystal mused, as there did not seem to be a road.

'I guess, to you. I know nothing different. You must find our way of life as odd as I do yours.'

Just as Kaipo predicted, an hour and a half into the journey, they found a vacant building that appeared to have once been a farm.

'Why would this be empty?' Crystal asked, thinking it would have been snapped up in England.

'People die or cannot financially keep it going.'

The house was not suitable for sleeping in, as it was filthy and had nothing inside. So, they settled for the barn, which still had bales of straw, to rest and eat. It was now late into the afternoon. Exhausted from the heat and journey, Billy fell asleep with Diesel, who had plopped beside him.

'My village is close by.' Kaipo's voice was shaky, reflecting how she was feeling.

'Why not stay here the night and face the village in the morning?' Chris suggested. 'We're all shattered.'

'Kaipo?' Crystal prompted, as she looked like she was mulling it over. 'I think it's a good idea.'

'OK, you're right. Tomorrow, we will be fresher.'

Billy woke a few hours later. After eating, he found a great game of jumping and rolling in the straw with Diesel, who yapped excitedly, destroying the peace. Thankfully, after a few hours of disruption, they fell asleep again.

Crystal carried him to the back of the barn so he would not be disturbed, kissed him on his head and joined the other two.

'How many brothers and sisters have you, Kaipo?' she asked, wiggling into the straw to get comfortable.

'Four brothers and a sister. I am the youngest. So it was easier for me. My sister is only one year older. We were very close. She was married before me. I often think of her. It would be great to meet again.'

Sleeping in the straw was itchy and uncomfortable. By morning, they all, except Billy, had red bites covering their bodies.

'Oh my god!' Chris hollered from the other side of the barn. 'You won't believe where I've been bitten!' He came back scratching his crutch, a look of horror on his face.

The two women burst into fits of giggles.

'It's not funny! I'm in agony. It's not just one bite, it's loads!'

'Well, leave them alone. Otherwise, they'll fester. Crystal tried to look serious but then burst into laughter again when she looked at her friend, especially when Chris huffed and stormed from the barn.

The break had given Kaipo time to gather herself. So, once they had eaten and drunk, she took a deep breath before walking out the door and leading them through twisting tracks to her home village.

Before entering, they covered their heads with scarves, thankful Chris was with them. With his tanned skin, he would pass for a local and not raise too much suspicion.

'How do the people survive?' Crystal asked, seeing no shops or production in any way.

'They grow crops, fruit, even potatoes or farm animals. Or they make things to sell to tourists at the mainland. But we are relatively poor.'

'I thought your people were farmers,' Chris said.

'We live in a house in the village but have land on the outskirts.'

Although it was early morning, people were already out and about. They stared as the little group entered before dismissing them and going about their business. Groups of older men sat drinking coffee and women bustled about or sat on benches, gossiping while they sewed and weaved.

'Now what?' Chris asked.

'If my father sees me, I am in trouble. But he should have left for work by now.'

The houses were cubed and similar to the ones on Panchea. They were built at different levels up the mountain in monotonous rows. There was not the same art brightening the dull grey painted walls, giving each home an identity. In a way, Crystal thought it similar to the estate she had grown up in boring, sad, and poverty-stricken.

They weaved through the narrow streets that all looked the same, with Kaipo leading them. Without her, they would be lost.

'I think we're going around in a circle, everything looks the same!' Crystal's attempt at a joke was ignored.

'This is where my best friend lived,' Kaipo pointed towards one of the houses.

'How can you tell?' at her friend's confused look, Crystal quickly added, 'What happened to her?'

'I never saw her after I was married. I guess the same as me. Matched to some man from another village. I hope she found happiness. We would get into so much mischief when we were young.' Kaipo looked sad and heavy.

They stopped at a larger single-story building, not much bigger than three residential houses.

'This is the village school.'

Through the window, they could see children sitting cross-legged on the floor. Unlike Crystal's schooldays, when the youngsters were noisy and disruptive, they intently listened to the teacher. It appeared to be just one large room. A partition divided the boys from the girls. The walls were brightly painted with animals, a world map, and writing, possibly an alphabet. The outside space was fenced and concreted. The outer walls were painted in what were once bright colours. They were now faded by the sun. A Snakes and Ladders crept up one large square of bricks, and a net for ball kicking was also painted on the wall; it was sadly chipped and flaky. On the floor were washed-out squares for hopscotch and white lines of a track. Kaipo explained they used that for a type of bowl game with stones. In one corner was a pile of rotting logs for climbing. It all seemed so paltry.

'What age do you leave school?'

'For large families, the eldest daughter leaves between nine and eleven. They need to look after the youngsters of the family. The boys stay until they are sixteen. Our society does not believe girls need education as they are to be married and produce children. In my mother's day, girls did not attend school at all, only boys. However, with Western intervention, they are now allowed to.

'So, boys are separated from girls?' Chris asked.

'We are not allowed to mix. lunch and arrival times are separate. Girls start school at seven am. The boys eight. But school ends at eleven for girls and twelve for boys.'

They left the school, leaving Crystal to ponder on her privileged childhood. She had wasted such precious opportunities when there were children in the world who had none. She should have done as her parents wanted, gone to college and university.

Not far from the school, through a few more narrow streets, they reached the house Kaipo grew up in. It looked the same as all the other houses they had passed. A track through the middle of the street separated one side of dull dwellings from the other. Behind was another track with more identical houses. There was no outside space for children to play. They stopped at the beginning of the row. Most doors were open, and women sat outside on stools, peeling veg or sewing and chatting away. Kaipo pointed to the fifth house, which was, or once was, her family home.

'This is it. Where I grew up,' both her voice and body shook with emotion.

'Is it safe to knock?' Chris asked.

'No, we wait, see who comes in or out.'

It wasn't long before an older lady appeared. She chatted to her neighbour while shaking a throw, then disappeared inside again. A cat had followed her. It stretched lazily and yawned before flopping in the doorway to nap.

'That was my mother,' Kaipo's eyes were large with emotion.

Chris squeezed her hand. 'Would she not talk to you?' he asked.

'What if my father is inside? He will report me to the authorities.'

'How about if Chris and me ask for some water for Billy?' Crystal suggested. 'We've got to do something.'

'That is suspicious. I mean, why that house and not the first?'

They stayed silent while trying to think of a plan.

'Let's just walk past; we might be able to see inside,' Chris said, not knowing what else they could do.

260

They walked forward, receiving stares from the women, who stopped talking until they had passed. Billy began to struggle as they approached the house. He broke free from his mother's grasp and ran to the doorway, reaching out his hand to stroke the cat.

'PussPuss,' he squealed delightedly.

The cat looked terrified when he saw the toddler launching at him. Jumping up, he tore into the house with Billy in pursuit.

'Oh no!' Crystal gasped.

Chapter Twenty-one

They ran to the doorway and peered in. The older lady was crouched on the floor, talking to Billy. There did not appear to be anyone else in the room.

'Mamar?' Kaipo said quietly.

The lady looked up, alarmed, before putting her hand over her mouth; she squealed in shock.

'It is me, Mamar.'

Kaipo strolled forward, and the lady stood on shaky legs, cried out again, and threw her arms around her daughter. Both were sobbing uncontrollably. Crystal and Chris had tears as they stood near the doorway, not wanting to intrude on this moment.

'My baby, I thought you dead,' Chris whispered in Crystal's ear as he translated.

'How many times have I begged the gods for you to be here so I can apologise for not helping you. Tell you how much I love and miss you. I should have been stronger and stood my ground against your father. He was wrong making you marry that man. So many regrets, now my prayers have been answered.'

Letting go of Kaipo, she rushed to the door. 'Come, come,' she ushered them into the room before shutting out the neighbour's curious stares.

'Shall we go for a walk and leave you?' Chris asked Kaipo. 'You have much talking to do.'

She gave a slight nod and looked grateful. So, they left, taking Billy, who began screaming and protesting as they interrupted him while he was busy crawling under stools, looking for the cat.

'How's winkie?' Crystal asked once in the street, wondering where to wander.

'Very funny… Sore!'

'I thought you were walking funny.'

'I'm trying to scratch without being obvious.'

'I don't think I could stand living up a mountain,' Crystal said, changing the subject.

'Me neither. I hope Kaipo will be safe,' he fretted, worry clouding his eyes.

'You love her, don't you?'

'Well… I… think so. But she doesn't seem to feel the same way.'

'Have you told her?'

He shrugged, finding visual escape in his hands.

'Maybe you should.'

'Couldn't you? I mean, find out how she feels.'

'Oh, come on now. How old are we?'

'I know. But I don't want to scare her. We get on so well. I tried to kiss her recently and she freaked out.'

'Maybe her experience of the men in her life has put her off.'

263

'Guess you're right. I don't know. But you could feel your way forward so as not to frighten her.'

They were now perched on rocks at the edge of the village. People, not used to strangers, eyed them suspiciously.

'OK, I will,' Crystal agreed. Seeing the alarmed expression on his face, she laughed and added, 'Don't' worry, I'll tread as carefully as I would on a kitten.'

'Good grief, do you have to be so graphic!'

They had another wander away from the village and slightly further up the mountain. The landscape suddenly panned out into a flat country. Sheep and cows grazed on grass, and a few goats were seen on rocks in various places.

'This is a bit more peaceful,' Chris stated, feeling free to have a good scratch.

Crystal elbowed him and he stopped.

They returned to the house two hours later, hoping it was enough time. The door was open again and a gathering of people was bursting out of the small inside room.

Kaipo greeted them, her eyes sparkled with delight. 'This is my family. My brothers and my sisters-in-law, plus some of their children. They have all welcomed me home. My father died a few months ago.' She suddenly realised there was no sadness in her voice and quickly hung her head in shame. 'My family wants me to stay here and be with them.'

Chris looked panic-stricken, 'but you can't,' he blurted, 'They'll marry you off again.'

Kaipo did not appear to hear him as she continued. 'My eldest brother now lives here with his wife and children. My husband apparently did not die from the stabbing. So, I am still married.'

'But you have been in prison all this time for murder?' Crystal said in disbelief.

'Yes. Many women are. Until my husband agrees to take me back and forgives my defiance.'

'That's shocking!' she raved.

'There was much trouble about what I had done. My husband was furious and blamed my father for my lack of discipline and respect. He threatened to have my family evicted from the village and exiled from the country. The argument raved for many years. But after I was thought to die in the fire, my father offered my sister as a settlement. Apparently, after she was unable to produce children, her first husband divorced her, which again is a disgrace to the family. So, my poor sister took my place, and my family's disgrace was lifted. I can't imagine what she has been going through.'

'But what of your daughter?'

'She still lives with him; my sister is now bringing her up.' Kaipo, with a considerable weight in her voice, continued. 'There is no way I will be able to see my sister, let alone my daughter. It will never be allowed.'

'Course you will,' Chris said with a grin. 'He's now a bigamist; I'm sure he would not argue at you seeing her.'

'But he will have me locked up again. It is hopeless... My family said we could spend the night here. I'm afraid it will be on the floor, though.'

'I think Chris and me should go back to the barn and let you spend time with your family,' Crystal suggested. 'We'll come back tomorrow. But things are not all bad. At least we could maybe see your sister when he's not around. She'll let you see your daughter, surely?'

Kaipo looked doubtful. 'You do not understand. It is forbidden. We do not break rules like you would. Women are afraid of consequences.'

Crystal grabbed both her hands, 'You listen to me. We have one life to live. It's not for regrets. You need to shake off those mental restrictions and be a person in your own right. You can leave now or stay with your family and be under your brother's control. Or you can go find your daughter!'

Kaipo nodded slowly and swallowed the lump in her throat. 'I am so worried about my sister and so is my mother.'

'I don't think you should tell your family your intentions,' Chris advised. 'I mean, if that is what you decide, to try and see your daughter.'

They left with a promise to return the following morning. Chris was quiet and fretful. Crystal did not know what to say to console him. She grabbed his arm, receiving many horrified looks from the people of the village. She had forgotten that contact between men and women was forbidden.

'I don't think I can stand another night being bitten alive,' Chris said, trying to sound better than he felt inside. 'Think my winkie would fall off.'

'It's strange Billy never got bitten. I wonder why,' Crystal pondered.

'That's true. His blood must be sweeter. Or maybe they don't torture children.'

266

'Let's look in the house again. Maybe we can find a place to squat,' she suggested.

Darkness was already descending, and soon, they could not see. Inside was empty, apart from a concrete floor and dust. Ultimately, they decided to risk the barn as there seemed to be little choice. Billy was delighted as he ran towards the bales of straw, throwing himself onto a large pile. Diesel followed, and soon, the two were tearing around, playing chase the flying straw.

'Do you think she'll stay,' Chris burst out, unable to contain his fear any longer; even if it wasn't true, he needed reassurance.

'I don't know. It's all she's known. But how sad that she might choose such a restricted life when she now has the chance of freedom.' There was no comfort in Crystal's words.

'Women who don't conform are exiled. They have nowhere to go. It is terrible. I'm guessing Kaipo is afraid,' he said despondently, fearing the worst.

'How come the islands are so different in their beliefs,' she asked.

'The two have never really mixed. They don't share the same culture,' Chris explained.

They fell asleep, wondering what the next day would bring.

They walked back to the village after breakfast, the last piece of bread, and some cake. It was amazing to retrace their way through the maze of buildings without getting lost.

Kaipo opened the door, looking flustered but pleased to see them. Her mother served sweet tea while Billy ran off to find the cat.

'The family have decided it is best I leave. If my husband finds out I am here, he will report me.'

'How do you feel about that?' Chris asked, hoping she might want to return to the island to be with him and not just because of her family's rejection.

'I do not know. I will miss my family terribly. Especially my mother. But it is for the best.'

Crystal noted the disappointment in Chris's eyes, which he tried to hide.

An hour later, it was a tearful farewell as Kaipo and her mother sobbed in each other's arms again.

'I am just so grateful you are alive. Be happy and stay safe. I will be thinking of you and praying every day.' She kissed her daughter's hair.

Kaipo, through her own tears, managed a small smile back at her as they left. 'I will write,' she shouted back.

'Now what?' Crystal asked.

'I am going to see my daughter and my sister. It is close, about a mile or so.'

Her two friends raised their eyebrows questionably.

Kaipo laughed. 'I had a long talk with my mother. It is a story for another time, but you were right, Crystal, I need to live my life and shake off the weight of restriction.'

Soon, the land panned out into a vast expanse of greenery, with houses dotted around the landscape. They were individually built, painted in different colours and almost pretty. Each had its own area of outside space, most with animals basking in the sun. It was certainly not as poverty-stricken as the village they had left. Not so many people appeared to be around this time. It was still reasonably early, and the sun was already very warm.

Kaipo looked tense and nervous as they entered the village. 'I feel sick and am unsure how we do this,' she stammered.

'Where's your husband's house?' Chris asked.

Kaipo pointed to a large dwelling slightly higher up the mountain. It was isolated, away from the main part of the village.

Crystal was surprised, 'What does he do for a living as he seems more wealthy?'

'He lends money and claims it back with extra on top,' She explained. 'Well, what now?'

None of them had any suggestions, so they sat on some rocks with a good view of the house to think of a plan.

No one came in or out, so after an hour, they ventured closer. Kaipo's body shook and her breath came in short gasps as they approached. Crystal squeezed her arm to show her understanding.

No one appeared at home as they circled the house from a safe distance; however, the shutters on the windows and the front door were closed.

'Maybe they're away?' Crystal suggested.

Kaipo looked deflated at the thought.

Chris bowed to Billy, 'Now, little chap, we need you to run into the garden and knock on the door.'

The little boy stuck his thumb in his mouth and looked worried. He preferred being naughty without permission.

'It's a weak plan, but what else can we do? Crystal and me can pretend he's ours. You keep out of the way, Kaipo. At least we can find out if someone's home.'

'True,' Crystal agreed. 'Go on, Billy,' his mum reassured.

But the little boy's expression was sheepish. He shimmied behind her, clinging onto her trousers, almost pulling them down.

'OK, plan B,' Chris shrugged, grinning as Crystal hung onto her pants. 'I haven't one yet, though.'

'Why don't you stay out of sight, Kaipo, while Chris and I knock and make out we've lost our little boy?' Crystal suggested.

She nodded in agreement and grabbing Billy's hand, encouraged him away with Diesel. Safely out of sight, they approached the front door and knocked. It was not long before a young woman, swathed in a black dress, with her face covered, all but her eyes, opened it. An older man pushed her away. He looked as ancient as Sanskrit.

'I'm sorry to intrude. But our little boy ran this way and now we have lost him. Would you mind if we had a look around?' Chris spoke and Crystal stood dutifully behind him.

The man eyed the couple suspiciously. They got few visitors in these parts of the mountain.

Sensing apprehension, Chris added, 'We're visiting family.'

'OK,' the older man shrugged and slammed the door on them.

They walked around the house, calling Billy, who, upon hearing them, broke free of Kaipo and ran to his mother.

'Thank goodness,' Crystal said, grabbing his hand to play the part.

'Plan C,' Chris said once they were a safe distance away again.

Plan C developed itself, as the man soon left the house without the woman, who they assumed was Kaipo's sister.

'Now's our opportunity,' Chris scooped up Billy and began to walk towards the house.

'NO!' Kaipo objected. 'I go alone. You stay here.'

Taking a big breath, she went off. They watched while she banged on the door. The woman answered, and after what seemed to be a brief few words, the two cuddled before disappearing into the house, leaving Chris and Crystal to wonder what was happening. Thirty minutes later, Kaipo appeared and ran to where they were standing.

'He's due back soon. We need to hide. But in an hour or so, he will be gone for the rest of the day,' she puffed.

They dodged away to the edge of the village, where they could still watch the house, and sat on the ground.

Kaipo looked upset, 'My sister was shocked to see me. She was angry and blamed me for her life.'

'But why?' Crystal asked.

'If I had not stabbed my husband, she would not have had to marry him,' she explained.

'That's a little twisted,' Chris huffed. 'It sounds like she needs someone to blame. I get it, I guess. But I think the blame lays with your father, not you.'

Kaipo met his eyes as she nodded in agreement. 'She has such a terrible life with him. Her face is bruised, and her mouth is cut. Which is why he forces her to cover up. She is so unhappy and miserable. His other children have left home and only my sister and daughter live there.'

'Where's your daughter?' Crystal asked.

'At school. She will be home soon, and I can meet my baby. She is the only thing keeping my sister sane. She was so afraid I would take her as she looks at her as her own daughter.'

'What a predicament,' Crystal felt sad for both women. 'What do you think about it all, Kaipo?'

'My head is like a whirlpool,' she confessed.

'I'm not surprised,' Chris sympathised.

'I can't seem to find a solution. I do not want that monster near my baby. But I do not want to tear her away from my sister and break her or my child's heart. Besides, I have no right to. If I got caught stealing a child, I would be hung.'

'There has been a lot of emotions flying around. What's your daughter's name?' Chris asked.

'Aisha. It is such a pretty name.'

At that moment, they spotted the older man leaving the house. He walked from the village towards the road to catch the bus to the main town. They had hours before he was due to return. Kaipo's sister, Hemi, already had the door open and was waiting for them.

Hemi removed her headdress once they were inside the house. The bruises on her cheek and the puffy eye were purple; her lip was swollen and cut.

'Come with us! You and Aisha, come back to the island, where you will be safe and away from him?' Kaipo blurted out as soon as the door closed behind them.

They all looked at Hemi expectantly. If they left now, they would be home by evening.

Hemi hung her head, 'I cannot do that. It is my duty. I am a married woman.'

'Kaipo clamped her hands on her sister's arms. 'Listen to me, you can. Please. It does not have to be like this. Look at your face. You can escape and come with us.'

At that moment, the front door opened, and a pretty young girl walked into the kitchen. Eyeing the strangers suspiciously, she flicked her eyes from one to the other.

'Do not tell her you're her mother,' Hemi hissed, 'It will confuse her.'

'Of course not,' Kaipo hissed back.

She knelt on the floor near the child, who was looking at Billy with distaste. He, in turn, was pulling away from Crystal, feeling the need to cause havoc.

'Hello, Aisha,' Kaipo began gently. 'It is lovely to meet you. I am the sister of... your mother.'

The girl stared at her and then ran to Hemi.

'Go outside and play for a bit. Maybe take this youngster with you?' Hemi said, looking questionably at Crystal.

'Yes, course, but stay where I can see you from the window.'

273

The child grabbed Billy's hand and dragged him through the back door.

'She is beautiful,' Kaipo held onto her emotions, but her eyes were filled with pain. 'Please, there is time; come with us,' she begged.

'You know I cannot do that. I would be disowned by the family, as you were.'

'But father is dead. Mamar will understand. I know she would. She is worried about you living with that monster. What have you got that you will be losing? I bet you are not even allowed to see our family.'

Hemi hung her head. It was true; she was forbidden to see anyone or leave the village, even when her father died.

'We were once very close. We could be again,' Kaipo continued.

The shutters closed on Hemi's expression as she shrank inside of her soul. 'You need to leave. You have seen your daughter, now go.'

Kaipo was having an internal battle; several emotions rippled her heart. She wanted to shake her sister and make her see sense; she did not want to leave her daughter here. 'You will let him choose a marriage match for my daughter in a few years. Her life will be as miserable as yours. If you leave him, we could be happy and free. Just for once,' she said quietly, knowing it was hopeless.

'And if we are caught?' Hemi said. 'You know the consequences of that. I'm pregnant.'

Kaipo looked horrified. Pity flooded her eyes. 'But I thought you were barren?'

'Obviously not,' Hemi laughed dryly.

Kaipo turned to her friends and said, 'We need to go.'

Her sister lowered her head and did not even see them out as they left by the back door so they could collect Billy.

Kaipo knelt by Aisha, 'It was so lovely to meet you.'

The little girl nodded in agreement, 'Are you my Aunty?'

'Sort of,' Kaipo answered. Not trusting her tears, she rubbed the child's arm, kissed her head, stood, and quickly bustled away. Taking one last look back at the house to see her sister watching from the window.

She remained silent, lost in her battles, as they walked from the village to the main road, where they could catch the bus back to the port.

'That's heartbreaking,' Crystal said despondently.

Chris nodded; he felt as hopeless as his two friends.

Chapter Twenty-Two

They were back at the port by the afternoon, walking silently to the boat. Billy, exhausted from the long, hot journey, was carried by Chris. His head on his shoulder, he was almost asleep. Diesel dragged his legs, walking behind them. He still limped slightly from his broken bone. When tired, it was far more noticeable.

Slowly, debris from bombed buildings was being cleared. The city still looked dismal and sad. They were careful to avoid going anywhere near the prison or the army base, which meant a longer walk around to reach their destination. People in camps were still lodged on the streets, looking lost and despondent. As they walked past a small group sitting on the floor, Chris nudged Crystal and nodded toward a man in the doorway of what was once a shop. It was Masa, sitting cross-legged and hunched with his head down. His clothes were filthy, and a beard was growing fast. He held a stone in his hands, which he twisted agitatedly, oblivious to the world around him.

'What should we do?' she whispered.

Chris shrugged. 'There's nothing we can do. We certainly don't want him back.'

Crystal felt dreadful. Was this her fault?

'Leave him,' he advised and began to walk again.

Crystal fumbled in her pocket to draw a few notes from her money. She went to Masa and held it towards him. He snatched it without looking up and knowing who had done this.

Kaipo gave a small sympathetic smile and grabbed her friend's arm. 'It will be good to be back on the island.'

'Will you ever return to see your family?' Crystal asked once they were out to sea and heading home.

'I do not know. It has been painful. My life is so removed from them. I could never go back to how things were. I will miss them, though. Somehow, I have to live with losing my baby and knowing she is destined for a life of misery. That will not be easy. I want to go back and steal her away. But I would not get far, as my sister would report me before I even left the village.'

'Let's hope your husband dies a horrible death soon.'

'CRYSTAL! That is a terrible thing to say,' Kaipo was shocked. 'You must never wish bad. It will come back on you.'

'You're just too nice,' she grinned.

'What would happen if he did die? Would your sister be left in peace? And the property belong to her?'

'The house and any money would go to his eldest son. He would probably move in and take over where my husband left off with his work. My sister would still be allowed to live there, though, and my daughter would be matched with whoever the eldest son decides.'

Although they had only been gone a few days, it felt like weeks. All three were grateful to be back, and everyone was pleased to see them. Crystal no longer felt people blamed her for the war. Chris was right; they had been grieving.

Mira threw her arms around her, 'I missed you so much. I have lost my sister. I cannot lose you, too.'

Even Ayan managed a small smile and eye contact with Crystal, who smiled back at him, pleased he may be coming out of his depression a little. He thumped Chris on the back, 'We fish tomorrow. Enough holiday. Food is getting low.'

Chris raised his eyebrows as Ayan walked away. This was such a move forward.

Billy was also pleased to be home; he did not object when Crystal took him to her hut and undressed him, ready to bathe. The little boy was filthy and so was she. She carried him to the stream and dumped him into the shallow water, where he squealed and giggled. They played a game of chase while Diesel lay on the bank to watch and nap. Puss, unusually, appeared, having dragged herself from the bed and made a significant gesture of sitting bolt upright with her back to them. This was punishment for being left. When they returned to the hut, Puss followed, climbed on the bed and again sat bolt upright with her back to her mistress.

'Oh, Puss, you're hilarious,' Crystal laughed.

Much to Puss's disgust, she ruffled the fur and kissed the prim head. This horrified the cat, who threw herself upside down and began to wash vigorously with her tongue, combing her fur back in place.

Crystal was mortified to find Sanskrit still hunched by the fire. She looked questioningly towards Mira.

'I am worried. We sit and hold her hand constantly, talk, and try to encourage her to eat, but nothing helps. It is like her soul has died.'

Crystal sat next to the older lady and took hold of her hand. 'I'm back. I've missed you.'

Sanskrit looked up with glazed, far-away eyes, which brightened. 'Maya! You're back. I did miss you. Where have you been?'

278

'It's me, Sanskrit. It's Crystal. Maya died. She's not here anymore.' The words were too hard for her to hear as they cast pain into the older lady's eyes.

She turned away, back to the fire. It was heartbreaking to see.

'You must not give up. We need you. We all love you. I know you're in there somewhere; come back to us!'

Once home, Kaipo became very subdued. At night, she slept by the fire instead of the hut. During the day, she disappeared for long walks alone. Chris and Crystal assumed with many thoughts to process she preferred to be alone.

It was a few weeks later when Crystal bumped into her in the woods. Kaipo finally looked a little more at peace with herself. They went to sit beside the stream and soak their feet to cool themselves. It seemed a perfect opportunity to speak about Chris.

'How you feeling?' Crystal asked. Trying to plan how she would get around to the burning issue.

'I don't know. Still so muddled. I feel like a big chapter in a book has not been finished. I need to know the ending.' Kaipo confessed.

In for a penny, Crystal thought. 'You know Chris thinks the world of you. I know he would like to be closer?'

Kaipo was a little taken aback, 'Well... I...' she stammered.

'He's a good man, so kind and gentle.'

Kaipo flushed and looked away.

Crystal laughed. 'You've feelings for him too, don't you?'

'Yes, but I thought he wanted to be with you.'

279

'Goodness no. He's like a brother. I love him dearly. But not in that way. The same as he doesn't love me like that.'

'But when we came to the island and at the party, he was all over you.'

'We're just close friends. Honestly, there's nothing like that between us. Please believe me. It's you he thinks of, I mean in that way. Not me.'

Kaipo began to grin widely. 'Do you think so? But I am a married woman.'

'For goodness sake. That wasn't a marriage. It was another type of prison.'

The next day Crystal found Ayan at the cliff top, staring out to sea. Sitting, uninvited, beside him, she took his hand in hers.

He squeezed in acknowledgment without turning. 'You're a good person, Crystal,' his voice was gentle, causing her heart to flood with warmth.

'And you're a good man. The people need you. They also need Sanskrit. You're both cogs that turn our little world. Without you, we'll drown.'

Ayan turned, his eyes trying to digest her words. 'I've missed you.'

He put his fingers to her face, slowly caressing her skin. Crystal startled, pulling away, but Ayan's hand at the back of her head prevented escape, his lips found her own. The kiss was gentle at first, until the passion burned urgently within them. Every trouble melted as they lost themselves in their desire, just like when trying to escape on Panchaea. This was more powerful, as to Crystal, it cast them into the universe, losing their entwined souls amongst the mysteries of creation, until nothing existed but the two of them.

After, they lay exhausted, naked in each other's arms and safe in those pain-free moments. Ayan kissed and stroked her hair as he held her. never wanting that moment to end.

Suddenly, he pushed her away with force and jumped up.

'That should not have happened!' his eyes were loathing and disgusted. 'It was your fault!' he spat at her.

Crystal jumped up, too, shocked and then profoundly hurt. 'How dare you!' she shouted, with her fists clenched and forgetting her nakedness.

'Keep away from me. Do you hear me!' he snarled. 'You're a witch.' He turned and stomped into the woods, his stance stiff with anger.

'You're a pig, Ayan. Do you hear me? A PIG!' she screamed after him.

Crystal was crushed; she sank onto the ground and began to sob as though her heart was breaking. The hatred and loathing in his eyes were too much to bear. Then guilt and shame joined the hurt; she had disrespected her friend.

'What's wrong?' Kaipo asked when Crystal returned to the camp some hours later.

'Nothing, I'm fine. Just upset about Sanskrit.'

Kaipo was unconvinced, but Crystal looked away and tidied the hut, which did not need tidying.

'Mmmm,' her friend murmured, the sound full of suspicion. 'Ayan came thundering back about an hour ago. He was in a terrible mood?' she was prompting and knew something had happened.

Crystal wondered why her life was always so transparent.

'Really, did he?' she said, as lightly as possible and left the hut, not wanting to engage in conversation anymore. She sat by the fire.

Sanskrit looked over to her, 'You should not have done that.'

Crystal was startled, 'Done what?'

'You know. You should not have done it. Now you're pregnant.' Her eyes diverted back to the flames.

The words had sent a shiver through her spine; did the older lady know what had happened? What if she was pregnant? She could not stand anymore. She left and went swimming in the sea to clear her head.

Chris was sitting on the beach when she came from the water. She sat beside him, grateful for someone who wouldn't ask or judge. But he did, like Kaipo, sensing something wasn't right.

'What's wrong?' he asked.

'Oh, for god sake!' she snapped. 'Nothing's wrong!'

'OK… OK, don't snap my head off. You just seem a little upset, that's all.'

With that, she burst into tears. Chris pulled her into his arms, allowing the sobs to subside. 'Tell me. What's happened?' He cooed as though she was a child.

'I can't,' and the tears came again.

'Well, I can't help if you don't.'

'I'm pregnant!' she blurted.

Chris pushed her at arm's length, his eyes wide with shock. 'But how?'

She could not help laughing then, 'Well if your parents didn't explain, there's no hope for you.'

'Not Ayan? Please tell me you didn't. Not while he is so screwed up.'

'It wasn't like that. It just happened out of the blue.'

'Well, knock me down with a feather!'

At that, Crystal began to laugh. 'You come out with some weird stuff.'

'How far gone?' he asked, more serious.

'A few hours.'

'WHAT!'

'It happened a few hours ago and Sanskrit said I'm pregnant.'

'For god sake, Crystal! The woman's head has gone to live on Mars. There's no way she could know that. She was probably mumbling about Maya again. She said the same to me a while ago. She said... You're bad getting pregnant like that. I thought I was a miracle man for a moment.'

She began to laugh. It made sense; Sanskrit probably thought she was telling Maya off when she got pregnant.

283

'All the same. You need the morning-after pill, just in case.'

'Is that right! I'll pop to England and get one then.'

'I'm being serious. There's a herb that does this. I mean it stops a baby from coming.'

'You're kidding! That would be fantastic. What is it?'

Chris's shoulders sank and he looked slightly guilty. 'I don't know.'

Crystal stared at him in disbelief, 'You plank! Why the hell tell me about it then!' she raved, wanting at that moment to thump him.

'Mira'll know. You'll have to ask her.'

'Oh Yeah. What a good idea. "Oh, Mira, I just bonked your brother-in-law after the death of your lovely sister. Can you advise?"

Chris gave an amused grin, 'You've got a point. I'll ask her.'

'What will you say?'

'I'll think of something,' he jumped up, pulling his shoulders back and headed for the camp to find Mira.

Crystal wiped her tears and followed him, keeping a safe distance away but within earshot. She pottered around the camp, fiddling with the fish baskets and rearranging herbs. Chris was already speaking with Mira, who was close by. The two looked towards Kaipo and Mira grinned knowingly.

'You are bad. But I understand,' She laughed. 'You need Black Cohosh root.'

'Fantastic,' Chris said in relief. 'What does it look like and where do I get it?'

284

Mira shook her head, 'You won't find it here. Back on our home Island, you would. But, think that's out of the question.'

Kaipo wandered over to them, wondering why the two were looking at her. Panic filled Chris's face and he began to stammer. Crystal's heart missed a beat, so she lowered her head to the fish baskets again.

'What is wrong?' Kaipo asked them.

'Nothing,' Chris gushed. Quickly, he grabbed her arm and tried to lead her away.

'It's OK, Chris,' Mira said gently, 'Kaipo needs a friend at a time like this. I will help if I can.'

'What do you mean, losing my child?'

'No. Although I am deeply sorry about that. 'I mean the love accident.'

Chris looked towards Crystal, his eyes full of pleading for help. She shook her head, her eyes equally pleading him not to betray her secret.

'Love accident?' Kaipo needed clarification.

'It is OK. It can happen to any of us if we get carried away. We can all slip up. I mean...' She leaned closer, 'I slipped up with my firstborn.'

Kaipo gaped from Chris to Mira and back again. She drew back her hand and slapped him around the face before stomping off into the woods.

'Oh god!' Crystal covered her face with her hands as Chris, flushed crimson, threw her a filthy look before running after Kaipo.

The situation deteriorated further as Ayan appeared and assessed the scene. He looked at Crystal as though her head was a window, and he was looking inside, reading the situation. His eyes were cold and accusing, so he was still blaming her. Crystal could stand it no longer, so she ran from the camp to try and rectify the damage she had caused.

She could hear the argument blazing before she found her two friends. Chris was trying to explain, but his words were coming garbled as he attempted to protect Crystal. She was overwhelmed that he had stood by her and loved him all the more for it.

'It's all my fault, Kaipo,' she cried on her arrival.

They stopped and looked her way.

'Chris was asking for me. I made him promise not to tell anyone. I'm sorry.'

'Why? What do you need something like that for?'

Crystal flushed and lowered her gaze.

'Oh, Crystal! You never!' Kaipo gushed, regretting her words as they had left her. Her friend probably did not need judgment at that time. She looked back at Chris; her anger had dispersed.

He put a finger under her chin to lift her head so he could look deep into her eyes. 'I love you, Kaipo. I'd never want to hurt you. I'm sorry,' he said gently.

Her eyes were flooded with love as he pulled her into his arms, and they became united in their own secret world.

Crystal smiled and turned away, tiptoeing through the undergrowth as silently as possible so as not to disturb the moment for them. She was elated that they had now maybe removed the barriers and hopefully will be happy. They were both such lovely people.

Luckily, Mira did not suspect anything was different from what Chris had told her.

'Shame, I know Sanskrit has some in her magic box of treatments,' she said aloud and then shrugged, going into her hut as Tiare was crying.

Crystal doubled back and followed her. 'Could you show me?'

Mira looked surprised, 'But I thought it was for Kaipo?'

'It is. I can discretely offer it to her. She won't be so upset maybe coming from me.'

Mira nodded, understanding as she rocked the baby to calm her. 'I'm not sure what it looks like, though. Only Sanskrit knows these things. I know a little about medicines, but not a great deal. Still, let us go and look.'

They went into Sanskrit's hut and lifted the lid on the wooden box. Inside were hundreds of packages, dated and methodically placed in order. Mira shuffled through.

'Well, it is a root. So, it could be any of these.' She gathered about five possible packages. 'Let us take to Sanskrit. You never know.'

'Black cohosh root?' Mira said to the older lady, holding the packages before her. 'Which one?'

Sanskrit blinked, her gaze blank as she looked at the packages, before returning her attention back to the fire.

Mira sighed, 'it is hopeless.'

'Black cohosh root,' Sanskrit said, lifting her hand and pointing to one package. 'How many times have I told you? You never learn.'

Mira laughed. 'It's true, this one, ' she held up the small bundle. I remember, now, she said. Maya was always the clever one. She remembered them all.' Her eyes clouded with sadness for a moment. She leaned forward and kissed her grandmother's head. 'Thank you.'

The lucid moment had gone, as her eyes had blanked once again.

Mira handed the package to Crystal. 'Tell Kaipo to put a small amount in hot water twice daily. It will stop a baby from coming. But bring the rest back. You never know who else Chris will spread his seed to.' She laughed and went back to her hut.

The tea tasted disgusting and bitter, making Crystal gag as she forced it down twice a day, persevering for a week, just hoping it would work and reasoning that she probably wasn't even pregnant.

Chapter Twenty-Three

Crystal awoke in the early hours to find a silhouette of someone standing by the bed, staring down at her. She threw her hands over her mouth to stifle a scream, wishing Kaipo was there. She still slept beside the fire, now with Chris, where they held hands all night. The two were sickeningly inseparable. Even the elders became gooey-eyed as they 'awwwed' when the two passed, glued together.

'Sanskrit?'

The old lady turned and walked back through the door. Billy moaned in his sleep. The noise had disturbed him. Crystal jumped from her bed, pulled on her clothes and ran from the hut to see her disappearing into the woods. Going to Chris, she shook him.

He moaned and turned over, 'go away,' he mumbled.

'It's Sanskrit, she's wandered into the woods. What if she falls off the cliff?'

Chris moaned again, untangled himself from Kaipo, who was still asleep, and jumped up, still bleary-eyed. They ran into the woods. It was very dark, but the full moon offered a fair amount of light, just enough to see the trees swaying and rustling in the slight breeze. They stared into the darkness, trying to spot the woman. But she was nowhere to be seen.

'I'll check the cliff edge. You look around the woods,' Chris suggested. 'On second thoughts, go get Mira; she'll know what to do.'

Chris sped off towards the cliff and Crystal returned to the camp.

'Mira, Mira,' she called, the loudest whisper she could manage, without disturbing anyone else.

There was no response. Taking the plunge, she went inside, thinking that her friend would not mind under the circumstances.

'MIRA! it's Sansk....' Crystal stopped as shock blasted into her core. Ayan was in the bed with her.

They sat up and stared back, devastated to have been caught.

'Crystal!' Mira stammered.

'Sanskrit is wandering. She's disappeared into the woods. Chris is looking for her at the cliff edge.' Her voice was flat and toneless as she threw the worst look of hatred she could muster toward Ayan,

swallowing her stomach contents, which threatened to explode from

her at any moment. She turned her back, attempting to block out the scene.

'Oh No!' Throwing the sheet aside, Mira leaped from the bed.

Ayan woke the rest of the camp, and everyone began to search for Sanskrit, leaving a few behind to mind the children.

An hour later, the older lady was found on the beach, paddling in the sea. She was cold as Mira threw a cover around her shoulders and led her back to the campfire. Sanskrit mumbled incoherently; she began to cry, sobbing as big tears streamed down her face. They made her hot tea, sweetened with Mulethi and another herb to make her sleep. Once warm, Mira led her into the hut and helped her to bed, where she slept most of the day. Sanskrit was to be watched more carefully in the future, day and night.

'Maybe she needs a doctor,' Crystal suggested to Mira.

'Crystal, I need to explain...'

'You don't have to. In fact, last night said it all. I don't want to talk about it,' she snapped.

'But I...' Mira called after her.

Crystal rudely raised her hand to stop the words as she marched away, unceremoniously dragging Billy, who began to scream in objection. It was time for school to start and the children would be waiting.

Passing Ayan on her way, her shoulders bristled, and she threw him a look of loathing. He looked burned and sheepish, or was it guilt; she could not decide. Crystal vowed never to speak or even think of him ever again. She was deeply hurt and wounded. Her life would never be happy again. Everyone was lost to her: Sanskrit, Maya, Mira, Will, and now Ayan. If it were possible, she would leave and never return.

The hurt inside her was overwhelming. Each day was worse and more painful. It ate away and was mentally crippling, so much so, at times, she doubled in agony and screamed when far enough from the camp not to be heard. Crystal hardly slept as she paced the floor at night. If she did, her dreams were vivid, again seeing the camp people being shot. Will bleeding, his body rotting in a pit. Or Sonya calling for help and crying. Other times, they were full of images of the burning women at the prison, their bodies melting like wax, leaving skeletons standing in their place. They always finished with Ayan and Mira locked naked in each other's arms, laughing at her. When she tried to swallow food, it stuck in her throat, lay heavy in her stomach, and more often than not, she was sick.

Chris and Kaipo did not seem to notice; they were too embroiled in their new romance. She was pleased about this, not only for the lovely couple, who deserved happiness but also because she wanted to be left alone.

Diesel and Puss were the only ones who knew how she suffered. The dog would look up with big, sorrowful eyes, watching her. At times, he whined and nudged her with his nose as she cried silently into his fur. Puss slept on her pillow, purring to try and lull her to sleep like she had once done. When it did not work, the cat would rub her nose with hers and follow Crystal everywhere.

Crystal no longer talked to Mira unless she had to. Her friend was also hurting. She looked pathetic and lost without the bond that had kept her going since the loss of her sister. Crystal had taken some of the grief away. She had made her laugh and kept her positive when she sank into a depression.

Mira tried hard to speak to Crystal, but she was cold and dismissive. Not knowing what else to do, Mira waited until her friend went to wash at the stream and followed her, knowing there would be just the two of them.

'Please, Crystal. Let us speak. I know you think I disrespected my sister. Me and Ayan took comfort in each other's grief. The pain was gone just for that time when he held me. I was not meaning to be disloyal to Maya. I love my sister.' Mira was trying to get these words out through her tears and shame.

Of course, Crystal thought; Mira knew nothing about her own encounter with Ayan, just that she was being judged. Her resolve softened and she put her arms around the sobbing woman.

'Oh, Mira, don't cry. I wasn't judging you, honestly. I understand.' She felt even more animosity towards Ayan. He had used and broken two women. The man certainly was a pig.

'I thought you hated me for taking comfort with my sister's husband,' Mira sobbed, her eyes red and swollen.

'I don't think badly of you. I understand it helped your grief. Made you feel closer to your sister. You've lost your husband and your baby, too. Don't cry. It's OK. We're still friends.'

'But why was you so angry, if you understand?'

'I was just shocked seeing you both … well… I don't know. Let's forget it and put it behind us. It's hard enough battling the sadness without each other.'

Mira looked relieved as she dried her eyes and turned to leave.

'Mira,' Crystal called as an afterthought. 'If you and Ayan want to be together. Then nothing should stop that. Maya would understand and be pleased for you. You must do what makes you happy.'

'Do not be silly, Crystal; It can never be that way with us.'

Crystal needed to be alone to think. She no longer sat on the cliff edge; it was too much of a painful reminder of her last time there. Her favourite spot had now been soiled. She found a rock on the beach instead for her quiet time, often paddling and watching the waves gently caressing the sand as they drifted to the shore.

'Guess what!' Chris scrambled beside her, nudging with his bottom to move to allow room. 'You'll never believe this in a million years.'

'What?' she said flatly, annoyed at the intrusion.' I've been speaking to Ali…'

The mention of his name jerked the pain again, as bile rose in her throat as she fought not to be sick.

'His sisters, my cousins, live in the same village as Kaipo's sister! Can you believe that?'

Crystal looked at him in surprise. 'But surely you knew where they lived?'

He laughed, his face full of excitement. 'I had no idea. It's not something we've ever talked about. He's going to write to them and see if they can help. You never know; Hemi might welcome an ally. I've not told Kaipo, though. I can't,' he confessed.

'But you mustn't keep secrets.'

'What if I get her hopes up only to crash them from a great height?'

'That's true. She's only just getting her head around it. But it's lying. She will be angry if she finds out,' Crystal said.

'Maybe you're right. I was going to wait and see what they say first. But I'll speak to her later. She's looking after Billy and Tiare at the moment. I thought I'd leave her to it.'

They sat for a while, both with their own thoughts. Until Chris broke the silence.

'Are you alright, Crystal?' he said gently, expecting her to bite his head off. 'It's just you're so pale and have lost weight. I'm worried about you. We both are.'

She smiled at him, 'I'm fine. Honestly, I'm just a little sad. I miss Maya and Sanskrit, that's all.'

He squeezed her hand, 'Crystal… You're not pregnant, are you?'

His words were like thunderbolts as realisation burst into her head. When was her last period? She began to panic that what Sanskrit had said was right, but she couldn't remember. The disgusting root had not worked.

'Don't be silly,' she scoffed too quickly, causing Chris to raise his eyebrows suspiciously.

If she was, no one must know, at least not until she got her head around it and there was no choice but to spill the beans. Working out the timings, she realised it had been almost two months since they had made love.

'OK,' Chris patted her back before returning to the camp. 'I'm here if you need to talk.'

Sanskrit's mental health deteriorated more as each day ticked by. Everyone found this difficult to cope with. Not to mention missing their guru and medicine woman. Rohan and Mr Slap seemed to take this worse.

'We have known each other for so long,' Mr Slap told Crystal as they sat on each side of the older lady beside the fire. 'Sanskrit was such a beautiful girl. I wanted to join with her.'

'I did too!' Rohan shouted, finding a vacant stool and pulling it closer so he could join in.'

'Why didn't you?' she asked.

'She was destined to become Sanskrit, not to join with a man. Besides, we were only five,' both men giggled.

'I don't understand. I thought that was her name and that she had married?'

Rohan and Mr. Slap grinned conspiratorially, showing few teeth between them. They were enjoying telling the story and reliving memories of their past.

'Her name was Samaira,' Rohan began. 'Apparently, when she was born, her mother had a vivid dream. She went to the Sanskrit to ask for it to be interpreted. An astrological chart was drawn up. The planets and stars in the chart showed her new baby was to become the new Sanskrit once this one had passed.'

'Wow!' Crystal was stunned, she never even imagined.

Mr Slap picked up the story from there: 'When Samaira was just six years old, she was taken to the holy island.' He pointed to the right of where they were sitting. No one is allowed there, unless, of course, you're a holy person or to learn medicine.

'I've heard about it, vaguely.' Crystal said, looking in the direction of the pointed finger. 'It must have been terrible for a child to be left at such a young age. But surely, she married as she had children.'

'No one knows,' Rohan continued. 'Sanskrit never told how she had a daughter. Rumours flew, of course, as they always do. There were two stories. A holy man made her pregnant. The other was that a baby girl was found on the holy Island's rocks one day. Samaira took the infant in and bought her up as her own.'

'It's so much to get your head around,' Crystal said, staring from one man to another and then at Sanskrit, imagining her as a beautiful young woman. 'What happened then?'

'When our Sanskrit died, Samira returned to the Island to take over. She brought the child with her. Pretty little thing she was. The girl became pregnant when she was sixteen and unmarried, which is frowned upon in our culture. She died giving birth to the twin girls. Samaira was heartbroken, but she became a mother and grandmother to them. Now, one has died and I guess it has sent her mad.' Mr Slap continued, looking wretched. 'We have lost everything; it is too much. Now, we are losing Sanskrit. There will never be another; there cannot be with our homes stolen and our people dead.'

Crystal shimmied her stool closer and put her arm around him. 'It's all so terrible.'

'Our civilisation is dead; this is all that is left.' Rohan added, shaking his head despondently.' I will not be sorry to leave this world.'

'We need a party!' Crystal burst out. 'Music, dancing and good food. We need cheering up!'

Mr Slap patted her leg, 'You are right, young un. We need to get drunk.'

She giggled, 'good idea.'

No one was initially keen, but after a deep ponder, they warmed to the idea. It was too late in the day for that evening, so it was decided for the next afternoon once school was finished.

It was the first since Crystal's welcome home party when she had returned to the Island. It started a little morbidly, as they remembered the last when Sanskrit had danced with Rohan and Maya was laughing and singing to the music. After a few alcoholic drinks, the gloom lifted, and the people sang again. Chris asked Crystal to dance and even Mira did with Mr. Slap.

Ayan watched, his eyes never leaving Crystal. She could not interpret his expression, but other than the odd stare of loathing, she ignored him.

The following day, when Chris went to take the boat out to fish, Crystal asked to go with him and one of the other men.

'What about school?' he was surprised; she had never shown interest before. Crystal usually wrinkled her nose at the smell of fish.

'I've asked Kaipo to cover me. She's good and can teach far more than me. I just fancy doing something different. I want to learn how to drive the boat.'

'Why?' Chris was puzzled; his friend had been acting strange lately.

'Another feather in my cap. Besides, you never know when the skill might come in handy.'

He laughed, 'I'd hardly call it a skill. There's nothing much to it. But OK.'

Chris was right. There was little to boat driving as long as she remembered to turn on the battery first. There was only the left lever to accelerate and reverse and then the steering wheel to drive. Parking between two other boats took a bit of negotiation and she managed to hit one of them, causing Chris to put his arms over his head and cringe mockingly.

'Pull it into reverse. You're going too fast,' he hollowed over the noise.

'How on earth do you know where to go and how to get back?'

'Well, put it this way. Panchaea's over there,' he answered, pointing to the left of the Island, 'And the mainland, that way,' he pointed straight ahead.

'That's as clear as mud,' she laughed. 'So, you just drive in a straight line and hope you reach the right place?'

'Something like that,' he linked her arm as they returned to the camp. 'It's good to have you back, Crystal.'

She stopped walking, 'What do you mean?'

'You've been really odd for weeks. Something has been wrong. Normally, you'd tell me about it. It's something to do with Ayan, isn't it? I know you're in love with him. But you'll tell me in your own time.'

She sighed to give her time to collect herself and stop any tears from escaping. No words would come, so Crystal looked away and continued to the camp.

Billy came running, his arms stretched out. He was almost three years old and certainly a little man. Crystal scooped him up and kissed his forehead; he was getting heavy.

It was terrible to see Sanskrit just stand and wet herself. The older lady, who had once been so proud and respected, had lost her dignity. When this happened, one of the other ladies would lead her away into a hut and clean her up. Seeing her like this upset them all.

A week later, Crystal woke feeling unwell and sick. There was a mild pain in her stomach. But she had this happen when pregnant with Billy. Running her hand over her usually flat stomach, she was upset to feel a slight bulge already. It was early, and everyone was still asleep, including Billy, who was usually bouncing around the hut by that time.

Going outside, she tiptoed over the sleeping bodies towards the fire to boil water, ready for the morning tea. Ayan was sitting on a stool outside Sanskrit's hut.

'Crystal,' he stood up and walked towards her. 'We need to talk.'

'I've nothing to say to you,' she snapped.

'I'm sorry. Please hear me out. I didn't mean to hurt you.'

'Just leave me alone, Ayan!' It seemed significant to now use his full name.

'You're stubborn, but please, meet me later, on the cliff edge. Let me explain.'

Her eyes blazed as she stared into his, 'Why's that? So, you can take what you want and dump me again. Use me, like you always have?' she hissed with conviction.

He looked hurt, as though she had slapped him around the face. Leaving the water, Crystal marched towards her hut, needing to escape. She cried out and doubled over as a gripping pain wrenched her stomach.

'CRYSTAL!' Ayan called out, shocked and alarmed, staring at the blood that flooded from her, wetting her trousers.

Kaipo, who had just woken up to the commotion, gasped in horror. She leaped up and ran to her friend.

'Mira!' she called, come quickly.

Mira ran from her hut, assessing the situation in seconds. Reality fell into her head as she looked at Ayan, who had frozen in disbelief.

'She could find no words; it was not the time. But she shook her head at him, her face full of anger and disgust. Now she knew why Crystal was so upset and her heart broke for her friend's suffering.

They led her into the hut, Kaipo quickly carrying a sleeping Billy, who moaned, out to Chris.

Pulling off Crystal's pants, they took away the fetus and cleaned the blood with water brought to them.

'I've lost the baby?' Crystal sounded small and pathetic.

'I'm sorry, it's gone. Maybe for the best, eh?' Kaipo said gently, stroking the hair away from her friend's sweating forehead.

Crystal nodded, her eyes full of pain. Mira bought a warm liquid for her and made her drink. It was sweet and comforting; it took away the pain and sent her into a deep sleep somewhere safe, where she no longer hurt.

Mira left Kaipo sitting beside Crystal's bed to watch her. She went to Ayan, who was looking distraught and hopeless. She drew back her hand and slapped him around the face as hard as she could. No words were needed; she could find none and it was not necessary. The slap had said it all.

Chapter Twenty-four

The sun had not yet risen, and daylight was just beginning to break as Crystal carried Billy to Maya's grave, where she laid blue flowers on the earth before the cross.

'You seem to have been the string knotting us all together, Maya. I miss you.'

Crystal choked back tears as she took her son, Diesel, and the few belongings to one of the fishing boats. Gritting her teeth, she turned the key to ignite the engine, hoping no one from the camp would hear.

Crystal left the Island, hoping that the direction Chris had pointed would lead her to the mainland. Her heart was heavy, and she was sad, but she tried not to shed any more tears. It was time to leave; there was nothing left for her here.

Saying goodbye to Puss had been difficult. They had been through many good and bad times together, but the cat would be happier living with the people she knew. She had kissed the silky fur, waking her up. Puss had chirruped and rubbed her nose on Crystals. Her green eyes looked sad and tearful, or had she imagined it?

'Puss, you've been the best friend I could ever have. You've got me through some bad times and now we have both lost babies. I'll miss you. But you're safer here, and I cannot take you with me.'

The cat yawned and went back to sleep, purring gently.

The evening before, she had sat with Sanskrit, knowing she would never see the older lady again. Crystal knew that her time was near. It was unbearable to watch every day leading up to her last.

'I'll miss you so much,' she kissed her head noting there were steal streaks of black hair amongst the grey. They had shared fine memories that would stay with Crystal for life.

Driving the boat to the mainland was scary as the ocean panned out monotonously in front of the boat. She could be lost at sea and never found again. She wished now that she had quizzed Chris more on navigation, but to do so would have made him suspicious.

The sun was beginning to rise and the camp would be waking up.

Thankfully, Crystal saw the mainland in the distance; she had done it. The next challenge was to park the boat safely, which was not her most excellent skill.

It was some hours before anyone noticed Crystal's absence. At first, they assumed she was bathing at the stream or had gone to the cliff edge to be alone. Since the miscarriage, she had been even more withdrawn and quiet. They were all concerned for her. Both Chris and Kaipo had spent time with their friend. Trying their best to draw her from the depression that ate her away. Everyone blamed Ayan and he blamed himself. He was shamefaced and riddled with guilt; it seemed there was nothing he could do to put things right. Mira ignored him, Chris was cold and even the older men shunned him. He took the punishment; it was deserved. Even Sanskrit, in a lucid moment, seemed to condemn him.

'I thought better of you, Ayan. You were once a good, honest person.'

He considered leaving the camp for a while, maybe staying with his mother and sisters, to give space to the situation. But he could not bear to leave Crystal while she was so unhappy and sad.

It was when school started that they really noticed her absence. Kaipo went into the hut, noting her belongings had gone, even the stone she kept on the small table as decoration. Then she saw the paper on the bed next to the sleeping cat. It was a letter. She took it to Chris, and everyone gathered while he read, stopping at times to swallow his sorrow.

'Oh Crystal!' he said, as he skim-read first.

'What, tell us?' Mira prompted.

My darling, sweetest friends.

I'm crying writing this. As you now realise, I've left. It's hard for me and breaks my heart to go, but it is for the best. I need to find a new life with Billy and Diesel. I'll miss and will never forget any of you. I love you all, except Ayan—he is a pig!

Ayan shifted uncomfortably. Blood had drained from his face, which was full of disbelief and panic. Everyone's eyes were on him, accusing and blaming. Chris looked down again and continued to read.

Mira, thank you for being such a wonderful friend. You and Maya welcomed me when I first met you. You made me feel so at home and one of your group. You are more of a sister.

Kaipo, You too. We went through some times together, didn't we? You saved me when we were in prison and on the streets. I pray one day, you will get your daughter back. You and Chris have something special. I'm pleased, you both deserve every happiness life has to give. You've been such a special friend.

Chris reached up his hand and gripped Kaipos as she sobbed.

If Sanskrit is ever coherent, tell her how much I thank her for spending so much time with me. She has been my mother and grandmother.

Please look after Puss. She's very precious, although snobby. I cannot take her, and it has been hard leaving her.

Chris, what can I say? We've laughed so much. You're the brother I never had. Take good care of Kaipo.

I'll miss you all, Rohan, Mr. Slap (I never did find out your real name), the elders, and the children. You are precious to me. I hope one day we'll meet again.

I love you all,

Crystal, Billy, and Diesel.

Also, I'll leave the boat parked at the mainland port, with the keys hidden under the seat. I'm sorry to do this, but I could see no other way.

There was not one dry eye amongst them.

Mira looked at Ayan and said, ' You need to put this right! You cannot let her go. We all know you love and want to be with her. So do something!'

Everyone nodded in agreement.

Mr Slap stood up pointing an accusing finger towards Ayan. 'Go find her. Bring her home!'

Crystal was nervous about approaching the aid worker station; there was a risk that she would be recognised, but there was no choice. The queue was not as long as when she was last there with Ayan all that time ago. With Diesel safely secured with a rope around his neck, she walked to the desk, coughing to hide her trembling.

'My name is Sarah James. I've been stuck here since the war started. I've lost my passport; I want to return to England.'

The man eyed her as he spoke in a clipped, matter-of-fact voice. 'So where have you been until now? Why did you not come forward sooner.'

'I've been staying with family in a village called Ukatira. I was pregnant when I came here four years ago. My son has never had a passport. So, I thought it was impossible to go home.'

'So, you're not English?'

'I am. It was my husband's family. He was killed fighting in the war.'

'So, have you a birth certificate with you?'

'I have, with my parents in England.'

'You'll have to come back tomorrow. I need to find out what we can do.... Next!' he shouted.

'Please, could I make a phone call... to my mother?'

'I'll see what I can do. Stand over there... Next!' he shouted again.

As she stepped away from the desk, the young man spoke to his colleague, who looked her way and nodded before turning to the next person.

Soon, she was led into the Army headquarters, which made her shake with fear as she looked around, expecting to bump into Lieutenant Warner at any moment.

'We can give you ten minutes to make a phone call, ' the lady told her, opening an office door and pointing to the phone.

After thanking her, Crystal freed Billy's hand, who immediately found a pile of papers on the desk fun to pull apart. The only phone number she knew by heart was her friend Layla's mum, Janice. Her mother had never written one on the letters sent. She dialled the number, which, after a few rings, was answered by Janice, who was shocked to hear from her.

'Crystal!' she shrieked. 'Where are you? We've been so worried. Your mother is beside herself.'

'I've not much time. I'm still here, but I'm trying to get home. Have you my mum's phone number? Oh, by the way, It's Sarah now.'

She could hear Janice fumbling with something before reading out her mother's number. 'Stay safe... Sarah. It'll be so good to see you again.'

Crystal dialled the number and thankfully, her mother picked up the phone.

'It's me, mum. ' As Janice had done, her mother squealed down the phone and burst into tears.

'Listen, Mum, I'm trying to get Billy and me back home.'

'Please, god!' Mary breathed, trying to control her sobs.

'I need my birth certificate. But at the moment, I've no address to forward it to. Have you still got it?'

'Of course,'

The aid worker banged on the door, indicating time. Billy tore some of the paper in half, 'Billy, NO!' Crystal chastised.

'Mum, I've got to go. I'll call again as soon as I can. I love you.'

She hung up the phone and scooped up the papers from the floor, hiding the torn sheets in the middle of the pile. 'I hope they weren't important,' she told the little boy.

'Is there somewhere I could stay?' she asked once outside the office.

'There is the hotel we all stay at. It is in the next village, so amazingly survived the bombing. It's not much, but it's that or the streets.' She led her from the building and pointed to the bus stop.

'How far is it to walk?'

'Mmmm, about forty-five minutes.'

They waited for the bus, which weaved a different way up the mountain this time. The village was surprisingly very pretty. Before the war, it was used by holidaymakers. It even had a few little shops selling souvenirs. Crystal guessed they did not sell much these days, but she found a few toys for Billy, two cars, and some rubber animals. He was thrilled, especially as he no longer had to share.

'No dogs!' the receptionist shouted as Billy, Diesel, and Crystal entered the foyer.

The aid worker was right. The hotel was very run down and needed painting, as the walls were grimy. But this was not surprising after what had happened.

'OK. I have someone who can take care of him. But I need a room,' she lied. There was no way she was leaving her loyal dog with anyone.

The receptionist handed over a key and pointed the way to a room one floor up.

Crystal thanked her and left the building, under the glare to ensure she did, before going to her room. She spent the next hour peering through the window to wait for the receptionist to disappear. Finally, she went into a back room, closing the door behind her. Crystal rushed through the foyer as fast as she could, puffing as Billy was so heavy now. Along with carrying her belongings and dragging Diesel, she was finally through the door and safe away from the scrutinising eyes.

The room was basic, with a double bed, a dressing table, and a wardrobe. The bathroom was shared along the corridor. When Crystal went to look, she found it had a bath. It was too tempting after all this time not to soak in warm water. Taking Billy and Diesel with her, she turned on the taps, undressing herself and the little boy. They climbed in and soaked. Billy was hooked, as he splashed and threw water everywhere, giggling delightedly. He wasn't too impressed with the soap as Crystal scrubbed at his body and hair before tackling her own.

After the bath, she left Diesel in the room, telling him not to make a noise and went in search of something to feed them. They waited down the corridor to ensure the dog was quiet; dutifully, he was.

Billy and Crystal sat in the little restaurant, where she ordered from the menu three tuna sandwiches, a cup of tea for her, and juice for Billy. The little boy wrinkled his nose, not liking the taste of the tuna. He managed a few mouthfuls before Crystal scooped the rest up for Diesel.

That night, they slept, all sharing the double bed. Crystal got up in the early hours and stared out of the window over the mountain. Few lights flickered in the distance, but large pockets were in darkness. Already, she missed the Island and the people, wondering what had happened. Were they as sad as her? They would be alright; it was the right decision.

Dodging in and out of the hotel daily with the dog was challenging. Her money was getting low as they had already been there for a week. There was still no news about a flight home. The journey back to the city was difficult. The buses were always late and over crowded. Without Billy, she would have walked. Crystal had managed to speak to her mother again; the birth certificate was on its way to the hotel address. It could take some time, as the post was slow getting through since the war. There was no postman, so she attended the post office near the port each day to check if it had arrived.

The boat she had borrowed was no longer moored there. Someone had taken it back. It was her last link with the Island.

The aid worker advised that she needed to register Billy's birth for a certificate. It was the only way to get him a passport to travel.

'You could have stolen him for all we know.' It was the same toneless young man she had first spoken to.

'You can see he's English!' she argued.

It was hopeless; she was just going around in a circle.

When she left the aid station, she spotted Veda on the other side of the road, walking with a younger lady, who she assumed was her daughter. Crystal tried to dodge away, but it was too late; she was spotted.

Veda threw her arms around Crystal, receiving many disapproving stares from passers-by.

'It is so good to see you. What are you doing here?' The woman gushed.

'I'm trying to get home to England. But it's impossible with Billy, as he has no birth certificate.'

Veda gently pushed her away and bent down to the little boy. 'Oh my goodness, you are a grown man now! I cannot believe it.'

Billy giggled and went all shy. He hid behind his mother's legs, so they all laughed.

'You must come and stay with us until your flight.'

Crystal looked at the young lady; she was so like a female version of Ayan, 'I can't. I need to be close to the aid station. It's so far away.

'Nonsense. We have a car. It takes no time at all. We have come to try to find my son Masa. We've seen him a few times and spoke to him. I clipped his ear. But he is a silly man and prefers the streets with alcohol to his family.'

She grabbed Billy's hand and led Crystal to a car. There was no refusing her, as they drove to the hotel and Crystal checked out.

'Do you drive?' the sister, who was called Lalita, asked, 'If you do, you can borrow the car anytime.'

'I can, but no way am I driving these mountain roads,' she laughed, shuddering at the thought.

'I was devastated to hear about Maya. She was the kindest, gentlest soul. She was like a daughter to me. I wanted to come back and be with my boy. I'm still considering it once I sort Masa out. How is Ayan coping?' Veda asked.

'He's fine!' Crystal clipped, not wanting to discuss him.

Veda gave a slow nod as though she was looking through Crystal into her core. It was then that she wondered if the woman knew more than she was letting on. Luckily, Billy caused a distraction as he bounced on her lap. Excited to be in a car, he was desperate to get to the front and play with the controls.

'And Mira?'

'She has taken it hard; she is grieving badly and always so sad.'

They reached the village in about twenty minutes. The house was large and very pretty, but it was not close to Kaipo's sisters.

Lalita took Crystal to a beautifully decorated bedroom. She did not mind when Diesel followed them as she patted his back and made a big fuss of him.

'What will you do with him when you go home.'

'I'm taking him with me,' Crystal smiled, patting his coat too.

'You may find that difficult. They don't allow animals out of the country easily.'

At dinner, once Billy was fed and asleep, Crystal filled Veda in with all the news of the Island. She was devastated to hear about Sanskrit.

'Now Crystal, tell me what is wrong?' Veda asked, handing her a glass with some sort of alcohol in it. 'Something has happened, hasn't it?'

The kind words were too much and the liquid, which burned her throat, caused her head to swim and her emotions to burst to the surface. She poured out the whole story, even telling Veda about when she and Ayan were on the Island together. The woman listened without interruption, except for the odd nod or groan of sympathy, to the slow story as Crystal sobbed and had to take breaks. 'Now I need to go home and begin my life again,' she finished with an emotional sigh.

Veda stayed quiet for some time after Crystal finished.

'You still love him, don't you? Even though he has been a pig, I agree. But those feelings can't be wiped away.'

Crystal took another large swig of her second glass. Her voice was becoming slurry; even she could hear it.

'I do,' she sobbed pathetically, 'he was my world.'

'And he loves you. I saw that from the first time I laid eyes on you. That is why I had a hard time giving you a chance. I was afraid you would come between Maya and Ayan. But sadly, she has gone and you could be happy together.'

'But there's no way I could ever be with him. Not now. Besides, he does not want to be. He betrayed me with Mira.'

Veda laughed, 'If you don't know men now, you never will. Their heads are ruled by what's between their legs. Get off your high horse and forgive his stupid weakness. But are you sure he did betray you with Mira? That does not sound like the two people I know.'

Crystal laughed through her tears and nodded. They were in bed together.

313

Chapter Twenty-five

The next morning, Crystal woke with a thumping head. Billy wasn't there. She found him in the kitchen with Veda and Lalita, his breakfast spread around his mouth. Two other people were sitting around the table, deep in conversation. They stopped as she entered. The man stood up and offered his seat.

Veda introduced the couple as Koa and his wife Radha.

'Pleased to meet you,' Crystal said, plopping gratefully on the seat. 'Are you Veda's other daughter?' She shook the outstretched hands across the table.

Lalita had poured her a tea and handed her two painkillers, which she gratefully swallowed.

'No, my other daughter lives close by. Her husband has returned from the war, so I am staying with Lalita while she is alone,' Veda explained. 'These people are friends from the island. They live on the mainland now and help with the war, and Koa works with the government. Lakita is a refugee worker. She advocates for women's rights here on the mainland. At times, she has helped women escape from the country. She is trying to help Kaipo's sister. Or rather talk her into running away to the Islands so she can be safe.'

'How's it going?' Crystal asked thankful someone, was helping.

'Not too good,' Lakita answered. 'She is a very frightened woman. It is difficult to fight against the way some people have been conditioned from childhood. But I think we are getting there.'

Koa began to speak, 'I understand you want to go home to England. We can help you. I have been responsible for helping many people stuck here since the war started.'

314

'Can you?' Crystal was hopeful.

The man laughed, 'I can indeed. I understand what has happened. Veda has convinced me you are innocent of war crimes. She also said, if your decision becomes reality, you might change your mind and not want to go.'

Veda's stare was intense, as if willing Crystal to decide to stay and be with her son.

'I want to go home and start a new life,' Crystal said hesitantly, her heart flittering and sickness gurgling at the thought of leaving Ayan for good and never seeing him again. But it was how things needed to be.

'OK, it will take about a week. I will arrange passports for you and Billy. It will not be an easy journey. We can only get you out of the country. You will need to arrange flights once you are away from here.' Before leaving, he took a photo of both of them, which was difficult as the little boy was covered in jam.

'My real name is Sarah James,' she told him. 'I want to be known as this from now on. Oh, and I'm not going without Diesel,' she shouted as they made to leave.

Koa laughed and nodded. 'You make our life difficult. But your dog will go too. However, he will need certain vaccinations for his passport. Have you money?'

'I've a few hundred pounds.'

'How on earth do you get to know such influential people?' She asked Veda, who had surprised her so much.

True to his word, Crystal had no idea how, but four days later, Koa visited again, alone this time. He slapped down an envelope. Inside were the passports, including one for Diesel with his photo inside the front page. The vaccinations are fake for the dog,' he explained. I am not sure of the UK laws regarding animals. However, I am assured these will be enough for him to be able to get him to your home. You are booked on a cargo ship leaving the port in three days,' Koa grinned. 'It will sail to several countries to collect and unload. You can take your pick which you decide to get off at. It will not be a comfortable journey, but hopefully, you will get home eventually.'

Crystal did not feel pleased. She was heavy and desperately sad. 'Thank you, all of you.'

Koa nodded, smiled, and left.

Crystal saw Hemi bustling along the road a few days before her journey. She dubiously approached the woman, who was panic-stricken when she saw her.

'Please, Hemi, leave your husband; you'll be safe on the island. You'll find happiness. Do not ruin your life with such misery.'

Terrified, the woman lowered her head and rushed away.

Crystal climbed into the back of the car. Billy and Diesel were already strapped safely next to her. Lalita was driving them to the port.

Veda turned in the passenger seat, 'Are you sure about this?'

Crystal looked at her hands, wiped her eyes, and nodded, afraid to speak and become a jabbering wreck.'

When they arrived at the port, she spotted a little fishing boat moored, knowing it was from the island. Crystal hurried into the port before anyone spotted her, leaving Veda and Lalita to catch her up.

Ayan was standing inside, with Chris, close to the check-in desk. Her stomach lurched, and sickness engulfed her. She just knew that Veda had betrayed her confidence. She threw the woman a look of hurt and disgust. Veda shrugged and grinned guiltily. Panicking, Crystal darted toward the lady's toilet, dragging Billy and Diesel with her. It was too late; Ayan rushed forward and grabbed her arm.

'Please, Crystal! Before you go, give me a few moments. I love you. I can't live without you. Don't leave me?'

She looked into his eyes; they were deep and sincere, full of the love she had so craved from him. Giving in, they found a seat, and Crystal said nothing, allowing him to speak freely, as she looked down at Diesel, nervously stroking his fur as a distraction from the pain.

'It wasn't what you think... with Mira and me. She was so lonely after Masa and losing her sister. We were sharing our grief. Most nights, she cries; if I hear, I go and hold her until she sleeps and see to Tiare if she wakes, just to give Mira rest. That night, I fell asleep too. It would never be that way between the two of us. She loves my brother and misses the man he once was... I was riddled with guilt that I loved you as well as Maya. She knew I did,' he laughed nervously. 'She was a wise old soul in a young body. Maya told me that one day we would be together... When she died, I felt so bad and disrespectful, loving you, I could hardly look at you. That guilt escalated for what we did on the cliff. It was my fault and I blamed you. It was too soon and wrong. You knew that, too. How could I live with myself? I tried to blame you for bewitching me, but it was because I was angry with myself. What I did was wrong. And then you lost our baby, I hated myself even more. I've caused you so much pain. I love you. One day, I want you to be my wife. Come back with me. I need you, we all do.' He finished; it was like a long-rehearsed speech that he may have said repeatedly before it was right.

Crystal looked up meeting his pleading eyes. She had no doubt he had meant every word.

'When we made love on the cliff top that day,' he continued. 'It was the most wonderful thing I've ever experienced. It was like we were thrown into the universe and only the two of us existed. We were as one. It was just like when we were at the sacred ground together.' He was fumbling now as if his speech had a few add-ons.

Crystal was amazed; he had felt it, too. The pure love that maybe no one in a lifetime would ever get to feel. She looked around to see Diesel and Billy staring expectantly at her and then Veda, Lalita, and Chris.

Ayan took her hands in his and leaned forward. The sparks flew through her body, making her breathless, safe, and loved.

Crystal, with all her strength and determination, pushed him away.

'I've loved you for a long time, Ayan. I think I always will. This sort of love is nothing I've ever felt or am likely to again. But no. I'll not stay. I'm going home, where I belong.' She stood up, grabbed Billy's hand and Diesel's makeshift lead, cuddled each of the little party, and walked away.

Ayan stared at her in disbelief, not knowing if he should cry or beg.

Crystal turned at the barrier for the last time. 'When you think things are going well, life comes with a great big kipper and slaps you around the chops.' But she could not decide if that was for herself or Ayan.

Chris walked forward and put his hand on his shoulder. 'Come, we'll watch the boat leave.

They ran out of the port to the water's edge, leaving his mother and sister to catch up.

'You're so stubborn, woman!' he shouted to Crystal as she stood at the ship's edge, surrounded by huge dirty containers.

Billy reached out his arms towards Ayan, and Diesel began to whine, terrified.

'We had our clothes on!' The men, still loading the container, turned to look his way. 'If you hadn't turned your back, you would have seen. We were dressed.'

The men began to smirk, nudging each other. Ayan did not care.

Crystal was trying to process this.

'You are a Pig Ayan,' she finally shouted, looking mortified that she had maybe made a mistake, but it was too late.

'And you are a stuck-up Princess! But I still love you.'

Veda finally caught them up, 'Sometimes Ayan, I think I gave birth to two idiot sons.' She was holding a package, which she handed to him.

Ayan looked at the contents with glazed eyes. It was a ticket and his passport for the container ship. He threw his arms around his mother and squeezed, kissing her cheek.

'Mira and Tiare?'

'I will return to the Island and take care of them until you return. Be happy my son.'

THE END.